The PILGRIM'S PROGRESS
—— for the ——
21ST CENTURY

A Modern Adaptation of the
JOHN BUNYAN CLASSIC

DAVID HARAKAL

Publishing support for the first edition provided by Ignite Press
5070 N. Sixth St. #189 Fresno, CA 93710 www.IgnitePress.us

ISBN: 979-8-9863408-0-7
ISBN: 979-8-9863408-2-1 (Hardcover)
ISBN: 979-8-9863408-1-4 (E-book)

For bulk purchase and for booking, contact: David Harakal (DHarakalAuthor@gmail.com).

Library of Congress Control Number: 2022909818
Cover design by Aasman Iqbal | 99Designs
First Edition Edited by Elizabeth Arterberry. Second Edition self-edited.
Interior design by Kathy Lee

SECOND EDITION

*I unexpectedly felt God call me to write this adaptation
during a church service. I pray my efforts bring Him glory.*

*My wife sacrificed our Saturday mornings for years, the only time
I could carve out to write. Thank you, Suzanne, for your love, support,
and encouragement.*

*Thank you to my sister, Cora, for editing and reviewing the 600+ Scripture
references for applicability, my son-in-law, Treston, for his
early theological review, John Murchison, for his diligent review of
and suggestions for questions, and our faithful friend, Ellie, for her
kind critique and thorough review.*

Extract from John Bunyan's Original "Apology"

When at the first I took my pen in hand
Thus for to write, I did not understand
That I at all should make a little book
In such a mode; nay, I had undertook
To make another; which, when almost done,
Before I was aware, I this begun.

And thus it was: I, writing of the way
And race of saints, in this our gospel day,
Fell suddenly into an allegory
About their journey, and the way to glory,
In more than twenty things which I set down…

This book will make a traveller of thee,
If by its counsel thou wilt ruled be;
It will direct thee to the Holy Land,
If thou wilt its directions understand:
Yea, it will make the slothful active be;
The blind also delightful things to see…

Wouldst read thyself, and read thou knowest not what,
And yet know whether thou art blest or not,
By reading the same lines? Oh, then come hither,
And lay my book, thy head, and heart together.

Contents

Preface

John Bunyan wrote *The Pilgrim's Progress* from prison between 1668 and 1672. An allegory about the Christian faith journey, for hundreds of years it was second only to the Bible in popularity.[1] My goal in this retelling, 350 years after the initial completion of Part One, is to answer the question, "If John Bunyan wrote *The Pilgrim's Progress* in a 21st century American context, what might he have written?"

I sought integrity with the structure and intent of the original while addressing theological issues Bunyan did not experience or wrestled with to a lesser degree or in a different manner in 17th Century Puritan England. This update adapts the original for societal and travel contexts that will resonate with the 21st century reader and changes many names to more current forms, sometimes to modify the nature of the character as well. There are some chapters or sections which are wholly new to address sinful natures more widely expressed today. Some of Bunyan's original Scripture references I thought were a stretch given the passage's broader scriptural context, and thus I either omitted or replaced them. I also added references.

In this update to *The Pilgrim's Progress*, as in the original and other updates, each character's name carries with it the essence of their nature. This creative means of characterization plays on the reader's expectations and biases as it draws one into the text, true to an allegory. Per *The American Heritage Dictionary of the English Language*,[2] an allegory is "[t]he representation of abstract ideas or principles by characters, figures, or events in narrative, dramatic, or pictorial form." Given this definition, the only character who changes is Christian. A Christian should change and develop as the Holy Spirit forms them into the likeness of Christ through sanctification, with its ebbs and flows, fits and starts, and periods of temporary backsliding. Presented as the author's dream, the reader only knows what they hear or see, with no insights into unexpressed thoughts.

Structurally, the largest overall deviation from the original is merging Part Two into Part One to create a single story—Christian and his family quest towards Celestial City together. I functionally ignore Part Two and its specific events. I changed the number and gender of children and aged them to give them voice. I also added some couples to those Christian meets along the way, where Part One of the original had almost exclusively male characters. Bunyan wrote in a time where the role of the man as the head of the household differed from my day. As a husband and father, I could not imagine a walk of faith without inviting my family and updated the text accordingly.

Any student of the original will note immediately that I excluded most of the poetic interludes. I found these distracting from the storyline.

My two hopes for the reader are:

1. I believe I join Mr. Bunyan's desire as I pray that readers will fall in love or more in love with the Holy Bible and the Author thereof, that this update will drive one to study the referenced verses and all Scripture; and
2. I hope the reader will want to read or reread Bunyan's original.

I pray this update will reflect Paul's desires in Ephesians, "and also for me, that words may be given to me in opening my mouth boldly to proclaim the mystery of the gospel."[3]

Note: All Scripture references are from the English Standard Version,[4] unless otherwise noted.

CHAPTER ONE

Pleasantown

I arrived home exhausted from a long day and night of international work-related travel. The house was silent and dark; even my night-owl teen-aged children were asleep. To preserve the silence, I sat on the sofa nearest the door to take off my shoes, and fell fast asleep, my tie still tied. In my sleep, I dreamed.[5]

My dream started at a large, elegant home, as if I had stepped onto a movie set. A middle-aged man in a custom-tailored suit in dire need of dry cleaning[6] sat at a turquoise picnic table[7] in a well-manicured, weedless expanse of lawn under an ancient, Spanish-moss-hung oak. He struggled to sit upright as the straps of the beautiful glove-leather backpack cut into his shoulders.[8] When he opened his pack, I expected to see heavy books or stacks of papers and a thick laptop, but it was full of the weight of the sins he carried with him. He wept as he read the Bible on his smartphone. This man looked unaccustomed to shedding tears. "I've done everything I was supposed to do. I'm a good person. What more must I do?"[9] he groaned.

When he had regained his composure, he spoke his truth[10] to himself.

"I am a wealthy, self-made man. My family looks to me to lead them, to model the life we must present to those around us. I am a problem fixer, not whiny and needy. God has rewarded me with a good life, a beautiful wife, and three incredible children. Pull yourself together, Christian. Time to show them the confidence and poise they expect."

"Dad's home!" his daughter gushed as he walked in the door.

The setting sun visible through expensive Belgian lace curtains, he joined his wife and children, who were already seated for their evening meal. Each member played their part of their picture-perfect lives as scripted. No one commented on the bulky backpack weighing Christian down at the table.

After dinner, the family retired to the living room and melted into the country-chic sofas and chairs. Christian barely held back tears as he commanded the room, each of his listeners surprised and concerned. "I can't maintain this charade any longer. When I try to keep up appearances, it adds to the painful weight of the sins I carry. Christiana, children, I know Pleasantown is home. God has blessed us with comforts and health and good standing here.[11] We love our friends and they love us in return.

"As I read through the Bible, it convicted me that the town is destroying itself, its laws and norms so contrary to scripture. If we stay, it will destroy us with it."

Christiana fumed through tears. "You are so consumed with growing your business, making a good impression at church, and networking in the community that you ignore your family's needs. We tried to tell you our home was doomed, but you wouldn't even entertain the idea! Have you not noticed the burdens we carry?"

"I want the best of everything for you and assumed your packs were heavy because of the rich leather. We must portray the right image! Now I realize that each of us carries physical weight that reflects the burden of our sins. When I dug through my backpack earlier, the sheer volume of my offenses overwhelmed me, going back to how I disobeyed my parents, through the years where I placed my faith in my own abilities alone or blamed God for our poverty early in my career, to the ways I have treated you with disdain, Christiana. I am sorry—you all deserve better.

"We will leave first thing in the morning and figure out how to lighten these bags on the way."

The Pilgrims packed well into the night for their uncertain journey, shuttling back and forth to their climate-controlled, immaculate garage to pack their large, top-of-the-line SUV that looked like it belonged to a U.S. senator or powerful CEO of a large company. After prayers together, each tossed and turned most of the night and slept little.

"Christian, we must warn our friends of the imminent destruction of Pleasantown before we leave, especially the DoWells," Christiana pleaded over breakfast. "We have known each other since before the children started school. We always talked about church things with them. I'm sure they will recognize the tragic state of Pleasantown after we share what God has shown us through his Word. It will be nice to share their company on our journey."

The family hurried through the well-maintained lawns; they arrived as the DoWells finished breakfast at an antique farmhouse table on their deep, covered veranda. The children left for the outdoor sofas in the sitting area on the other end of the porch as the parents settled at the table, enjoying the breeze of the ceiling fan. None of the DoWells seemed to notice the heavy bags their friends carried.

After brief pleasantries over fresh-squeezed orange juice, croissants, and lattes, Christian got to the point. "As I read through the Bible, I am convinced Pleasantown has doomed itself to destruction—a modern-day Sodom or Gomorrah. We want to find a place where people live out the truths of Scripture. You are our oldest and closest friends, and given how often we have spoken of God and church, we thought you would want to join us.

"You look surprised. Am I correct to assume that you don't share our concerns?"[12]

"We love your family, but I'm afraid you are way off base here," Mr. DoWell condescended in a concerned, patriarchal tone. "I've talked to other people who put too much confidence in those outdated words in that ancient book. Pleasantown is renowned for its tolerance. God will continue to bless you with prosperity and health because of your tolerant lifestyle. There's no reason to leave when you have everything you want here."

Christian and Christiana tried to show their friends from Scripture how the highest worldly values of relative truth, or "tolerance," and comfort, cannot satisfy one's deepest needs and desires.[13]

The DoWells listened, stone faced with arms crossed, before Mr. DoWell excused himself. "It's getting warm. I'll go get us some of my wife's famous lemonade."

During their continued pleadings with Mrs. DoWell, her husband was on his phone inside. At times, his voice was loud enough for those on the porch to overhear.

"This is Child Protective Services, right? Our neighbors, the Pilgrims… Yes, Christian's family… Yes, they are a great family, or so I thought. Anyway, I think they mean well, but I'm afraid they have become religious fanatics: closed-minded and intolerant. They are trying to convince us to leave the safety and comfort ensured by the policies set down by our city council… I agree, ours are the most tolerant in the state.

"Listen, I'm worried about the children. They are at the age that they need the inclusive curriculum just introduced by the school board to help them as they determine their identities without the constraints of outmoded beliefs. But, even more, the Pilgrims are one of the most well-respected families in the town. If they are allowed to leave, their departure would set a dangerous precedent that we cannot allow. With some re-education, I'm sure we can protect their family."

Mr. DoWell returned with a crystal pitcher full of cold, sweet refreshment, and filled his guests' matching glasses. The Pilgrims downed theirs as Christian tried to cover their hasty exit.

"We are not ready for Sunday School tomorrow and need to run some errands to get ready. I apologize that we cannot stay longer. Maybe we can continue our conversation next week?"

With additional pleasantries, Christian and Christiana gathered their children and said their goodbyes.

Their neighbors gone; Mr. DoWell collected his family. "Let's learn from what Mom and I discussed with the Pilgrims. I've repeatedly bragged about how Mr. Pilgrim led his family. They are good people. They go to church most Sundays. Mr. and Mrs. Pilgrim teach Sunday School classes and their children help with Children's Church. They don't add stuff from the Bible that would conflict with the inclusiveness and tolerance curriculum approved by the school board.

"As far as I know, they have never broken the law or hurt anyone. They are wonderful neighbors, always ready to help, and give money to causes that are important to them. We volunteered together at various events, and they always seem tolerant and pleasant.

"I'm not sure what has gotten into them, but I bet their 'errands' are such that we'll never see them again. It's so sad when people become religious fanatics. I hope you kids will learn from their mistakes. When you work hard to earn a good life and all the comforts that come with it, plus the respect of your friends and neighbors, you don't just throw it all away on a whim.

"There they are in their driveway now. Just wave as though it was any other day. I've notified Child Protective Services and I don't want the Pilgrims to get suspicious."

Backing their land yacht out of the garage, the Pilgrims set out on their journey, listening to an Audio Bible they downloaded to the vehicle's audio system.

They stopped at the first rest stop outside out of town.

"I don't know where we should go, but wanted to stop before we got too far to discuss the conversation Mom and I had with Mr. and Mrs. DoWell. I was surprised at their lack of interest in what we have learned and tried to share with them from Scripture.[14] To be fair, I would have agreed with them as recently as a few days ago.

"I convinced myself that I was leading you to be good people. Our friends, people at church, and my business associates affirmed this—without exception. But I now see I have led you to a false confidence in our own self-worth. Our Savior confers his value to us through faith in his crucifixion and resurrection alone. I deceived you as I did myself, that my goodness was my path to Heaven.[15] I know that is wrong, but the problem is that I'm not sure what is right!"

Christian led his family in reading the Bible for direction as they discussed what to do and where to go. Deep in study, they barely noticed the car that pulled into the rest stop. A clean-cut, distinguished older man without a single white hair out of place got out and approached them.

"Good morning. My name is Good-Guide. You look lost. I was sent to help you."[16]

"Welcome! Odd. Somehow I know we can trust you.[17]

"I tried to lead my family in righteous living, but as we study the Bible, it convicted us of our sins and, now that we understand the consequences we will suffer, we are terrified.[18] These weighty burdens we each carry are incontrovertible evidence that will condemn us at the time of trial on the last day, as presented in Scripture. The resulting judgment will be unbearable.

"We have always believed we were good because we did good things and, therefore, deserved an eternal reward. None of us has ever gone to jail for breaking the law, or even had to visit the principal's office at school. But now we know our good deeds will not save us."[19]

"You are wise to look to Scripture, for the answers you seek are there—when taken in context. It not only convicts of sin but provides the way out. What is your plan?" Good-Guide's tone demanded a response, yet conveyed great love and kindness.

"I don't have one. I'm leading my family like sheep without a shepherd."[20]

The answer was as simple as it was confusing, "Escape the wrath to come."[21]

"Thank you, but I'm not sure I know much more than I did before. I sensed the need to leave, but where do we go?"

"Your final destination is Celestial City, which is a long and arduous journey. To get there, you must first stop at Narrow Gate,"[22] Good Guide directed. "I just sent you a pin, but if you lose your cell signal, simply proceed towards the bright light.[23] Do you see it way over there?"

All nodded like a family of bobble heads.

"Knock on the door when you arrive, and your host will welcome you and provide further instructions."

"Thank you," Christiana said with a beautiful, genuine smile as the family got back into the SUV, which their daughter had named "The Chariot."

CHAPTER TWO

Challenged

Christian followed The Chariot's directions towards Narrow Gate. The route took them back through their neighborhood, where friends and acquaintances ran out to stop their departure. "Leave the windows up. Our neighbors mean well, but will play on our love for them to distract us."[24]

He selected a country gospel station from the satellite radio to drown out the noise. "Smile and wave. We don't want to be rude, but we cannot engage with them."

When they finished singing along to "The Old Rugged Cross,"[25] Christiana reflected, "I have heard that song so often before, but today it has new meaning."

Without a backward glance,[26] Christian drove on.

"Pleasantown traffic betrays the town's name. Today it is terrible. We have escaped our neighborhood and our well-meaning friends who tried to detain us, but are now only two-thirds of the way through town and mired down in stop-and-go traffic. One of our favorite restaurants is just ahead, on our way, so I am going to stop for lunch."

* * *

It was crowded, and they met more people who tried to coerce them not to leave. News travels fast in small towns. They could overhear discussions as they passed,[27] some even debated whether they should call the police to prevent their departure. A few mentioned slashing their tires to keep them from making "a terrible mistake."

Soon after they were seated, Obstinate and Flexible joined them, uninvited but welcomed. Obstinate chided them. "Did you plan to leave without saying goodbye? I thought we were friends. Our children have known each other since they were in diapers, and yours do so well in school. You would be crazy to leave the comforts you enjoy, which you have earned and deserve; your exquisite home, your good friends, and Pleasantown's profuse entertainment options. You live the life most people crave. We love you and don't want to see you throw all of this away for some crazy, misguided adventure."

"Friends, the old me was a peacemaker, unaccustomed to causing controversy. I prided myself as a great compromiser. My 'win-win' scenarios were legendary," Christian shared. "But the Bible showed me I have not been a good friend to you. I allowed myself to be misled. My desire for comfort over confrontation added to the burden of sins that I carry. What you say, and what we were taught here, seems true, but is not. We have been chasing our tails.[28] The people of Pleasantown doom it to destruction.

"You and Flexible have been good friends to me. Join us on our path to Celestial City,[29] where we will find eternal peace and contentment in the presence of our Savior."

"What? You want us to leave well-deserved comforts, family, and friends who love us? I was born here and have lived here all my life. My and my wife's extended families are here. I worked hard to earn my position, am well regarded, and well established," Obstinate shot back.

"You love good things here, things we also love. Join us and discover what is infinitely and eternally better.[30] What is good is keeping you from what is better, and leads to death." Christian implored.

"How can you walk away from the certain goodness we enjoy here to chase some perceived 'better' goodness? In what world does that make sense? That is crazy,"[31] Obstinate countered.

"We pursue a city which is not only greater, but certain and eternal.[32] Would you read the Bible with me to see for yourself?" Christian urged.

Obstinate mocked him. "It sounds you have opened the door to the crazy house. To even consider abandoning the blessings of Pleasantown for some promise you think you found in an outdated book no one reads anymore—at least, no thinking, rational person—confirms your insanity. Come to your senses. We can go back to your house and help you unload the SUV so you can get back to normal."

"Thank you for your offer, Obstinate, but we seek what we know is best. We will not turn back."[33]

Looks-Good, the Pilgrims' older son, jumped in. "Mr. Obstinate, you are kind and generous, so I expect you will find the path we travel easy. You know my mom and dad. They are smart and reasonable. People respect their decisions."

Obstinate shifted his attention. "Flexible, I'm afraid Christian and his family are beyond reason. His lunacy has infected the entire family. They trust that silly old book for advice, and ignore the sage counsel of those who love them. We have no choice but to leave them to their own fate."

Returning his focus to Christian, he continued, "Even in your foolishness, we love you and your family. When you realize the error in your decision, we will welcome you home and help you relearn what you should not have forgotten."

"You might be right, Obstinate," Flexible replied, "but I have to consider Christian's offer. Everyone holds him in high esteem and he has a great family. His children are strong leaders and loyal friends to our kids at school. Your wife and the young women in our neighborhood all love and respect Christiana. What if these promises are true, and something far better than what we know is waiting for us?"

"Flexible, there is no wise answer for a fool.[34] Are you seriously willing to join in this nonsense? Listen to my wisdom[35] and leave the Pilgrims to their little endeavor."

Christian joined in the fight for his friend's future. "Flexible, I am learning a new way to love my friends, to speak even if it may lead to disagreement. Come with us to share the glories promised in seeking and finding truths in Scripture. Contrary to what Obstinate says, I do not rely on my own wisdom,[36] but on the truth of the Bible. It is as relevant today as when it was written thousands of years ago. I do not ask you to trust me, but the Author of Truth and Creator of Peace who died to provide you with everything good."[37]

"Obstinate, I value our friendship and your position in our city, but I want to try Christian's path and see how it goes."

"Flexible, you make a wise choice. A man named Good-Guide has directed us to Narrow Gate, where we will learn additional details for our journey," Christian encouraged him.

Obstinate threw his napkin onto his plate, pushed his chair away from the table, and bolted up from his chair so that it fell backwards. "Flexible, you will regret this. I will not waste my time in the fellowship of fools, and I will definitely not succumb to religious fanaticism." He stormed towards the door.

Soon he returned, cool headed, now with a kind demeanor. "I'm sorry for that show. It is not like me. You must have touched a nerve.

"Because I am kind hearted, I will wait for all of you to come back to your senses and care for your homes until you return. Good day."

They finished dinner. Christian paid the check and left a generous tip.

Looks-Good parted the crowd to allow his family and Flexible to pass, as they made their escape suffering their neighbors' taunts and verbal abuse.

CHAPTER THREE

Flexible's Journey

"This will be a grand adventure, Mr. Flexible," bubbled Joyful, Christian's ready-for-anything daughter, as he joined them in the SUV. "I am so excited you chose to join us!"

"Joyful, I love how you embrace life and opportunities. This is not our usual family trip," Christiana said to her daughter before turning her attention to their guest. "We are thankful that you chose to join our quest to Celestial City. What's on your mind?"

"I am thankful that I can speak freely with you. Like Joyful, I love the idea of a noble journey with good friends, and always look for what is new and different.[38] What can you tell me about our destination and what should I expect on the way?"

"The Bible answers both questions. We can read it together," Christiana offered.

"Do all of you *actually believe* that everything in the Bible is true?"

Self-Disciplined, Joyful's younger brother, addressed his question. "We do now.[39] Mom and Dad read us Bible stories all growing up, so we thought we knew all there was to know because we knew all the stories. But we never read it cover to cover. Truth be told, and I hope I do not dishonor you, Mom and Dad, we used it only for advice on how to be 'good people' and do 'right things.' Now when we read it, the Author shows us his truth.[40] Now we know that right beliefs drive right actions,[41] not vice versa."

"Well spoken, son. And, to the contrary, your integrity honors us.

"I'll add that the Author can only speak truth,[42] and we were unwise not to place our confidence in it before now," Christian regretted.

"Okay. Back to our journey," Flexible continued. "What is so special about this 'Narrow Gate' that you are each willing to walk away from everything you enjoy to find it?"

"Narrow Gate is only a waypoint. Our goal is Celestial City, where Scripture promises the faithful eternity with the Loving Protector,"[43] Christian shared.

Flexible sat back in his seat, scratching his head. "Seriously? That's it?"

"Oh no! Those who enter receive crowns of glory and radiant clothing. They will shine like the sun![44] It will be so amazing!" Joyful exclaimed with her typical exuberance.

"There won't be crying or sorrow, we will never be hungry or thirsty, and the King will wipe away tears and guide us to springs of living water,"[45] Christiana added through tears of joy.

"Anything else?" Flexible asked.

Christian had a faraway look on his radiant face. "The Bible describes dazzling creatures, including seraphim and cherubim and myriad of those who will arrive ahead of us, each one holy, enjoying the eternal loving presence of our Lord in his everlasting acceptance.[46] Truly wise leaders with their golden crowns[47] await us there, as well as musicians playing glorious music and those who have dedicated themselves to the service of our King.[48] There will be heroes who were killed in just wars and those who were tortured and died for sharing their faith in the one who offers this eternal life.[49] All who are there will enjoy this great joy forever."[50]

"Who could say 'No' to all that? You've convinced me. How do I get in on this deal?"

"The Lord of that place tells us in his book that he offers it as a free gift. We just need to ask,"[51] Christiana blurted almost before he finished his question, beating out the others as she leaned in.

"Let's get a move on! Is there a traffic app that can help us get us through town faster? This sounds too good to wait," Flexible jumped in, never seeming to notice the great and growing burdens on the backs of Christian and his family, despite their squirming. Neither did he seem to sense his own.

* * *

Flexible's house was across town, so they headed there for him to pack.

Traffic was slow, which provided time for some additional conversation. Flexible probed. "Some of your word choice confuses me. You mention a 'Lord,' which I think refers to the leader of Celestial City, and a 'King.' Are they the same person? Is Celestial City in England, and a few centuries behind us?"

Christian chuckled before he answered. "Not quite, though I can see how that might be confusing here and now. Our destination is under God's rule and reign, and there is no better language to address his absolute authority over our lives."

The pleasant question-and-answer period ended when traffic ground to a standstill for a parade. They turned off the main road to find an alternate route, but The Chariot's navigation system crashed and soon they were lost in an unfamiliar part of town. As they crawled along, the air conditioner broke, and it got warm even with the windows down.

"Dad, will you please pull over as quickly as possible?" Joyful asked, ashen, holding her stomach. "The exhaust spewing out of the car in front of us and the heat have made me sick."

Christian turned off the busy road onto Melancholy Swamp Street[52] and Joyful bolted out of the SUV to a grassy area just in time. When she returned, The Chariot wouldn't start.

Flexible broke the uncomfortable silence. "I love you and your family, Christian, but this situation is probably a bad omen for your adventure. I was looking forward to a fun trip with good friends, but this must not be it. I'll just hop out, enjoy the festival and the parade, and return to the good life I know."

He disappeared into the crowd before anyone could respond.

"Dad, what if he's right?" Looks-Good speculated. "What if God is showing us we were wrong to try to leave? I'm also sick, hot, and miserable. I also don't like this backpack, which I cannot get off and is biting into my shoulders."

Self-Disciplined joined in. "Our lives have been great in Pleasantown. Maybe we should stay and try to share the Gospel with people here instead. What if the comforts we enjoyed here are blessings to reward our good choices and encourage us to stay?"

A man appeared at Christian's window. "Hello. My name is Help. Good-Guide sent me to you. I brought you some cold water and some snacks. I'm a mechanic by trade, so if you will pop your hood, I'll get you back on the road."

He worked on the SUV for just a few minutes.

"Give it a try now."

The Chariot sprung to life, the engine purring and barely audible.

"You should be good to go. I made a few adjustments to your air conditioning system so it should work better than it did before and put less strain on your engine. Is there anything else you need?"

"We want to go to Celestial City," Christiana offered, "and have been following Good-Guide's advice to go to Narrow Gate first. Stuck here, we are second guessing our decision. You must be trustworthy if Good-Guide sent you. What should we do?"

"You were right to leave. I can help you.[53] The Lord of Celestial City has called you to him. Had you stayed, you would have disobeyed him. One of the Lord's enemy's favorite tactics is to use good intentions and actions to lead people away from Narrow Gate and beyond.

"Do you see that barrier straight ahead? It keeps that street clear for emergencies. Mention that you are going to Narrow Gate and the guard will allow you to pass. Stay on that road and it will carry you to the edge of town. Navigation systems are overloaded in town, but will reconnect as you leave."

Looks-Good, always practical, asked, "Mr. Help, you seem to be in the know. If the traffic is terrible even when there isn't a festival, and if everyone has to pass through Pleasantown to get to Narrow Gate, why don't they just build an overpass, or a tunnel, or a transporter? That would be more environmentally friendly than people stuck in traffic spewing exhaust, and faster. My vote is for the transporter—just zap us from here to there."

"Interesting alternatives, Looks-Good. Snarled traffic definitely brings out the worst in people," Help explained. "The town council could address it and add lanes to existing roads or build an overpass, but the citizens will not tolerate the disruption that construction would cause. Citizens of Pleasantown do not think long term. They will forgo substantial future benefits to avoid short-term inconvenience. It is ultimately man's sin that makes the path to Narrow Gate difficult. Not that long ago, you were part of that majority. Many people have set out for Narrow Gate, but the awful traffic through this part of town has led them to reconsider their plans. Most have turned back, unwilling to endure inconvenience or discomfort."[54]

"Sounds like the traffic ends up separating the sheep from the goats,[55] or maybe the jeeps from the boats," Self-Disciplined opined, to the pained grins of his listeners.

"Many of us know the back roads and ways through town[56] that the traffic tools on navigation systems don't show, even when they do work. It was no accident that you broke down here, now."[57]

Tempted

The Pilgrims followed Help's directions and crossed town with no further delay or incident. Around supper time, they arrived in the town of Blessing.[58]

"Mom, can we stop here for dinner?" Joyful asked in her typical effervescent disposition. "I love this town. I know it is a tourist trap, but this will be the last time we get to visit. The displays are all so creative. It's like we could move in and live in the store. The owners are aesthetic masters."

"Suck-money-out-of-your-wallet masters would be more accurate," her younger brother corrected, earning him an elbow to the ribs.

Christiana supported her daughter. "I think that's a great idea, Joyful. A walk will be a pleasant break from sitting in the car."

After window shopping, the family went to Bless Your Belly Café for dinner, a quaint spot with its blend of over-priced food and comparably over-priced, beautifully displayed, spiritually themed items to collect dust in the home.

A well-dressed man in his early forties approached the table. His hair was perfectly quaffed, his bespoke suit perfectly cut to his fit physique. One would expect to find him modeling on London's Savile Row, not in a remote small town. "You must be the Pilgrims. Word travels fast on the faith community's social media and I expected you would stop here on the way to Narrow Gate. I have helped many traveling in that direction.

"I am Pastor Ear-Tickler, the founding pastor of Abundant Victorious Life Church. You probably recognize me from my top-rated social media channels. Those packs on your backs should not weigh you down. You need my latest best-selling book, *Heaven on Earth: Being Your Best You Now.* You will find the answers you seek there. This autographed copy is my gift to you," he said, handing them the book with both hands as if it were a delicate porcelain tea set.

"Thank you! We are headed to Narrow Gate on Good-Guide's advice, hoping to rid ourselves of these heavy burdens and find Celestial City," Self-Disciplined shared.

"You are too young to be weighed down by sin! You are good church-going people. I know that from the social media posts my staff shared with me. Sin should not distract you.[59] Good-Guide gave you terrible advice. My plan for you is far better."[60]

"Your church is huge! What an honor to meet such a successful pastor! I have made so many mistakes leading my family, but I want to turn that around. It seems God put you in our path for such direction and encouragement."[61]

"Of course he has. He wants you to be happy. I have no doubt that Good-Guide had good intentions, but he misled you. Toss off those heavy packs. You won't be happy with those things slowing you down and they will cause you to miss out on the blessings God wants for you."

Self-Disciplined jumped in again. "We've tried, but can't get them off. The few times one of us has managed to wiggle out, he or she always puts it back on without even realizing it!"

Pastor Ear-Tickler turned on the charm. "You make everything too hard. If you follow Good-Guide's instructions, you will miss the comforts that God wants for you. It is good that I found you, to save you from this foolish path you follow, as I have done for so many others.

"Pleasantown's notorious traffic jams are pleasant compared to where you are going, according to the stories I have been told by those who turned back. Christian, you are a loving, good father and husband. Why would you needlessly endanger your family in obvious contradiction to the good life God wants for you?"

"These burdens are difficult to carry, so when Good-Guide offered us a way out, I jumped at it.[62] Sins, our sins, pervade our thoughts. You are right. These packs have kept us from fully enjoying the good life. I went from one extreme to the other, from not caring at all about sin to caring too much. Thank you for your counsel," Christian conceded.

"Who told you the weights that you each carry are from sins? Those are just the effects of negative thinking and taking your focus off of the comforts God wants for you. You have a thinking problem."

"We've been reading the Bible and listening to it as we drive," Joyful answered. "And it has convicted us that our lives are full of sin that we've overlooked or ignored. Now that we see our inability to measure up to the standard of perfection that we heard and read, we're overwhelmed."

"How fortunate for you that you have met me. The Bible is a guidebook, not a rule book. Rational people do not take it literally and certainly do not try to follow it to the letter. God does not want people to think about sin and depravity. Those are downers. When I preach or post on social media, I'm careful to avoid those outdated thoughts. I focus on the love of God and his goodness, reminding my audience that God wants his people to be healthy, wealthy, and well regarded. He wants to favor you and honor you, like it says in the Bible.[63]

"Lest you worry about how to turn your lives around, I have the answer. God led you here at the perfect time. Our 'Be Your Best You Now' conference starts tomorrow! I want to bless you, to counteract the hurt Good-Guide has caused you. I will personally cover all the costs for your family to attend. Drive straight up to my church's Abundant Life Village Conference Center, Resort, and Spa.

"As you can imagine, my responsibilities during the conference preclude me from giving you the personal attention you deserve. I was confident that you would accept my generous offer, so I arranged for a member of my staff, Civility, the conference center director, to ensure all of your needs are met during the conference. This is my gift to you, further evidence of a good god[64] who wants you to be happy. Give yourselves a rest from that burden-generating tome you've been studying and enjoy *Heaven on Earth: Being Your Best You Now*, which is a suitable replacement, and far more encouraging."

"Thank you. We met you at just the right time. You are an answer to my prayer to lead my family better."[65]

On the short drive to the conference center, the family discussed this fortuitous turn of events.

"Dad, this is absolutely the right decision. It is so much more reasonable than that wild goose chase from Good-Guide," Looks-Good asserted.

"I'm always up for a new adventure, but I'm unsettled,"[66] Joyful shared. "I'm sure my spirit will calm down once we get there."[67]

* * *

"This place is amazing! Look at the tall trees, beautiful meadows, and especially the hip coffee bars. I'll never need to walk more than a few hundred feet for my half-caff caramel macchiato with vanilla almond milk. Maybe this is Celestial City! It fits my dreams of heaven," Joyful rejoiced. "We will know for sure if they serve pumpkin spice lattes even though it isn't fall yet!"

They checked in and received their room assignment. Christiana stayed to register them for the conference sessions as the rest of the family went to their suite.

On the handmade, country-chic wooden coffee table, the family read a note encased in a stone frame with all styles of crosses carved into it. "Welcome to the Country House Suite! Your home away from home was designed by one of the leading clothing and home goods designers. Note the rich, soothing colors throughout and the softness of the glove leather. You deserve these comforts. The designer is available to consult with you in person during your stay. Schedule through your concierge."

Christiana entered through the open door. "What is this? An open door? It must be a miracle! Christian, are you going soft? Where is your 'close the door!' mantra?

"I ran into some old friends from our days in the biker gang, Sugar Daddy."

"What?" all three Pilgrim children exclaimed, faces a mix of fear and awe.

"We may have to find new parents," Self-Disciplined suggested.

"I just wanted to make sure you were paying attention. Happy to know the three of you still have the capacity to listen at the same time.

"So, back to reality. I signed us up for the main sessions tomorrow, but not the optional ones to give us time to rest, reflect, and drink pumpkin lattes! I stopped and grabbed one for each of us, Joyful, and a black coffee for you, Christian. You boys are on your own because I ran out of hands."

Joyful shot out of her chair to retrieve this liquid gold from her mother, just as someone knocked on the frame of the still-open door.

"Come in," the family sang out in unison.

"Hello! I'm Civility, the center's director. Pastor Ear-Tickler asked me to care for you this weekend. God has blessed you to be here and start the life he has always wanted you to live.

"I noticed you registered for the main sessions only. Perfect. First-time conference attendees like yourselves find it beneficial to have time to read the resources God has created for your happiness, specifically our speakers' best-selling books.[68] I've provided you all these plus a few others by different best-selling christian[69] authors as a gift from the center and our church.

"I see you already have Pastor Ear Tickler's book. Wonderful. I have another copy for you, so that more than one of you can read it at a time. It forms the foundation for the entire conference, from God's heart through Pastor's hands. You should all read his book and skim through the others during your free time and then study them all more deeply before you return for the next conference."

"This is a beautiful, peaceful place," Christiana noted. "Why do we still carry these burdens, which seem out of place here?"

"Those burdens are part of your imagination, like sickness.[70] They exist only in your minds. That's not what God wants. Tomorrow morning's first session will probably help you overcome that misconception. I pray you will all rest well tonight."

* * *

After a sumptuous breakfast, Civility met them in the dining room. "Let's head over to the first session. God has ordained just what you need—it's about health. On the way, we will stop to get each of you your favorite drink, on the church's tab, of course," Civility invited them. His confident voice was a mix of a manager directing his staff and a salesman trying to convince a customer to purchase insurance.

The cool morning air, with the sun still low in the sky, plus a beverage refresh from a bubbly-barista-infused coffee shop, prepared the group for their first session. They found seats in the crowded, well-appointed auditorium, availability indicated by the unspoiled taupe journal and embossed pen centered on the cushion. Religious-themed music by one of Abundant Victorious Life Church's bands boomed and propelled them to their feet, sing-screaming with hands raised high, preparing them for their first speaker. From the back, the room looked like a wheat field on sensory overload, waving in the breeze.

"This is better than the last concert I paid to attend!" Self-Disciplined exclaimed.

The speaker was Pastor Good-Life, a mega-church leader famous on social media and so popular as a public speaker that most of the congregation of his home church would not recognize him if not for his giant smiling face on the commercial billboard outside. He was either born with a perfect facial bone structure or had a photographer with a retouch gift.

The concert paused until after the speaking session and the audience took their seats. Looks-Good informed his family: "What a gift! Famous pastors from different churches around the country come together to help people. I searched the internet for information about Pastor Good-Life. God has blessed him with a private plane and a villa in the Caribbean, even though most people in his congregation are poor. That goes to show how much impact he has in his community—they sacrifice to bless him while they wait for the day God provides the same for them, as Pastor Good-Life promises," shared Looks-Good.

The speaker's primary proposal was that any perceived health problem results from either lack of faith or a corrupted mind that perceives disease that is not there. He went on to explain that this lack of faith was sinful.

The Pilgrims left as soon as he finished speaking and got fresh drinks on the way back to their suite. After some time quietly praying and reflecting, Self-Disciplined broke the silence. "Pastor Good-Life's talk was certainly upbeat. His bouncing around the stage like he could barely contain his excitement was entertaining, but I don't think his views are consistent with the Bible, or at least what I've been reading. Scripture presents sickness as a normal part of life for a Christian[71] and even a blessing.[72] The pastor calling illness a sin really doesn't sit well with me."

Civility stopped by their suite just as Self-Discipline finished speaking.

"You should have some time now to reflect on Pastor Good-Life's uplifting presentation and read his book and others! He always leaves me spellbound. Those burdens you imagined when you first arrived have either 'fallen off' or at least gotten lighter, right? I still can't see them."

Christian and Self-Disciplined said, almost in unison, "No! They are heavier now than they were before the session!"

Self-Disciplined added, "There are also several discrepancies between what Pastor Good-Life presented and what the Bible says."[73]

"That's just because your faith is still immature and you are uniformed. Read Pastor Good-Life's book, *Faith: God's Prescription for Perfect Health*. I've read it and taught from it many times."

Joyful turned her focus to Civility, with an air of concern mixed with incredulity. "If mind trumps matter, how do you explain that big gash on your leg? I did some first aid training in Scouts, and by that coloration, it looks like it's infected."

"That's not an infection. That's just God expressing his pleasure with me through body art—a sign of his particular favor. Pastor Good-Life describes it all in his book. You really should read it."

Skeptical looks spread to more of the family's faces as they left to enjoy a bountiful lunch, after which they followed Civility to the next session. The topic was God's design for personal wealth, led by a well-known pastor who owned a successful investment company. The presentation was more of a sales pitch for the speaker's latest books than a sermon. Announcements before and after each speaker, along with abundant large print advertising, ensured the attendee was well aware of resources available from the bookstore throughout the conference.

They had time after the short session to read, study, and discuss what they heard before a supper they would have enjoyed in an expensive restaurant. The meal was followed by the main event, presented by Pastor Ear-Tickler himself, entitled "Your Best You Now."

Pastor Ear-Tickler spoke passionately as he detailed his view of God's design for people to enjoy the best the world offers during their lives. He developed compelling arguments attacking "unscrupulous religious leaders who created the idea of 'sin' to scare people," followed by his rejection of what he described as "a misguided belief that the best life comes after death,"[74] which he presented as "pacification for those who lack the faith to live their best lives here and now."

Back in their suite after the talk, Joyful collapsed into one of the overstuffed chairs, sobbing. "Dad, I feel more burdened now than at any other time on our trip. It's getting worse, not better."

Still not adept at offering comfort, Christian stated pragmatically, his arm around his daughter, "I sought a simple solution to a difficult problem. During the sessions, I was reading Scripture, comparing what I heard to what I read. Now I recognize that today has been nothing but false teaching.[75] We will leave before breakfast."

* * *

The sun not yet above the horizon, Self-Disciplined stacked all the books Civility had given them neatly on the table next to the stone framed advertisement as the rest of the family loaded the SUV. He had just placed Pastor Ear Tickler's autographed copy on top and they were about to leave when Civility met them.

With his best feigned compassion, he addressed the family. "Is there a problem? Pastor Ear-Tickler's presentation last night was compelling, but there is still more great content in today's sessions. Your suite and meals are still covered for two more nights, our church's gift to you while you recover from your travel ordeals. I apologize if that was not clear."

"Thank you for your generous hospitality, Civility. The facilities are exceptional, and every staff member has been hospitable, accommodating, and pleasant towards us. We are leaving because each of us feels the weight of our sins more intensely than when we arrived," Christiana explained.

"But we have time to walk through the teachings of these pastors together," Civility implored. "I noticed you accidentally left the books we've given you. Once you've read through them, these burdens will fall off like dust blowing in the wind."

Christian reasoned with confidence. "What the Bible teaches opposes what the pastors taught in the sessions we attended and what we gleaned while perusing the books you kindly offered us. We would be disingenuous guests to take advantage of your hospitality and gifts when we cannot endorse the principles they present. Either the Bible is true, or the teaching at the conference is, and we are placing our confidence in Scripture."[76]

"That's why we don't read the Bible," Civility countered. "Most of it is obsolete, outdated, and irrelevant for today's culture. God has inspired our speakers to extract the parts that still apply and mold them into the encouragement God wants people to feel.[77] Faith is living and dynamic and has to change with the times. Once you've completed reading the books we gave, you'll see what is true."

Christian gave Civility a love-filled hug. "Thank you, Civility. You are a wonderful host. We will not read those books, but do appreciate your generosity. We have a gift for you. You say it is outdated, but this is a copy of the Bible in which we each wrote you notes of encouragement, underlining verses that had special meaning for us. From what you said, I assume you have not read it. I wish we had a more well-worn copy to offer,[78] but we are newly on this path. I recommend you read it and see for yourself if God shows you the same thing you say he has shown these pastors.[79] While I pray our paths will cross again, I must return my family to our initial course. Our burdens are intolerable and worsening."

After hugs and goodbyes, Christian and his family got back on the road to Narrow Gate. They fasted, skipping breakfast and the excellent free coffee drinks.

"Holy Spirit, please motivate Civility to read the Bible we have left him. Please stir his heart with the truth of your Word and draw him to you," Christian prayed, after which they took turns reading aloud from Scripture in The Chariot.

CHAPTER FIVE

Not Narrow Gate

Christian turned off the road they had been following.

"Dad, I don't think this is on the path that Good-Guide showed us, the one you said you would follow, is it? I don't see that bright light anymore." Self-Disciplined wondered aloud.

"I had an idea. One of my old college buddies lives here. He was like a mentor to me. It's not that far off the path, so I thought it would be good for us to get his thoughts. From what I see on social media, Pastor Legality lives a pure life, devoid of the burdens that weigh us down and will probably lead to scoliosis or fused disks or some other back problem. He just follows all the rules in Scripture, which sounds easy enough. I think he can help us process what we experienced at that retreat and show us how to follow the Bible more obediently."

Parked across the street from his modest, well-kept home, they pulled up his website, "Twelve Steps to Guarantee God's Acceptance." The website banner read, "Follow these twelve steps to guarantee entry into Heaven."

"Dear, glancing through these steps, it starts out with regular reading and praying, which is right, but it doesn't leave much room for error. I see the appeal, though, because it is all things we can do with enough discipline. Scrolling through the topics, they all seem biblical, but I'm not sure I could follow the list as faithfully as your friend seems to," Christiana lamented.

"I agree with Mom," Looks-Good added. "This website is full of expert advice. Everything your friend suggests is under our control. If we just work harder, as Pastor Legality says, we can guarantee our entrance to Heaven. No doubts. People do their part, then God has to do the rest. That makes complete sense! Simply driving along the narrow path Good-Guide recommended is too easy. How could we possibly get to Heaven without working for it? Dad, you always say that nothing in life is free."

"Looks-Good, that sounds right, but I cannot even muster the courage to go knock on the door," Christian replied, his head on his chest.

"My burden weighs me down so that I'm not sure I can still carry it. It would be impossible for me to measure up to my old friend. In reading his posts, he doesn't make mistakes and counsels others how to follow all the steps perfectly.[80] I don't think our old friendship is enough for him to condescend to speak to me because I am so far from his goodness.

"Further, that conference I took us to is the opposite of what we just read on his site, adding to my shame and guilt. I can't get any of this right."

Good-Guide pulled in behind them,[81] got out of his car, and came up the sidewalk to Christiana's open window. "Why are you here? This is not on the road to Narrow Gate. It has only been a few days and you have twice set out on your own path."[82]

Christian did not hold back. "We stopped for lunch in Blessing and Pastor Ear-Tickler invited us to an all-expenses-paid conference at his church's beautiful Abundant Life Village Conference Center, Resort, and Spa. We had heard about the place, and given that it was free, beautiful, and the conference promised an easier way to relieve us of our burdens, I'm ashamed to say I led my family astray.

"Instead, the weight of our sins increased, and while we were still there, I realized I had made a dreadful choice, so we left early. Do I get some credit for leaving once I realized it was wrong, when we still have two free nights available to us?

"We read from the Bible and prayed when we recognized our mistake, and I decided it would be wise[83] if we visited an old college friend. He is the pastor of a rapidly growing church and, from all I can see, is devoted to Scripture. It wasn't far out of the way and I hoped he could offer us sound advice on how to live our lives rightly. But when we pulled up here, guilt and shame overwhelmed me when I realized how far short I fall from living the good Christian life that he leads."

"How foolish you have been to pursue these two opposite paths, both of which contain corrupted elements of truth.[84] Let's go grab lunch and I will show you the truth from the Bible you missed."[85]

Good-Guide led them back to the correct road, where they soon pulled into the parking lot of a diner. They sat in a large corner booth where he shared Scripture's truth.

"Do not reject him who speaks to you as Israel did. God did not spare his chosen people from punishment when they rejected his earthly messengers, prophets like Elijah and Isaiah. How much worse to reject his Holy Word inspired by the Holy Spirit.[86] Let's read from Hebrews, 'but my righteous one shall live by faith, and if he shrinks back, my soul has no pleasure in him.'[87] This is where you've led your family, Christian. You shrunk back to ways that made sense to you, looking for shortcuts to rid yourselves of your burdens," Good-Guide said as he pulled a handkerchief from his jacket pocket to dab the tears from his eyes as he spoke. "I love you all enough to share this harsh reality with you, not to shame, but to teach."

Christian lamented, "I failed. I have not only ruined my life[88] but led my family astray in the process!"

"You made some atrocious choices, but you and your family are not without hope. The Son of God is our Great Pastor, our High Priest. Jesus was tempted to stray as you were, though he never did, and he invites you to receive his grace and mercy.[89] He is ready to forgive all of your sins.[90] Don't be faithless, but believe."[91] Christian straightened himself in his chair, his shoulders relaxed with peace in his face.

Good-Guide continued, "To avoid repeating the same mistakes, not to shame you, let me recount the missteps you took:

> *The first wrong turn you took led you to Pastor Ear-Tickler, who does not speak for God, nor does any other man. He tells people what they want to hear, which makes him popular with those who value the lie of mankind's "innate goodness." His teaching makes God into a celestial Santa Claus whose only role is to give you what you want so that you can stay focused on you, while assuaging or negating the cost of sin. This is cheap grace, a false hope.*
>
> *Next, you turned the opposite direction to your friend Pastor Legality, who prescribes a contrary approach. He follows and promotes the rules he finds in the Bible so that he can earn salvation, teaching that God then owes the obedient person salvation on his merits. This denies the grace Jesus died to offer.*
>
> *Each promises a way to avoid the hard work of correcting sinful thoughts and behaviors, of replacing selfish desires with a desire to live for Christ alone. It is this painful transition that leads to sanctification for the one who follows the way of truth.*
>
> *Both extremes will lead one away from the true but harder path I instructed you to follow, and result in focusing on oneself, not Jesus.*

These men teach doctrines you must not simply forget but learn to despise.

The first error that both of them taught is that there is a different way to your destination, bypassing Narrow Gate. You ignored my counsel and chose a path that seemed more pleasant to your sensibilities and was better aligned with your worldly desires, as Pastor Ear-Tickler taught. Conversely, you must reject the idea that you can live righteously enough that God owes you his favor, as Pastor Legality would have taught you. The life of obedience without faith you see on his social media posts negates any need for the Cross of Christ. Neither of these men can relieve you of your burdens.

The second, and more grievous, error is that each implicitly rejects the Cross as offensive. You must value what Jesus accomplished through the Cross more highly than life itself. Scripture tells us that those who would save their lives will lose them, and those who follow the Great Pastor, the King of Glory, according to their own terms, cannot be his disciples.

Ignoring these false teachings is not enough. You must loathe them. Their aim is to please man, not God. Many read books like those from the conference or the information you found on your friend's website, not the Bible, and either trust in their own perceived goodness, which is contrary to our fallen nature, or rely on their good works to earn salvation. Either leads one away from the path to the truth.

Stepping back to his car to get his water bottle, Good-Guide gave the Pilgrims a little time to reflect.

"What an emotional roller coaster. I was distraught, then encouraged, but with this summary I'm more anxious now than I was before! We may have crossed a line and can't go back now," Christian said to his family. "I'm ashamed and angry that I followed the lies of Pastors Ear-Tickler and Legality so readily, but I'm also frustrated that Good-Guide would set us on this difficult path, which he knows is too hard to follow."[92]

Looks-Good whispered to his sister, "I don't see what Dad's so worked up about. We've all lived good lives and I'm sure we'll get to this Starry City place just fine. I'll be glad when he quits stressing out and we can enjoy our vacation."

Good-Guide returned. Choking back tears, Self-Disciplined asked Good-Guide, "Are we beyond hope? We barely set out on this path and have already left it twice, without a second thought. At this rate, we'll never get to Narrow Gate, let alone anywhere beyond it. We all agreed with the decisions Dad made. Are our sins so great that we are beyond forgiveness and that is why we can't stay on the correct road?"

"You speak rightly that your sins are great. The truth is that they are greater than you realize. You have not only foolishly followed unwise paths that were forbidden to you, deciding that your ways were better, but in doing so you rejected what was good.[93] Even so, he at Narrow Gate will be pleased to welcome you.[94] He understands the path is hard and full of distractions. Do not be led astray again.

"Let me pray for you. 'Father, please give Christian and his family perseverance as they travel to Narrow Gate and beyond. Please keep their minds focused on you. Thank you for your grace in forgiving their mistakes thus far.'"

Christian turned on the navigation system and announced to his family, "We will not stop again or speak to anyone[95] until we reach Narrow Gate."

CHAPTER SIX

Narrow Gate

The navigation system led them to Narrow Gate, and, true to his word, Christian neither stopped nor veered from the route, though it was a long drive and there were several side roads to entice him.

Their destination was an ancient brick and stone building, not large, yet heralding a sense of gravity.

"Dad, I think we've seen this before on our vacation a few years ago," Joyful said, her face pensive. "It was at a distance, and I remember thinking that it looked foreboding and intimidating.[96] Now, being led here by Good-Guide,[97] it looks warm and inviting.[98] Isn't that weird? And look up there. Carved in the stone lintel, it says, 'Welcome to Narrow Gate. Knock and it will be opened for you.'[99] Interesting."

"I feel like we are not worthy to be admitted,[100] but on Good-Guide's counsel, we should knock. If we are allowed in, which I in no way deserve, I sense we will have reason to sing lasting praise," Christian shared with his family.

They all beat on the huge, imposing door at once, rattling its hinges. A muffled voice replied. "Who is there? How did you find me? What do you want?"

Christian responded in a timid, quavering voice. "My family is fleeing the pending destruction of Pleasantown, seeking Celestial City,[101] to live there in peace. Good-Guide told us we would be welcomed and find further guidance here. En route, we have made many mistakes and fall on your mercy."

The door swung open, and the inhabitant grabbed each shocked Pilgrim, all but throwing them into the building so that they ended up on the floor in the entry.

"After your vigorous knock, your timid voice surprised me. I hear even the most reluctant summons. You followed wise guidance. I welcome you here and hope you will feel like family.[102] My name is Good-Will. I apologize for my aggressive welcome. The Beelzebubs,[103] a street gang, roam this area to keep people from getting here, even to the point of killing some. I never know how close they are to my guests, so I cannot take any chances. But you are safe from them inside this building, on the grounds and beyond."[104]

Joyful's whole body shook as she spoke.[105] "That's terrifying! I'm so thankful we're here and safe. Dad, thank you for bringing us."

Christian held her as Good-Will continued. "Notice the open door opposite where we stand," directing their gaze to the fragile glass-paned patio door so different from the door through which they just entered. "It will be open to you always. In fact, no one can shut it."[106]

Christiana breathed a sigh of relief. "I sense that the troubles we have endured were worth it[107] to be here now."

With condemnation, Good-Will asked, "Why did you come alone? Where are your friends?"

"We did try to bring some," Looks-Good exclaimed, eager to show their new acquaintance the right things they had done. "Our best friends next door called the police to keep us from leaving, and then Mom and Dad talked to a couple of friends of theirs, Obstinate and Flexible. Obstinate called us foolish and left. Flexible joined us initially, but when we got stuck in traffic, he gave up and went home."

"You are responsible only for the ask, and in that you were faithful. Unfortunately, that is all too common," Good-Will resumed the tone of a loving father. "People like Flexible consider Celestial City's glory of so little value that they are unwilling to endure even minor inconveniences or challenges, which grieves me."

"We were also sad about Flexible, but, if I'm honest, my decisions were not much better. At the first offer of an easier path,[108] I led my family away from life and towards death," Christian regretted. "As we read the Bible, we realized we were on the wrong path, so I took us to the opposite extreme. We were about to visit my friend Pastor Legality to learn how to master works-based lives leading to the same end when Good-Guide intervened. Without God's mercy on us at that point, I doubt we would be here. Thank you for opening your door to us."

"My pleasure. All whom Good-Guide sends here are welcome. I turn no one away.[109]

"I expect you met Pastor Ear-Tickler first. The enemy of our Lord has used him to lead many astray. Ease and comfort offer all-too-common enticements to depart from the often-difficult route here.

"You would be like many if you believed your past actions and decisions would keep me from opening the door to you. I believe I heard that in your timid voice when you arrived. Let's take a walk in the back garden."

Strolling together through the manicured English garden at a relaxing pace, Good-Will continued. "You see the road there, past that house? That is the road you need to follow. Notice how straight and narrow it is here."

"What a relief given our often-twisted path to get here!" Christian responded. He bowed his head to avoid eye contact before asking sheepishly, "Is that the only path, or can I still choose a wrong one?"

"Oh, there are many side paths that might seem promising, some wide, some crooked, some that will appear better. The difficult and narrow path[110] is the only one that will lead you to the end set for you."

"Can you help us remove these burdens? The pain is excruciating and they keep getting heavier. We tried, but failed," begged Joyful.

Good-Will's fatherly voice encouraged them. "You must endure a while longer. When you leave here, you will stop to learn from Interpreter. He will help you understand Scripture and show you excellent things.[111] The walk to his house at the far end of the garden will refresh you. You need not hurry. Your packs will give you less discomfort here."

CHAPTER SEVEN

House of Visions

Rejuvenated after their stroll through the garden, the Pilgrims sauntered down the long, tree-lined gravel drive. Christian knocked several times on the mansion's imposing mahogany door. Though they could hear the effect of the large brass knocker echoing inside, no one answered. As they turned to leave, a voice slipped out of the intercom. "Good day. Who is knocking, and how may I help you?"

Christian answered, "We are a family of five from Pleasantown. Your neighbor, Good-Will, recommended we seek you. He said you would show us excellent things that would help us on our journey to Celestial City."

The tall, imposing door opened slowly. A diminutive older man welcomed them, wisdom personified. "Please come in. I am Interpreter. Please forgive my delay in answering the door. I was preparing my home for you.

"It is good for you to be here. Good-Will called and shared your story. What I show you will help you on your way, and I am happy to do so.[112] Pay close attention to everything that you observe and experience here." As he finished speaking, Interpreter turned on all the lights for them to see more clearly.[113]

He first led them into a side room, where he showed his guests the portrait of a man with a serious disposition, not scowling but painted to impress upon the viewer a sense of importance, dignity, and courage.

A world map behind him, his gold-crown-adorned head lifted, and his eyes looking towards Heaven, he held a Bible in his hand, with the word "truth" painted on his lips in many languages.

Self-Disciplined noted, "I get a weird sense from this portrait that the man is offering me something I need and want, but I don't know what it is—or how to ask for it."[114]

Joyful, with her artistic nature, was most enthralled. "The painting looks ancient, but the map is current. How can that be?"

"The one in the portrait is the exceptional man who can sire grown children,[115] struggle alongside them as they mature, and nurse them until they are ready for solid food.[116] He is looking to Heaven for direction, with the Bible in his hand and the law of truth written on his lips, to show that his work is to bring to light what is dark to the sinner.

"Notice that he has the world behind him with a crown over his head, standing as if pleading with men, as Self-Disciplined noted. This signifies his turning his back on the present age in his great love and devotion to his Father's service. The crown above his head foreshadows the glory and honor he will receive in the time to come. Most people miss the detail you caught, Joyful. The map is always current.[117] Though the subject in the portrait is from the Ancient of Days,[118] his love and devotion never fade.

"The reason I started here is to show you the only man who the King of Celestial City has commissioned to lead you, which he may do himself or through others. Take this to heart and encourage each other along the way, as you will meet some who will claim to lead you along the right path, but who, if you follow them, will lead you to destruction."[119]

From there, Interpreter led the family into a richly appointed but dusty sitting room; so dusty, in fact, that it seemed never to have been cleaned, in marked contrast to the room they just left. He called for a cleaning team, who began sweeping and feather dusting, which raised such a cloud of dust that the family could barely breathe. Addressing a gracious lady standing nearby, he asked her to bring a sprayer to mist the room. As she finished, the dust subsided, and the cleaners made it spotless straight away.

"How are we to understand this, Interpreter? As one who prided myself on keeping a tidy home, I'm curious if there is something I missed in my quest for cleanliness," Christiana inquired.

"The dust represents the original sin of Adam and the inward corruptions which have defiled the whole person. The living room represents the heart of the person whom the grace of the Gospel has never cleansed. The cleaning team who swept and stirred up the dust represents the law, whereas the gracious lady who sprinkled the room represents the Gospel.[120]

"You noticed that when the cleaners swept, it was worse than when they left the dust alone. The message is this: obeying the law will not clean the heart of sin, and adherence to the law alone has the opposite effect. It causes sin to grow in the soul.[121] While the law uncovers and condemns sin, it lacks the power to overcome and subdue it.

"Once the gracious lady sprinkled the room with water, the dust settled, and it was cleaned with ease. The Gospel conquers sin, washing the heart clean through the believer's faith, by the grace of Jesus alone, preparing a dwelling place suitable for the King of Glory to inhabit."[122]

Interpreter led the family into another elaborate room furnished with two comfortable chairs. A child was seated in each one. "Carpe Diem" was embroidered on the older child's shirt. He seemed discontent and anxious, while the younger child, "Contented"[123] embroidered on her dress, sat reading a book, calm and peaceful.

"Why is Carpe Diem so unsettled?" Joyful asked. "They both look like they have everything they need. I love children, and seeing one discontented makes me sad."

"The children's parents believe they should preserve the best they have for their children until a future time when the children can be prepared to enjoy their gifts to the fullest extent. Contented is satisfied in the waiting, but Carpe Diem wants everything now."

The parents entered the room and, yielding to his pleadings, gave Carpe Diem everything for which he asked, the treasures of his young heart.[124] It thrilled him to revel in his bounty, as he scornfully laughed at Contented for her lack of good things to enjoy. As the Pilgrims watched, he consumed all the treasures his parents had to give him. Contrary to the joy he clearly expected, he appeared less satisfied and more disgruntled.

"These children represent two kinds of people. Contented represents those willing to wait for a promised future. Carpe Diem represents those who 'seize the day' and live lives consumed with the here and now. He and those like him value what they can experience or consume today over the eternal treasures available to them in Celestial City. Worldly proverbs like, 'A bird in the hand is worth two in the bush,' carry more weight than the Bible's promises for the life to come."[125]

Looks-Good joined the discussion. "Got it. So Contented is smarter. She is willing to give up lesser things for greater things, and she seeks things of lasting value over those that are temporary. Lesson learned. Next?"

"You are partly correct, Looks-Good, but be patient," Interpreter acknowledged, his voice and demeanor betraying doubt in Looks-Good's motives. "To expand on your point, it is not just long-term or greater value that Contented seeks. She waits for what will be of infinite worth. While Carpe Diem laughed at his sister's lack, she found lasting satisfaction.[126]

"The Bible tells a story of a rich man who, like Carpe Diem, enjoyed good things in life, and contrasts this with a poor man named Lazarus, who patiently did without. But in the end, Lazarus was comforted while the rich man was tormented.[127]

"This does not imply that all who are rich are condemned, nor that all who are poor will be blessed. A rich person may fixate on what they have, and a poor person on what they want. In both cases, they elevate the material over the eternal."

"I remember hearing something about giving up what we cannot keep to gain what we cannot lose,"[128] Christiana replied.

"While not a perfect fit for this context, you are on the right track. What we see and touch and feel and consume are temporal; what our senses cannot perceive is eternal.[129] The challenge is that, while we may know this to be true, tangible things are so close to our 'natural' desires that they overshadow the future promises which then seem unable to satisfy our current wants or needs. The result is that too often we give in to satisfying our fleeting desires at the expense of what lasts forever."[130]

Moving to the living room, the party watched a man try to extinguish a fire in the massive fireplace. He tried fire extinguishers, water, sand, wet towels, and many other methods, but the fire blazed brighter and hotter with each attempt.

"The fire before you is the work of grace that has ignited in a person's soul," Interpreter explained to a sea of perplexed faces. "The one trying to extinguish it is the Devil. You notice that the more he tries to put it out, to remove what God has planted, the brighter it burns. But there is more happening that you cannot see from here."

Directed around the wall of the fireplace, they found a small room where wood was stored. Interpreter continued. "As is common with grand homes of this era, this space was built to be out of sight from the public side of the living room. Notice the man adding wood, coal, kerosene, and other flammables to the fire. He represents the Holy Spirit, who fosters and fuels the work started in the soul through the grace of God bought by Jesus through his death and resurrection.

"The Devil uses lies and temptation to try to undermine the spiritual growth of the follower of Jesus, but our Lord preserves the souls of his people.[131] You could not see the Holy Spirit working when you entered because it is often hard for one tempted to sense the work done on their behalf."[132]

The party left there and climbed a flight of stairs, where they stepped out onto a balcony overlooking a magnificent ballroom.

Joyful gasped, captivated by the look of the guests, all dressed in gold. "I feel like I've just stepped onto a movie set for a ballroom scene from a Jane Austen novel, only grander.

"Can we please go down there?" she asked, dancing and clapping her hands.

"Where else would we go, dear Joyful?" Interpreter smiled.

"Do you have a crowbar, Mr. Interpreter?" Self-Discipline rolled his eyes. "We will need one to get Joyful to leave this ball."

Joyful sneered at him as he moved out of her reach.

The ornate imperial staircase swept the small crowd to the doors of the ballroom, where a crowd waited to enter. No one approached the keeper of the lists, who checked names against a large book opened on the stand in front of him. Formidable armed guards protected the doors, ready and able to restrict entrance by force if necessary, as one would expect at an event for heads of state and other dignitaries.

While most people avoided eye contact with the guards and kept their distance, one man confidently walked up to the keeper of the lists and proffered his name. Before confirmation, this guest rushed towards the doors, taking the guards by surprise. He ultimately overpowered them—receiving a few painful blows in the process—and joined the guests at the ball.[133]

The Pilgrims watched those inside welcome the man with joy,[134] singing out to him, "Come in, come in! Enjoy the eternal glory you have won."

They brought him beautiful gold clothes, and soon he was lost in the crowded party.

Christian sought confirmation. "I think I get it, but please correct me. The man was seeking Heaven and the social secretary had to confirm that he was invited.[135] Right? But the guest didn't wait and rushed to the door in his excitement to be welcomed into eternity, convinced that his name was recorded because of his faith in Jesus for salvation. Still correct? However, even though Jesus's righteousness earned him access through his faith, he still had hardships to endure, represented by the battle with the guards. Yes?"

"All correct. Well summarized."

Looks-Good blurted out, "Wow. Thanks. We have learned a lot! We need to get going now, if you will please just show us the way."

"I still have more to show you," Interpreter replied with a look of disappointment mixed with sadness.

In contrast to the bright lights and finery of the ball, they descended a dingy stairwell used by servants. In a dank corner of the mansion's basement, Interpreter showed them a room. The padlocked door constructed of rusty iron bars and the scalloped shelves on the walls looked like a wine cellar converted long ago into a prison cell. In the darkness sat a man. When Christiana and Joyful saw him, they were moved to tears. He sat, head down, eyes on the ground, hands clenched, a picture of hopelessness and dejection.

"Why are you showing us this man?" Christiana asked. "What are we supposed to learn here?"

"Ask him."

"I'm sorry to see you look so forlorn. Why are you here?" she asked in the tone of a woman mourning the loss of a friend.

"I wasn't always like this," he responded, looking at them for the first time. "At one time I was handsome and had everything going for me. I went to church almost every Sunday and sometimes other days as well, enjoyed praying, and even did my best to share the Gospel with others.[136] My wholesome life and personality drew people to me. At that point, I was confident I would live out eternity in Celestial City. I could not have imagined I would end up in a place like this."

"What did you do?" Looks-Good accused him.

"How did I end up trapped in this cell without hope? My new 'faith' was just excitement for something different with new friends to enjoy. I neither confessed with my mouth nor believed in my heart who the Lord is,[137] and did not seek the Author of the Book I didn't read. My desires for the things of the world overtook my desires for God, and in this, I sinned against his goodness. I traded my no-longer-new friends for a completely different group. Because I had never given my life to Jesus, I blasphemed the Holy Spirit by attributing his works to Satan[138] so that I could remain winsome to my new friends. My heart is now hardened beyond repentance."

Christian turned aside to ask the Interpreter if there would be any hope in a case like this. The interpreter addressed the question to the man in the cell.

"Do you have any hope at all that someone will release you one day?"

"None at all."

"But our God is always ready to forgive the one who turns and repents, offering hope to all,"[139] Christiana pleaded.

"But I have crucified him again in turning away after once having chased after him,[140] and I have despised his righteousness.[141] I have disregarded the blood he shed for me, and insulted the grace of the Holy

Spirit.[142] In doing so, I have become an enemy of God, shutting myself off to his promises. Even though I'm distraught, I have no desire to change."

This confused Self-Disciplined, compelling him to ask, "If you started down your path with great joy, or so it sounds, what could have drawn you away that you ended up like this?"

"I was jealous of all the things that my old friends did that were forbidden to me, and didn't want to miss out. I sought the delights and pleasures that I could enjoy in this world to the extent that I rejected the joys and pleasures God offered me, both in this world and in the one to come. Now, the memory of them only brings me more misery. My heart is hard now—stone cold. I don't want that old life, but I don't want God either."

At that, Interpreter led the family away with a warning to them all. "Let this man's misery be a constant reminder to you. Remember where he started, where he is now, and how he arrived there."

"Dad, I think we should pray," Self-Disciplined announced. "Lord, please help us as we continue along the way you have set out for us.[143] Please stay close to us."

Looks-Good, however, seemed lost in thought and showed no evidence of hearing that prayer.

"I have one more thing to show you before you continue on your way."

This time they ascended the grand staircase up two flights of stairs to the floor housing the family bedrooms. They turned into the first room and observed a man rising out of bed, shaking as he dressed, prompting Joyful to ask Interpreter what disturbed him.

"Ask him."

"Sir, may I ask why you are shaking?"

I had a most disturbing dream.

The midday sky turned black, followed by a terrible storm full of terrifying lightning and deafening thunder. The clouds rushed through the sky, and then I heard the blaring sound of a trumpet. A man in radiant white clothing was sitting on a gleaming white cloud, attended by thousands from Heaven arrayed in flaming fire. The whole of the sky became a burning flame. He issued a bold command to all the earth: 'Arise, you dead, and come to judgment.' Graves opened, boulders crumbled, and the dead came forward. Some expressed joy, looking upward in anticipation, while others tried to hide under the mountains.[144] Then I saw the man on the cloud open a book and call all the world before him. They did not come too close because of a great flame which shot out from him, creating a space like a courtroom between the judge and the accused.[145] The man seated on the cloud then commanded his attendants, 'Gather those who have rejected me, and cast them into the burning lake.'[146]

I was almost overwhelmed by the sulfurous smoke, the heat from the burning coals and molten earth, plus the cacophony of hideous sounds from below, worsened by the pitiful cries of the masses brought forth to be thrown into the lake.

The man then commanded those attending him to gather his faithful followers, which they did and carried them away.[147]

I, however, was neither gathered into the clouds nor cast into the lake of fire, so I tried to hide. But the man on the cloud kept his eye on me. My sins flooded my mind, so that my conscience accused me.[148] Then I woke up, trembling as you found me.

Christiana, always the loving mother, asked, "What most frightened you in your dream?"

"I thought that the day of judgment had come and I was not ready for it. But what jarred me most was that I was left, with the mouth of the pit of Hell opened right before me, my conscience afflicted, believing the Judge disapproved of me."

"The Bible promises relief to the repentant sinner," Self-Disciplined reminded him.

"Of course! I believed the lie that my savior would condemn me after I had placed my faith in him because I could not forgive myself! Thank you for that encouraging truth and the certain hope it offers!"

Relieved, Interpreter moved them to a comfortable ground-floor sitting room surrounded by large windows overlooking the manicured estate. A servant brought them iced tea and cold lemonade.

"Remember all you have seen here. If you do, it will help keep you on the correct road. Though you will not see me, I will be with you for the remainder of your journey to comfort you and lead you to Celestial City through Good-Guide.[149] You may sense me more than hear me, though I will share warnings and reminders.[150] Read your Bible, as that is how I will most often provide guidance and direction.[151] Discuss what you have seen and heard with each other.

"When you are ready, your vehicle is parked outside, filled with gas and loaded with snacks and drinks. You cannot miss the initial path forward. One last warning before you leave. You will come to a hill where you will undoubtedly stop. When you leave there, though likely euphoric, do not stop. Beyond the hill, a ravenous beast prowls."

"Thank you, Interpreter, for what you have taught us, for provision, and especially for your promise of continued support and protection for our onward journey."

On the short walk to the SUV, Christian spoke to his family. "We have seen things here that I cannot imagine seeing anywhere else—things that are strange, and yet I believe Interpreter when he told us they will be beneficial for our journey. We need to follow his advice and remind each other of these things, as I assume the journey ahead of us will be full of challenges. Let's get moving."

CHAPTER EIGHT

Relief

The road narrowed, with high walls on either side, the word "Salvation" painted at regular intervals in large, easy-to-read letters.[152] There were no opportunities to choose a wrong road.

They came to a small but steep hill with a cross at the top and an open grave at the bottom. This was the only place they had seen since leaving Interpreter's where there was a place to pull off the road and park.

"Honey, while we were at Interpreter's, my backpack was almost weightless. It felt so light that I had forgotten it was still there. However, with time to reflect on our life, I'm now even more burdened as I remember my personal and our collective failings," Christiana shared. Christian, Joyful and Self-Disciplined shared similar sentiments.

Opening the door, she continued, "I need help to get out. My pack is so full and heavy I cannot get out on my own."

Self-disciplined, struggling under the weight of his own backpack, helped his mother out of The Chariot.

Looks-Good did not even attempt to leave. "Aren't you coming? Are you not drawn to that cross at the top of the hill? I sense that there is something about this place that will lessen the increasing weight of my sins," Joyful pleaded with her brother.

"My burden is not heavy,[153] and I am not drawn as you seem to be. I'm also feeling a little carsick, so I'll just wait here for you to come back."

"Interesting. Your pack is as full as any of ours. Are you sure?" his brother asked.

"Really, I'm good. I'll probably just take a little nap or check my e-mail."

Another car pulled in and parked. An enormous smile on his face, Christian lumbered as fast as he could under the weight of his pack to open the door for Civility, struggling under his own weighty burdens.

"I am so excited to see you here!" Christian cried out. Christiana, Joyful, and Self-Disciplined also expressed their excitement as they struggled to stand under the weight of their bags.

"Thank you! Christian, God chose you to be the agent who started me on the path to salvation. The Holy Spirit drew me to read the Bible you left me. Through Scripture, he revealed to me how many people I had encouraged in sin, which weighed me down to the point I considered taking my own life. As I was gathering the means to do so, I opened the Bible to confirm that I was right to remove myself from the Holy One's presence because of the sin I had encouraged in others,[154] which I thought had to be unforgivable. To my complete surprise, what I found was that he not only did not want me removed, but he wanted me restored![155] I just left Interpreter's. It seemed like I must be years behind you, yet here we are together."

The party trudged to the top of the hill with great difficulty, helping each other and stopping often to rest. As they reached the foot of the cross, their backpacks were so full with the weight of their sins that they almost toppled over backwards. Kneeling, they each prayed.

"Jesus, I do not deserve your forgiveness, but you promise it to all who ask. My burden is intolerable. So I ask you, please forgive me for my sins. Holy Spirit, please change my heart to turn from my sinful desires and run to Jesus when I am tempted."

Before they realized what was happening, the straps on each sin-filled bag snapped. The packs rolled down the hill into the open grave.

None of them saw their pack again.

Rejoicing, Self-Disciplined captured the moment perfectly. "Thank you, Jesus, our High Priest! You have taken away our sins."[156]

They sat at the foot of the cross, still surprised at the immediacy of their lightness. Through eyes blurred by the tears continually welling up,[157] they sat admiring the cross and praising him who died on it.

Suddenly, three shining beings appeared. The Pilgrims and Civility trembled and Christiana almost fainted. With frightening voices, the heavenly host said in unison: "Do not be afraid. Peace be with you."

After which the first said with authority, "Your sins are forgiven."[158]

The second replaced their tattered and dirty outfits, which they had worn since their journey started, with clean, radiant, stunning attire.[159]

The third gave each of them a sealed envelope.[160] "Do not lose this. Each of you will be required to present it at the gate of Celestial City."

"I'm a new man, with new joy and peace I did not know existed," Christian beamed.

Civility added, "Thank you, Christian, for being obedient to God's call to challenge me to find the truth in Scripture. I feel the urge to get going and look forward to seeing you in Celestial City."

* * *

As she entered the SUV, Joyful asked her brother if he was feeling better.

"I'm okay. I ended up just sleeping most of the time. Thank you for asking. I just never felt the sense of burden the rest of you did."[161]

Joyful continued, "I'm really sorry you didn't join us. That was the most incredible experience. Jesus took away my sins forever and I feel more alive now than ever before!"

CHAPTER NINE

Rebuffed

They had not traveled far when Christiana pointed out three men asleep in the grass on the side of the road, chained together at the ankles like prisoners on a work crew. Christian announced to his family, "I am compelled to stop and try to help those men. Because of all we have been through, I want everyone to know the joy I feel! Civility must not have seen them, or I'm sure he would have stopped."

Christian exited the SUV and woke the men. "Good afternoon! Who are you three?"

"We are three friends whose personalities complement each other. I am Oblivious. This is my friend Lazy, and our friend Presumption."

"Friends, this place is not as safe as it looks. There is a ravenous beast that prowls these parts, looking for prey to devour.[162] If you do not get up and move forward, you are easy targets. I have some tools and can help you remove those chains."

Oblivious replied first, "We've been asleep for a while and are clearly fine. We don't share your sense of danger. Thank you, though."

Lazy added, "We might move on after a bit more sleep, maybe not. I'm not sure why you would even have such silly worries. If there were danger, someone would have told us."

Presumption ended the conversation, "'If something is to be done well, one does it oneself'[163] is what I always say."

With that, they all lay down to resume their slumber.[164] Shaking his head in disbelief, Christian got back into the car.

"Dad, are these guys crazy? Did you tell them they risk becoming beast snacks? How can they be oblivious to the danger pursuing them?"

"Self-Disciplined, son, I tried. I'm perplexed. If some stranger warned me of danger in an unknown land and offered aid, I would take it. What surprised me most was their tone when they rejected my offer of help, like I was the crazy one! I don't know what else to do for them. If they don't want sound advice, I can't make them take it, so let's go," Christian answered.

* * *

Christian had driven only a few miles when he spied a couple drop down into the street, having climbed over the wall. As they approached, he spoke to them through his open window.

"Hello, fellow travelers! Tell me a little about yourselves and your journey."

"I'm Tradition, and this is my partner, Hypocrisy. We are from Self City and are going to Celestial City to receive the praise due to us in honor of our upstanding lives."

Looks-Good interrupted from the back seat, "Why did you climb over the wall? We were told that the people who don't come through the gate to get to the road are robbers or thieves."[165]

"Are you serious? Do we look like robbers or thieves? The gate is too far in the opposite direction. Our town is much closer to this spot. It doesn't make any sense to waste time just to go through the gate, thereby doubling the distance we would need to cover. People from home have climbed over at this point for as long as anyone can remember. It's part of our tradition, even documented in our town statutes as an acceptable practice.[166] Here we are, all on the same road to the same place. Does it matter how we get here? Looks to me like we're all equal," Tradition argued.

"We walk in obedience to the laws of the loving protector, the Lord of Celestial City, and follow the Bible's instructions to guide us. It sounds like you rely on your wisdom or that of your town's elders, that you discount the guidance that the protector set out in his Word.[167] I worry the gatekeepers will not admit you when you get to the city," Christian challenged in a no-nonsense yet loving tone.

"We are good, law-abiding citizens," Hypocrisy jumped in. "You follow the laws you believe are true. We follow the laws we believe are true. We aren't really different. What is most important is that you believe something is true and obey that truth."

"If following the law alone will not save you,[168] following your own view of what is true will certainly not! You have broken the law and are trespassing because you entered without the gatekeeper's permission," Christian countered.

Hypocrisy abruptly changed topics. "Where did you get those beautiful clothes? I have never seen anything like them. Did you get them near here somewhere? Would I be correct to guess that you had other clothes that would have shamed you where you are headed, maybe a little too racy for you 'good people'?"

"Agents of the Lord of Celestial City gave us this clothing as a token of his kindness, replacing outfits that had become worn out and dirty. These are not just comfortable but comforting. He gave them to us freely and we hope they will further identify us as those whom he has chosen through no merit of our own. His messengers also gave us sealed documents to present at the gate of the city to vouch for our identity. Not coming in through the gate, I'm concerned you will not have these necessary items," Christiana said.

With his arms crossed and a look of pity on his face, Hypocrisy shook his head as he turned his back on the Pilgrims. As he walked away, he mocked them over his shoulder, "You do you. We will be just fine and catch a ride with someone a bit more open-minded. See you there."

With that abrupt end to the conversation, Hypocrisy and Tradition stormed off.

CHAPTER TEN

Three Choices

After several hours on the road, Christian pulled into a parking lot to get out and stretch. Everyone piled out to fill their water bottles from a beautiful fountain flowing with clear, cold water,[169] centered in a lush, green, well-maintained lawn.

As they pulled out to continue their journey, they came to a sign which read: "Difficult hill ahead." The road soon split into three, the middle one steep yet straight, narrow, and unpaved, without guardrails.

"Honey, let's remember the instruction to continue on the difficult and narrow road this time," Christiana said to her husband through a sheepish grin. That is the path the family took. The Chariot struggled up the hill.

Looking in the rear-view mirror, Christian commented, "I see our recent acquaintances and their new friends weighing their options at the split. Tradition and Hypocrisy seem to have caught rides with a pair of motorcyclists. I wish we were back there to help guide them, though I imagine none of them would listen."

"You take the left, I'll take the right," one biker said to the other. "These roads all have to lead to Celestial City. It doesn't matter which one we take. Plus, these roads are paved and smooth, whereas the middle one is unpaved, which would be hard on our bikes. We will see who gets there first and compare our adventures when we meet up again."

"Plus, we don't want to follow that fanatic Christian," Tradition added with a grimace. "That looks like his car on the middle route. We can be sure he is on the wrong path."[170]

None of them could see the road signs that had fallen into the bushes. From above, one could see that the left road was named "Danger" and the one on the right "Destruction."

The pair that took "Danger" ended up lost in the woods and never made it to Celestial City. The pair who took "Destruction" enjoyed a pleasant ride until the driver missed a sharp turn, careened over a cliff and into a ravine, both of them dying slowly and painfully from their wounds, unable to help each other.

For the Pilgrims, the road forward was difficult. As the SUV edged up the steep hill on the dirt road, there were times it moved backwards, its wheels spinning. Inching forward, The Chariot's engine overheated under the strain.

"I need to pull over to give the engine time to cool," Christian groaned. "Not far ahead is a grove of trees where it looks like some kind soul has put some benches. Maybe we aren't the first people in this predicament!"

The Pilgrims got out and settled onto the comfortable benches, each with a plaque on it which read: "A Gift from the Caretakers." After reading their Bibles, one by one each fell asleep, their books falling out of their hands.

It was late in the day when they all awoke abruptly and bolted to the SUV. Back underway, Joyful shared, "I just had a strange dream. In it I heard this voice from Heaven say, 'Learn from the ant, you slacker! Observe its ways and become wise.'[171] Did anyone else have the same dream?"

"The way we all woke up at exactly the same time and ran to The Chariot together, I have to assume so," Looks-Good snarked.

Self-Disciplined quipped, "Reminds me of a saying by Will Rogers, 'Even if you are on the right track, you'll still get run over if you just sit there.'[172] Looks like none of us wants to meet that train."

At the top of the hill, they met two people in a car coming from the other direction. Both vehicles rolled down their windows.

"Hi. We're the Pilgrims. Where are you two going? It looks to me like you are heading backwards," asked Joyful.

"Hello. I'm Fearful, and this is my wife, Doubtful. We were going to Celestial City, as I assume you are, but the further we went, the more danger we encountered, so we are going back home where it's safe."

Doubtful jumped in before Fearful finished speaking. "Just down the way some big, rough-looking troublemakers were milling around, blocking the lane to the only place to stay we've seen in a while. It felt like an ambush! Fortunately, we were able to back up and escape. I recommend you avoid that place!"

"As frightening as that sounds," Christiana responded, "we can't go back. Our home city will be destroyed. In Celestial City, we will find eternal safety. While we do fear death moving forward, we have a promise at the end. If we go back, we face certain death. On the map, it looks like we have to go down that lane to stay on the narrow path. We will face what lies ahead and trust God to carry us through."

"Good luck. You'll need it!"[173]

Parting ways, Christian continued forward while Fearful and Doubtful sped away in the opposite direction. Looks-Good, white with fear in the back row of the SUV, cried out, "I'm not sure I'm up for much more trauma. What if the group on the lane is more of those Beelzebubs Interpreter warned us about? Maybe we should go back and at least see if there might be an alternate route."

Self-Disciplined tried to encourage them. "Dad, Looks-Good, the best way for us to steady ourselves for the road ahead would be spending time in the Scriptures. We can take turns reading. I'll start with Psalm 9. Wait, where's my Bible? And my envelope?"

"I can't find mine either!" Joyful panicked.

They all looked frantically for their Bibles and documents.

"Looks like great minds think alike. I put my envelope with my Bible, knowing that would be the place I would least likely lose it, but when we jumped up and ran back to the SUV in such a panic after our dreams we must have left our Bibles near those benches back there."

The road was wider where they were, so Christian could turn around. Going downhill gave The Chariot's engine time to cool down. They found their Bibles and envelopes right where they had been just before darkness settled in. They sat together closely on one of the benches.

"I keep failing you all when I'm supposed to be leading you. I'm ashamed of my fear and lack of faith, my foolishness for falling asleep when I wasn't even tired, and allowing the journey to become more of my focus than the destination,"[174] Christian cried.

"I think God is changing Dad," Joyful whispered to Self-Disciplined through her own tears. "I've never seen him cry before. He never showed any emotion, which had to be hard on Mom."

"Dad, we've lost this day, between napping and back-tracking," Looks-Good said matter-of-factly. "Why don't we just lay back down on these benches and spend the night? They are comfortable, which is why we all fell asleep in the first place. We have blankets and sleeping bags in the SUV."

"No, we need to make up for lost time now and find a suitable place to stop. We have to overcome the fear of the warnings given to us by Fearful and Doubtful with faith. That we have to travel on in the dark is our own fault, brought on by our sinful sleep."[175]

They took turns reading to each other from the Bible to stay awake and encourage each other until they turned at a sign advertising Lodge Beautiful.

Lodge Beautiful

The SUV squeezed between the window-height walls on either side of the lane, only inches separating the stones from the doors. When they finally arrived at the gatehouse, the invitation of the beautiful lodge in the near distance was contrasted by a menacing group of hoodlums milling around in the immediate foreground.

Sweat on his forehead, Looks-Good gulped, "Now I'm awake! That must be the gang Fearful and Doubtful mentioned. Maybe they were right and we should have listened."

Christian lowered his window as little as possible to communicate with the guard.

"I am Watchful. I see the crowd frightens you. Is your faith so small?[176] You are where you need to be.[177] The ruffians near the lodge test the faith of those who desire to stay here, and drive away those who lack it. They work for us. Those whose hearts the Lord of Celestial City is refining need not fear. Continue through the covered passage into the courtyard and check in at reception."

Before they got out of the SUV, Self-Disciplined shared, "We have come through some scary stuff unscathed, and I believe what we have read is true, but I can't seem to shake this fear of what might be ahead."

The clerk at the reception desk offered them a warm welcome and shared some history. "This Lodge was built for the comfort and rest of those invited to Celestial City. Those who don't keep that goal in their hearts and trust in the Loving Protector of the realm to carry them there do not make it this far, or make it here but are too afraid to approach the guardhouse because of the gang out front,[178] or speed straight through without a second glance. How is it you arrive at this late hour?"

"My foolishness," Christian replied, hanging his head. "We fell asleep in the rest area on the other side of the hill, and when I awoke I was in such a hurry to get my family back underway that we left our Bibles and the envelopes given to us to present in Celestial City. It wasn't until we heard unsettling news about that gang you have out front that we turned to Scripture for comfort, only to realize we had left our Bibles in the rest area. We had to backtrack, which cost us a fair amount of time."

"You are welcome here. There is no fee for lodging or meals or anything else, and you may remain until you are refreshed and ready to continue. Our guests are family.[179] The proprietor asks us to interview each guest. Given the lateness of your arrival, we will interview all of you together."

He led them into the comfortable lounge and served them drinks and snacks. They were joined by a woman who brought a comforting presence, wearing a pleasant demeanor and a professional business suit.

"I am Discretion, and I will be your concierge. I pray each of you is comfortable. This interview is not an interrogation, but a means for us to know you better, to learn how we can serve you. Please allow me to introduce my colleagues Prudence, Piety, and Charity.

"Ladies, please sit among our new family members."

After individual introductions and small talk, Piety began. "You may speak freely here. Mr. Pilgrim, please share with us how it is you arrived here. What first motivated you to undertake this venture?"

"I heard in a dream that our city would be destroyed. On our way out of town, I stopped because I did not know where to go. God sent Good-Guide, who directed us to Narrow Gate. He gave us specific directions and implored us to trust the guidance we would receive there for onward direction. At Narrow Gate, Good-Will showed us many things. Three were most memorable to me.

"First, a fire in a fireplace representing the Holy Spirit feeding the work of grace in our hearts, overcoming the Devil's attempts to destroy it. Second, there was a man who had separated himself from the hope of God by trusting in his own sin—and holding on to it! And third was a man who recounted his dream about the day of judgment."

"Was there nothing else memorable?" she continued.

"He also showed us a magnificent palace with people in spectacular clothing," continued Joyful. "We watched a man wait in line, only to physically fight the guards to gain entrance and join the opulent ball. Though he entered by force, once in, the other guests gave him a royal welcome, as they exchanged his bloodied clothes for regal finery. Captivated by the finery and grandeur, my parents had to drag me away."

"After you left, did you experience anything else?"

Christiana joined in. "We climbed up a hill and looked up at a cross, and now in recollection I remember a man on that cross, bleeding. When we fell down on our knees at the base of the cross, the crushing burdens we had been carrying, which we had been unable to remove or lighten, fell off on their own and disappeared into an open grave. Three shining beings appeared out of nowhere, and the one on the cross became brighter than the sun.[180] One of the shining ones reminded us that Jesus has forgiven us our sins while another replaced our worn and dirty outfits with these beautiful clothes, and the third gave us each a sealed envelope." Each of them showed their envelope, except Looks-Good, who awkwardly turned aside to avoid eye contact.

"Is that all?" Piety made her final request.

"Those had the greatest impact, but there was more," Self-Disciplined shared. "Three men were shackled together asleep beside the road. Dad tried to wake them and warn them, but they wouldn't have it. Then a couple climbed over the wall onto the road. From the way they talked, theirs were lives of shortcuts. They each took a different road and we have not seen them since. Then, near here, we met two who were heading in the opposite direction because they were afraid that the gang guarding the entrance indicated more frightful challenges to come, and decided it was better to go back. Were it not for Watchful's encouragement at the guardhouse, we might have turned back also, but here we are, and thankful to be here."

"Thank you for that summary. We have a few more questions," Prudence began. "Looks-Good, do you ever miss home?"

"Yes, especially when I'm tired or we face something frightening. Life was much easier at home."

"And of the rest of you?"

Christiana answered, looking at Looks-Good rather than at Prudence, "I do, sometimes, but only with great sadness and tinged with shame for wanting what was comfortable over that which I now know to be eternal."[181]

"Christian, do you also long for those comforts you once enjoyed and wish you could return to them?" Prudence continued.

"Yes, but I don't want to.[182] When my thoughts are clear and I've been meditating on God's Word, I am sad when I reflect on them—sad that I found them so satisfying. I want to do what is right, but keep doing what is not."[183]

"Do you find times when it's easy to do what is right? If so, how do those times differ from when you struggle?"

"Absolutely! Those are the best times in my life. They come when I remember the cross, and look at the new clothing the shining ones gave me to signify my new life, or when I touch or remember the sealed envelope they gave me to secure entrance to our ultimate destination."[184]

"Christian, why does your family want to go to Celestial City?"

"When we started out, it was only to escape doom and destruction. We were simply running away from Pleasantown. But after the hill where our burdens fell, and the vision of our Savior on the cross bleeding to wash away our sins, we now seek Celestial City to live with him forever whom we glimpsed in his radiance on the hill, never again to be in fear or sadness.[185] At least we want our motives to be pure. The Holy One offers us the opportunity to be in his presence always, singing praises to him for all eternity. What can compare with that? I realize now that he removed my burden at greater cost to himself than to me, for which I will be eternally grateful."

Charity now joined in the interview. "None of you had close friends you could have brought with you?"

Joyful responded in an uncharacteristically sad tone. "We tried. Our next-door neighbors were very close to us and we shared our concerns about the imminent destruction of our city. But they thought we were crazy and even called the police to keep us from leaving."[186]

"Did the way you lived your lives encourage them to listen to you?"

This gave the whole family pause as tears filled their eyes. Christian accepted his responsibility. "I did not lead my family according to the standards set by Scripture. I modeled the life my family followed. We were 'good people,' doing 'right things', but lived for the praise of men, not to please God."[187]

Discretion ended their interview. "Thank you for your honesty and transparency. These two men will now show you to your rooms, where they have already deposited your luggage."

In their rooms, each laid on their bed fully clothed and fell asleep.

* * *

The following morning each awoke rested, well before dawn, followed by a bountiful breakfast, with fresh fruits, breads and pastries still warm from the oven, fresh-squeezed juices, rich coffee, and several tea choices. Each person had a favorite breakfast food available. Their hosts from the previous evening joined them to share information about the man who built the lodge.

"Wow. He sounds like a great military leader, a brave warrior. In the battle with terrorists who sought only destruction and death, you make him sound like a real hero. Terrorists and thugs have always scared me, but his example gives me great hope of conquering such a foe. Bring them on!" Self-Disciplined summarized before continuing.

"Now that you have told us the man in these stories and the one on the cross are the same, it all fits together. In our brief interaction on the hill, we experienced his willing self-sacrifice full of power and love, and for people unworthy of such on their own merits. I can only imagine how amazing it must have been for you three to get to sit with him and talk with him across this very table, and to hear his stories of elevating to royalty those whom the world considered worthless or useless, whom most people, including us all too recently, cast off as wastes of time.[188] His love for the great and the least is amazing."

After breakfast, they returned to the Peace Suite, which had at its center a beautiful, inviting sitting area, with large windows looking out on the rising sun. Comfortably seated in sofas and chairs with the bright morning light streaming through the glass, they each shared how close they felt they must be to their ultimate destination, which promised incomparable protection and peace.[189] They spent the rest of the morning reading, resting, and reflecting on their travels. In all of their discussion, no one addressed the bag Looks-Good still carried, and he did not complain about it.

CHAPTER TWELVE

Museum at Lodge Beautiful

Good-Guide joined them for a sumptuous lunch, then guided them on a tour of the museum complex behind the lodge. He first ushered them into a walnut-paneled reading room holding scrolls and manuscripts, ancient to modern, and began his guided tour.

Let's begin our tour at the beginning, with this book. It records the ancestry of the one who built the lodge. His legacy contains both earthly and heavenly components. You will find in this book that he is the Son of the Ancient of Days, but with no birth date associated with that sonship. He was born to a woman, but has always been.[190] You can read about his eventful but brief public life, which lasted only about three and a half years before his death in his early thirties. The book documents those he enlisted to join him as well.

Over here is a series of books from ages past to the present that chronicles what people willingly and even joyfully endured in service to this man. Before long, we will need to add new bookshelves for new books as they are added. There are stories of battles won against insurmountable odds, people who miraculously survived great torture, men and women who administered righteous justice, and others ranging from simple and commonplace to extraordinary.[191] Some of the protagonists initially hated the builder and even persecuted those who loved and served him, yet he joyfully welcomed them after they sincerely sought his forgiveness for these and other sins and expressed a desire to live a new life serving him.[192]

We have a section for history books and next to it are pro-phetic books regarding things to come. Something you will find interesting, but not surprising once you stop to consider it, is that the caretakers move books between these sections. When a prophecy is fulfilled, the book is moved to the history section. Some events described in the books about the future would terrify one who is not confident in the protection of him who is capable of conquering all.[193]

Last, but of preeminent importance, is this book, writ-ten before time began. The title is bold and clear, The Lamb's Book of Life.[194] Notice the lock on it.[195] This is the only resource unavailable to you, or anyone, until the end of time.[196]

"Thank you! We are all bookworms and thrilled for unrestricted access to the books available to us. This is like a dream come true," Joyful spoke for them all.

They delighted in their day spent in the library, bouncing from book to book, scroll to scroll, eagerly sharing what they found, with only a short break for dinner.

Though they had tasted only a minuscule portion of the rich mental nourishment offered, Good-Guide interrupted them. "I know you are not tired,[197] but it is time for each of you to enjoy the rest for which this lodge is renowned and for which it was created."

* * *

After another refreshing sleep and an exceptional breakfast—worth getting out of bed early to enjoy—one of the hotel staff led them to a great military storehouse.

Self-Disciplined broke the silence that came with the awe they experienced. "Dad, this must be the largest armor museum in the world. All the others we have visited contained ancient, battle-worn gear, with chunks out of the swords and shields. I remember you telling me how the evolution in military technology rendered it all obsolete. But this place feels like a staging ground, not a museum. All of this equipment is new and sharp, like someone has prepared it for a coming battle."[198]

Michael[199] replied, his presence startling them. "Good morning, and welcome to my rooms. You are adept in your assessment, Self-Disciplined. The day will come when this armory will be emptied for a great and final war, vastly different from the first war to end all wars.[200] Based on your astute observation, you also likely recognized that some of the armament is amassed by weapon type, but there are also individual groupings. These latter sets are custom sized to the person who will use them, and include protection for one's torso, once called a breastplate, a helmet, footwear, and a belt. A sword and shield complete the ensemble. These are for individual battles,[201] not the great war to come."

From there, he guided them to a separate building housing an outstanding collection of antiquities that they had read about in their Bibles. Moses's staff[202] was there, as were the hammer and tent stake which Jael used to kill Sisera,[203] and the fleece that Gideon used to validate God's instruction.[204] In a glass case was the ox goad[205] Shamgar used to destroy six-hundred warriors,[206] and next to it was the sling and the stone that David used to slay the giant Goliath.[207] They saw the donkey's jawbone stained with blood that Samson used to kill a thousand of God's enemies.[208] To see everything in the museum would take them days.

"Everyone, come over here!" Looks-Good blurted. "Everything else in this building looks old and beat up, but this looks brand new. Someone must have misplaced it. It should be in the armory."

In front of him was an ancient weapon, yet pristine and razor sharp. The plaque below it read, "The sword of the one who is faithful and true. For the final battle."[209]

As the family continued their study, Self-Disciplined's grumbling belly broke the silence. "Anyone else notice it's dark outside? I just did! Incredible! It feels like we just started. Breakfast was so filling it has carried me for the entire day. We could stay here for a week and not see everything. But now, my stomach tells me it is time to eat, and is rather adamant about it."

Supper lasted hours, punctuated by excited discussion recounting what each had seen that day, after which they retired for another evening of peaceful rest.

* * *

Charity came to their table as they relaxed over coffee, tea, and hot chocolate after breakfast.

"Have we seen everything?" Looks-Good asked in an impatient tone with a bored look on his face, drawing the ire of his family.

"Almost. I have one more thing I must show you. Please, follow me to the roof-top patio."

From their vantage point, one could see miles through the crisp, clean air. "Do you see the mountains over there,[210] those in the distance? They are the Delightful Mountains, which are close to Celestial City.

"Take note of the beautiful land around those mountains: forests, vineyards, rich farmland with all kinds of flavorful fruits and vegetables ready to enjoy. The springs are clear and cool. They source streams of pure water which require no filtration or purification. That is Immanuel's Country. All travelers to Celestial City pass through there. The farmers and ranchers who steward that land will care for you, and from there you can see the city."

"Let's go! That looks refreshing," Joyful almost shouted in her excitement. "I'm going to go pack."

Prudence stopped her and spoke to them all. "You are not ready yet. Remember the individual gear in the storehouse? You were likely so overwhelmed that I doubt you noticed, but each of you has a set crafted uniquely for you, made before time began.[211] The journey from here to Celestial City involves a battle that you must each be prepared to fight. You will meet enemies along the way who will hate you as they do everyone seeking the city, because of their hatred for the Lord of the city himself.

"Once you have been trained, you will each change out of your beautiful garments and put on your armor.[212] You arrived as tired guests, and will leave as warriors. Immanuel's country will welcome you soon enough."

They spent that morning in basic training, mastering these unfamiliar weapons in short order. They broke for lunch and then continued their training until a late supper, after which they went to bed, exhausted.

This schedule lasted six days, followed by a day of rest.

The day of their departure, Watchful met them.

"Have any other travelers passed through here recently, or are we on our own?" Christian asked him.

"Earlier today another young couple was here, Faithful and Dependable. They were more fully prepared for their onward journey and didn't need as much time to prepare, though I'm still surprised you didn't see them. They are not far ahead of you."

"Honey, that must be the young couple from church. They were newly-weds when we knew of them. I remember we envied their confidence and trust, though they were so much younger than us. Now I realize they had gifts we did not because we were only at church seeking glory for ourselves in the eyes of our neighbors," Christiana responded. "I hope we catch up with them."

Watchful left them with parting words of advice. "Your destination is safe, but the route is not. You must remain alert. The Lord of Celestial City has many ways to aid and protect those who serve him. Do not fear."[213]

They changed into their armor as staff members from the lodge filled The Chariot with gas and provisions. After lengthy goodbyes with many tears, they continued their journey. The road leading away from the lodge was far worse than the narrow lane entering it. Christian's knuckles were white as he navigated the treacherous road with steep ravines on either side. They had entered the Valley of Humiliation.

CHAPTER THIRTEEN

Battle in the Valley

Traversing the Valley of Humiliation, the SUV broke down—again. Almost immediately, a gang exploded out of the woods, shouting threats and brandishing weapons. With nowhere to run, the family gathered their swords and shields.

"Dad, who knew we would need our training so soon? I pray the Lord of Celestial City will help us.[214] This gang looks rough!" Self-Disciplined exclaimed.

As the gang closed in, they could see the leader's body tattooed with reptilian scales and each of his teeth chiseled to a point. One gang member was painted to resemble a lion, and another like a bear. Several of the gang carried torches.

The leader growled at them, "I'm Apollyon[215] and this gang serves me. These are the Pit Devils and you are in my kingdom. Where did you come from and where are you going?"

"The city we left, Pleasantown, will be destroyed. Our destination is Celestial City," Christian barked, his family wide-eyed with mouths open.

"You will travel no further. I am god here,[216] and could kill you right now with a single command, but I think your family could serve to me."

"There is only one whom we serve," Christian exploded. "I confess I have followed false gods. I emptied my life trying to satisfy the leaders of this world, and I learned that the reward of my hard work to make myself better on my own was death to my soul.[217] We swear fealty to the Lord of Celestial City alone."

Apollyon changed tactics and responded in a paternal tone. "You have no need to be angry. All who serve me began their treks with Celestial City in mind, but found my offer more appealing.

"You followed that remote, esoteric God sometimes, but you also obeyed other gods. If you commit to me, you will enjoy the benefits all of my people enjoy. Why would you forego what you really want in life? The path beyond is hard, and while I am powerful and able to lead with violence, I do not need to. We take care of each other in this community. Why not join us?"

"No. You are a liar.[218] We have learned the attributes of the true God from reading his Word and desire to serve only him—do his work, follow his leadership, enjoy his company, and live in his country."

"Have you forgotten what you have seen? Many whom you knew sought after him and came to horrible, painful deaths. Did you see him save anyone with your own eyes?[219] Don't let our initial interaction frighten you. You were dressed for battle and we responded in kind. We are one big, happy family. Every one of the Pit Devils is content serving me. Have you seen the Lord of the city, as you call him? Do you know anyone who has? Me neither. How do you know he even exists? Sounds like Santa Claus. You can see me. I'm here in the flesh. I have adopted this family. We eat and drink well, working together towards common goals. We protect and care for each other. I've not lost any of my family."

"Yes," Christian acknowledged, "many have died on the road to Celestial City, serving the Lord of that place. They exchanged what they could not keep for what they cannot lose.[220] The Lord's Word says some will be persecuted for pursuing our Savior and his righteousness, yet the reward in Heaven will be great.[221] We believe this is true."

"You are like all the others," Apollyon continued, trying a fresh approach. "You say you desire to serve him, but I think you are just trying to sound 'holy.' My servants live throughout the world and keep me informed. I know you took different paths than the one you were told to take. Others in our family would have led you down alternative paths as well, had they not been interrupted. You are pitiful. You want to be important and respected, to enjoy the praise of others, so you pretend to be brave, but that is just the armor you wear. Under it, you are just frightened little children."

Christian conceded, "Much of what you say is true. I have been unfaithful in ways your servants have not seen as well. We followed you and your ways more than you realize. We have been unfaithful and untrustworthy."

He then declared, "But the Lord we serve is faithful and we can trust him to forgive and welcome us back when we recognize our mistakes, confess them, repent from them, and return to him."[222]

In a rage, his voice deafening, Apollyon threatened them, "I hate the one you claim to serve. I hate his person, his laws, and all who follow him. I would rather kill you than let him receive any of your service. You have now led your family to death, Christian."

Several of the gang threw razor-sharp ninja throwing stars and knives. The family deployed their shields with the adeptness of trained warriors, stopping all the well-aimed projectiles.

"This road is still the King's and leads to Celestial City, and is therefore a holy path that we will defend," Christian retorted as he drew his sword and charged the gang, his family at his side.

It was soon clear that limited basic training alone could not prepare a family who had lived most of their lives in the comforts of suburbia. Hand-to-hand combat against fighters who lived by the sword required skill they did not have. The Pilgrims took many wounds in the initial skirmish, and the battle took its toll. As the family weakened, the Pit Devils fought with renewed vigor. Christian was overtaken, followed by each family member, with their sword and shield pinned to the ground by the heavy boots of an enemy standing over them, the point of a sword resting on each neck, prepared to end their lives.

"You haven't won yet. Our Lord offers us strength you do not see!"[223]

With that cry, Christian and his family overcame the strength of their adversaries, striking blows with their swords like battle-hardened warriors.[224] They reversed the trajectory of the fight. Apollyon and his Pit Devils fled.[225]

To the observer, Christian and his suburban family looked out of place in their battle gear, though it was custom made for each one of them. They looked to be no match for this gang experienced in street warfare.

Reflecting on their God-given victory, Christiana was the first to speak. "The Pit Devils had us in their sights, either to ruin our spirits with lies or our bodies with wounds. When you cried out to the Lord, I felt a renewed strength that I recognized was not my own."

"Me too! That was amazing!" Self-Disciplined beamed. "No superhero movie I've ever seen could measure up to what we did with God's help. It was real! In those movies, it's always just the hero in their own power. Like Mom said, I know that power did not come from somewhere inside of me. There's no way I could stand up to any of those guys, but when Dad cried out to God, I had not just physical strength that surprised me, but mental clarity and confidence."[226]

"I felt the supernatural energy God provided me during the battle, as I think we all did, but I'm not so sure the wounds we received aren't fatal. I still worry we won't make it," Joyful said, her spent voice a perfect representation of her damaged body.

A radiant being appeared, larger than life, in gleaming white armor, frightening each of them anew.

"Do not be afraid. I'm Michael and I'm on Team Pilgrim.[227] You each fought bravely and wisely, calling on Our Father for help. I trained you to develop skills that could he could use to win the battle and knew your training would be futile under your own strength. Without his care, your wounds will be fatal. But he who called you on this journey is faithful to complete it. I bring you a healing ointment extracted from the Tree of Life in Celestial City. Place it on your wounds."[228]

As quickly as he appeared, he was gone.

"He looked a lot different in battle dress than he did back at the museum!" Joyful said. "Back there, I thought he was kind of cute, but here he nearly scared me to death, showing up the way he did!"

"Always looking for a date," Self-Disciplined needled his sister. "Though he would make a pretty cool brother-in-law."

They helped each other to apply the cream to their cuts and gashes.

"I sure hope this stuff works." Joyful continued, ignoring her brother's comments except for a sneer.

While she was still speaking, the injuries were not only healed, but without scars.

"Unbelievable! Praise God!" they exclaimed in unison.

Each got back in the SUV and the comfort it provided. They sat, shared stories, and rested while they regained their energy with time and a healthy lunch.

"Time to see if we are stuck here or can move on." Christian turned the key in the ignition, and The Chariot roared to life, doing its part to move them towards their destination.

"I don't see any more danger looking forward, but recommend we keep our swords and shields within easy reach," Christian warned.

CHAPTER FOURTEEN

New Valley, New Dangers

The balance of the trip through the Valley of Humiliation was uneventful, except that the road continued to prove rough and uneven. It seemed they were in the clear, until they came to a foreboding road sign: "The Valley of the Shadow of Death."

"So much for our travels getting easier after leaving the Valley of Humiliation!" Joyful squirmed.

"Based on the map app, the only route to Immanuel's country is through there. Keep your swords and shields at the ready," Christian reminded them.

Though early afternoon on a cloudless day, the trees and vines encroaching on the road were so dense that it was as dark as a moonless midnight. Ahead, the headlights rested on two backpackers headed towards them. As they pulled alongside, Christian rolled down his window to talk to the pair.

"Shouldn't you be going the other way?"

"Absolutely not! We are headed back as fast as we can. Before your headlights brought some light, it was almost impossible to see where we were going. You are crazy to go that way. If you value your lives and your peace of mind, go back. You won't survive in there.[229] It is complete chaos—dark, full of strange wild animal noises, people out of their minds crying out, and demonic howls. We have never heard such terrifying sounds before."[230]

"If this is the road to Immanuel's country, then the destination will be worth any risk to get there," Self-Disciplined admonished.

"Don't say we didn't warn you."

Christian crept away as the backpackers let their eyes readjust to the darkness before crawling their way out of the valley.

The road followed a narrow ridge between two larger mountains, with less than a foot of clearance on either side. On one side was a ravine with a swamp at the bottom. If they were to go off the road in that direction, they would drown in the mire.[231] On the other side was a steep cliff. Given the darkness, one could not see the bottom of the chasm. Christian's white knuckles clenched the steering wheel to keep The Chariot centered on the road made slick from the rainforest-like climate. Eventually, the swamp on the one side gave way to molten lava with a horrible stench. The sounds emanating from the glowing surface added to the horror.

"From what we've read and images people have created over the centuries, if there is an actual Hell, that must be it!" Looks-Good cried out, eyes closed, hands over his ears, dripping sweat.

"I fear that these swords and shields will be of little use if we meet the owners of those cries. Praise God we have a more potent weapon that will prevail where these fail us, which is our only hope for success," Christian encouraged. "Let's pray."[232]

With this most powerful defense deployed, their ashen faces and tremulous voices belied the confident words.

Unearthly noises tormented them through the closed windows.

The sounds, sights, and smells that crept into the car were not their only concerns.

"Dad, I keep hearing these soft, convincing voices that I sometimes mistake for my own thoughts, suggesting evil things about the Lord of

Celestial City, the one I know we each love and for whom we are willing to die," Joyful quivered. "I'm trying as hard as I can, but I just can't shake those voices or thoughts or whatever they are. I'm afraid."

Christiana spoke the truth that saved them. "I thought it was just me, and didn't want to frighten anyone or plant seeds of doubt, but I should have shared this sooner. I felt the same attacks in my heart. When they came, I cried out in my spirit, 'Lord, save me,' and the Holy Spirit immediately reminded me[233] of what we read in God's Word. Though we travel through the darkest, most frightening places, we need not fear. The Lord will care for us."[234]

They took turns praying against their fears and anxiety.[235]

"Thanks, Mom! When I started praying, I remembered Scripture, some verses I didn't realize I knew, and those terrible thoughts ebbed away. Now I am at ease. Before we started this journey, I would have thought feeling peace in a situation like this would be unfathomable, but now it's almost like I expect it in this horrible, smelly place.[236] Am I the only one?" Joyful asked.

"Like you, Joyful, the Holy Spirit prompted me to pray against anxiety, which it looks like we all were facing, and the peace that God promises now seems to rest on each of us,"[237] Christian answered. "Look in front of us. The vegetation is thinning, and it is getting lighter. This artificial night is returning to day."[238]

As they passed into the bright, clear daylight, each looked back to survey what they left behind.[239]

"What the..." Looks-Good burst out, catching his breath with his mouth wide open. "That valley is even more terrifying than I had thought now that we can see it clearly! Those hideous demons were making those awful sounds! They are more heinous than I imagined. And look how jagged the rocks are at the bottom of the cliff on the other side of the road. No way we could have survived either of those fates if you had lost control of the SUV.

"Dad, I'm sure you noticed as you were driving, but I didn't realize the road sloped one way and then the other. We are so lucky that we survived that stretch of our trip!"

"Son, it was not luck that brought us through that valley, and certainly not my driving, though I've not been so focused in my life. I'm not sure I'll be able to peel my hands from the steering wheel for a while."

Christian responded after his first unstrained breath. "Lord, thank you for carrying us through the valley that we could not have survived without you. Thank you for letting us experience first-hand what you spoke to David: 'Even though I walk through the valley of the shadow of death, I will fear no evil, for you are with me; your rod and your staff, they comfort me.'[240] Thank you that even our small faith protected us from knowing the true extent of the dangers we faced and now see clearly. Show me how to lead my family in wisdom, placing my confidence solely in your guidance. Please forgive when I trust in my own abilities."

Christiana followed. "I agree with my husband's prayer. Thank you, Lord, for carrying us through that place. We know we survive nothing alone. Even our own thoughts were against us. There were so many places we could have died or succumbed to deception. As we live, you, Jesus, receive the glory."

CHAPTER FIFTEEN

Companions

Alarge hotel surprised them at the crest of a hill, not present on the map app.

"Dad, can we stop here?" Joyful asked. "Even though God has granted me much peace, I could still do with some rest, and I was only a passenger! You must be completely exhausted after that death-defying stretch of road."

"I think we could all do with some rest after those back-to-back valleys. I'll go in and see if they have any availability," Christian agreed, struggling to keep his eyes open.

"Praise God! Not only do they have rooms, but they upgraded us—for free!" The Pilgrims wolfed down supper, retired to their rooms, and were asleep almost before they were out of their armor.

* * *

Waking with the sun already well above the horizon, they started their day in the hotel lounge. Each sank with their Bible and a pastry into a mission-style chair or sofa upholstered with chestnut-colored glove leather facing a roaring fire in the large rustic-stone fireplace. Before they had read for long, Christiana turned to see friendly faces entering the room.

"Faithful, Dependable, I can't tell you how thankful we are to see you here! You are the first friendly faces from home we have seen on our quest.

God must have sent you to comfort us after what we've been through!" Christiana exclaimed as they all rose to share hugs before resettling into the comfortable lounge with their friends.

"I have to tell you that at church we always held you two in such high esteem! We were jealous of your peaceful and holy confidence. Though we were regular seat-fillers and pretty involved, we were too busy with the rest of our lives to make new friends. Now we realize we were actually unworthy of your attention," Christian shared with blunt honesty.

"We may have been farther down the path," Faithful responded, "but we certainly had faults we kept out of public view. It was only the grace and discipline of our Lord that had brought us to where you knew us then, still far from the image of our Savior, but closer.[241] I'm sorry we didn't get to know you at church, but I am thankful we have the opportunity to do so now!"

"As are we!" Christiana responded.

"You say you were jealous of us, yet you started this laborious journey before we did. Well done!" Faithful continued. "When we heard you were leaving town, we planned to go with you, realizing the way would most likely be dangerous and that there might be safety in numbers, but you left before we could pack. As we had missed joining you anyway, we decided to stay and try to get people to come with us.[242] Everyone at church had an opinion about your departure, and most were not favorable.

"Some wanted to send the police after you, saying that you were recklessly endangering your family. Some said you needed re-education, an appeal to your better judgment to remind you that Pleasantown was on the right side of history, promoting its self-defined progressive, open-minded, and tolerant values. Your friend Obstinate put a stop to that line of argument. We heard him more than once saying to someone, 'They are too far gone to benefit from re-education, and we are better off letting them go before they pollute the minds of anyone else.' People who didn't attend church had some profane alternative names for you, which I won't repeat. They wrote you off as crazy religious fanatics."

Joyful's kind eyes focused on Dependable, whom she asked, "Mr. Flexible joined us before turning back. How is he?"

"You are sweet to ask. His is a sad story," Dependable reflected. "After my initial excitement when I heard he started out with you, I learned that he decided the heat and traffic jam were a 'sign from God' that you were off your rockers and returned home. The worst part, however, is how the community treated him. Because he joined you, even for such a short time, he was labeled narrow-minded and intolerant. People he considered friends deserted him, the company he worked for fired him, and no one will employ him. Some accused him of hate speech, not necessarily for what he said, but, to use their words, 'simply because he had the audacity to lend credibility to the Pilgrims' wayward journey by agreeing to go at all.' We saw him one time while we were out for a walk, and moved towards him to visit, but he crossed over to the other side of the street to avoid us, hanging his head in shame."

"He seemed so eager when he first joined us. His return is like that part in the Bible that talks about a dog eating its own vomit and how a clean pig will go right back to the pigsty,"[243] Looks-Good added.

Christian grieved. "I failed him, too. I should have pursued him more diligently. Flexible started on a path to redemption, but will be destroyed along with the rest of the city. What about Obstinate? He said he would support all of us if we changed our minds, and that he would care for our homes until we returned."

"He was probably Flexible's prime abuser. He would go out of his way to debase and humiliate him.

"As for caring for your homes, Christian and Flexible, both succumbed to mysterious fires that the fire marshal 'investigated' but determined to be caused by faulty wiring. Right," Faithful sneered.

"But back to Flexible. His heart was not prepared to seek Celestial City," Faithful lamented. "Maybe you could have done more to pursue him, but I doubt the outcome would have been different at that time. You were right to encourage him and take him with you. His leaving was on his own account."

"Flexible is still not beyond the reach of our savior, so I will continue to pray for him," Christiana encouraged him.

"Thank you for that update. I'm sad to think our home is gone, but I guess it is our true home to which we are traveling. Please continue. I was going to ask you to share about your travels," Christian said.

"We knew the way to Narrow Gate without a map. That was an easy trip for us, and there wasn't any traffic. But when we arrived, as we walked towards the door, Lustful joined us and asked if we would speak with her. She was beautiful, elegant, and well-spoken. What shocks us, looking back, was how attractive she was to both of us, especially to Dependable, who has never struggled with same-sex attraction. As for me, I have never in my life suffered even the remotest desire to be unfaithful to my wife. I never even desired to be intimate with a woman before I was married. We were prideful in our prudence, and I realize that pride blind-sided us. Something about Lustful made it impossible for either of us to turn away from her."

"That's incredible. If anyone was immune to such temptation, I would have assumed it was you two! What happened?" Christiana gasped.

"God's kindness alone saved us from her pursuit. Honestly, on our own merits, in our own strength, we were ready to surrender to her winsome temptation," Dependable lamented. "The Holy Spirit gave us the ability to turn and run towards the gate.[244] As we ran away from her, she yelled hateful profanity that would make a sailor blush. Her vehemence exposed her true demonic nature. We both sensed that Lustful had planted a seed in each of our hearts, or, more likely, cultivated a seed of sin to which we had conceitedly assumed we were immune, even after being rescued by Interpreter."

"We presumed that would be the worst of it and that the balance of our trip to Celestial City would be uneventful," Faithful picked up, "but not long after we left Interpreter's we stopped for a rest in a peaceful meadow at the base of a hill where a kindly white-haired man walking with a cane joined us. I don't remember the exact conversation, but to the best of my recollection, this was how it went:

> *'Hi, my name is Adam. I live in Deceit, just over the wall and further down the hill. Where are you two headed?'*
>
> *'To Celestial City.'*
>
> *'That's still far from here. Why don't you come back with me and enjoy the good life?'*
>
> *'Which is?'*
>
> *'My days and nights are filled with the blessings of comfort and delights. Servants wait on me and provide for my every desire. I have three grown children who live with me: my daughter, Passion, her younger sister, Attraction, followed by my son, Accomplishment.[245] They are also gifted with hospitality. You are welcome to join us in these pleasures for as long as I live, which I expect to be far into the future. I seem to grow healthier every year, and I'm sure you would, too!'*

"Once again, the extent to which we were tempted surprised and frightened us. We were ready to 'fight the good fight'[246] and 'run the race with endurance'[247] when we set out on this journey, yet the temptation of a life of comfort and ease appealed to carnal desires we didn't realize we had suppressed. As we turned to join Adam in Deceit, the Scripture about stripping off our old nature and being renewed in our mind[248] came into both of our thoughts simultaneously.[249]

"We left him, feeling rude just walking away while he was still talking, but we had to ignore him as he persisted in his invitation.

"While we climbed up the hill, we noticed for the first time the cross at the top. What you didn't see at church," Faithful continued, "was that we, too, carried weighty sins on our backs. Sound theology told us that Jesus forgave us, but in practice we held on to them, fighting to follow the rules in the Bible for a salvation earned by our merits."

Dependable picked up their story. "About half-way up the hill, a man ran up behind us and knocked us down with such force that we both blacked out. When we came to, I asked him why in the world he attacked us like that, with no provocation. He barked that he saw us tempted to accept Adam's offer and hit us both again, this time in the chest, so hard that we both rolled down to the bottom of the hill.

"When we regained our senses, we begged for mercy. The man told us he did not know how to show mercy and knocked us down for a third time.

"Barely opening our eyes for fear of another beating, we prayed quietly so that we wouldn't give away the fact that we were again conscious, asking Jesus to protect us and forgive us for straying from him. Immediately, we saw a second man, dressed in white, who stopped the first from further attack. This second man, with holes in his hands, carried us to the top of the hill. While he was still holding us, our burdens fell off our backs and rolled down into an open grave, after which other heavenly beings offered us new clothes and certificates, evidence of our redemption, to carry with us to Celestial City."

"Neither of us has any idea what the initial violence was about, but we are relieved to have that all behind us!" Faithful added.

Self-Disciplined discerned, "The man who kept knocking you down must have been Moses, slaying you with the law that you thought you had been keeping faithfully as your means of salvation. Though you were good church people, by your own assessment, you trusted in the law, not grace.[250] The law is good to condemn, but not to save.[251] The one who carried you up the hill was Jesus, who saved you through his merit alone." The rest of the family listened to him wide-eyed and gape-mouthed.[252]

"Well done, Self-Disciplined! You and your family may have been behind us on your path to sanctification in Pleasantown, but it looks like you have now surpassed us! I'm embarrassed to admit you are correct. I had been leading Dependable poorly.[253] At the foot of the cross, after our Savior removed our burdens, he sent us on our way.

"It was late in the day and we didn't see anyone at Lodge Beautiful, so we kept driving. What a disaster that was! The road was terrible, and at the entrance to a valley, the car died."

Looks-Good jumped in, "Yep. That was the Valley of Humiliation. We broke down there too. There must be something in the air there that interferes with an engine's combustion or something."

"Could be, Looks-Good. I opened the hood to see if I could fix it as Dependable waited in the car with the windows down for some air, when a man named Discontent came up. He told us that the valley was dangerous and that we were foolish to go that way,[254] that there was a much easier way for us to find happiness. He said some of our friends back home—Pride, Arrogance, Self-Love, Pretense, and others—would agree with him that we should listen to their collective counsel and follow his advice. Pathetically, we were both tempted—again!

"The opinions of those friends had previously influenced much of our behavior and most of our decisions. As we started to consider the logic in his argument, we remembered Good-Guide's instruction to stay focused on the Celestial City and the Lord thereof. We tried to convince

Discontent that he believed lies and that the ways of the world were folly to the Author of Scripture, that God's desire is for a broken and contrite heart.[255] We told him we would rather be humbled at the feet of our Savior than have the complete support of our old friends.

"We could not have responded to Discontent the way we did had we not just been in the presence of our Lord on the hill. Even in that brief interaction, he strengthened us to pursue righteousness when our desires were moving us to old, wrong associations. We left Discontent, immediately severing contact with our tempting old friends. We removed them from our contacts, blocked their numbers, and unfriended them on social media. That was all good, but where we erred was not praying with Discontent, though we have often prayed for him since. In our haste and fear, we forgot that no one is beyond God's call to repentance."

"I'm so thankful you are here. We can learn from your humility and honesty. Did you meet anyone else?" Joyful asked.

Dependable addressed her question. "We met with one more, and she was our greatest challenge yet. Her name was Shameless, but she went by Shame. She was relentless. I'll do my best to recount what she said as accurately as I can:

> *Devotion to anyone other than oneself is idiocy, as is following the rules, laws, or guidance of any spirit other than one's own. Look at the great people of history, the world-changers. None of them were humble in spirit. Humility is just a euphemism for weakness. The path to success and wealth, power and influence, does not come from faith in some abstract deity. That's just a path to failure.[256] When you said you accepted the absurd stories in the Bible as true, rejecting the wisdom of secular scientists who can*

prove what they believe, I figured you might be beyond hope. You give thinking people a bad name.

Then, to make matters worse, you waste your time on Sunday mornings listening to teachings about archaic irrelevancies and singing boring, repetitive songs to the air, and even more time on weeknights gathering to study an outdated book of myths. Why don't you spend your time and resources like responsible, productive adults, who dedicate themselves to making a difference in society, who work hard and sacrifice to earn a better life for themselves and their families, who lead or volunteer for real causes like saving animals or championing the rights of pregnant women to do what they want with the tissue growing in their bodies?

"Dependable later told me that at this point my face flushed. Probably so, because I was ready to engage in battle and set Shame straight.[257] But my dear wife gently rested her hand on my knee, our 'secret code' to hold my tongue. In due time, when there was a break in the diatribe, she responded much more wisely, patiently, and with greater grace and humility than I would have.[258] Sweetheart, please share how you responded to Shame's attack."[259]

"I will try to quote myself accurately, and Faithful can correct me as needed:

Shame, you accurately portray the world's wisdom. Will you now please allow me to share what I believe? (She agreed with a nod, her arms folded defiantly.) Except for the knowledge of the person of Jesus the Christ, and faith in him crucified, I would agree with you. A day will come, and it is not far away, when we will each be judged less on how we lived than in whom we placed our confidence.

Faithful and I strive to live our lives to honor the one whom we serve. He expects us to live differently to reflect what he has done for us. The wealth we store up for eternity in Heaven[260] far outweighs any wealth we could enjoy during our lives on earth. Any sacrifices we make in this life for Jesus's sake and for the sake of sharing the truth of his life, death, and resurrection are wholly inconsequential when compared to the eternal life he promises us.[261]

We strive not to compare ourselves to the men and women who seek after even the best earthly things, nor to anyone but Jesus. While he is beyond compare, the Holy Spirit is making us look and live increasingly more like our Savior. Our only hope is the righteousness he earned for us[262] through his death on our behalf and subsequent resurrection.

"Though spoken with all the conviction, love, and passion I had, Shame heard nothing.[263] I was heartbroken." Faithful held his wife as she finished her story. "Shame tried other approaches, some bold, some subtle, but at last I put a stop to the conversation, noting that there was nothing she could say to shake our faith.[264] With that, she left. Her departure moved us to sing 'Amazing Grace,' reflecting that only God could have carried us through such an ordeal."

"Thank you for sharing that, Dependable," Christiana said, hugging her new friend.

CHAPTER SIXTEEN

Lip Service

"It's time for lunch!" Self-Disciplined blurted out. "Oops, sorry. That might sound insensitive. We just got to talking and never ate breakfast. I have learned so much from you, Mr. Faithful and Mrs. Dependable, but could we maybe eat? I'm pretty hungry."

As they entered the dining room, they saw a table set for all of them plus one who was waiting for them. Their unexpected host stood up and introduced himself. "Hello Friends. Call me Lip-Service. I took the liberty of having a table set for all of us. I enjoy good discourse and, based on the amount of time I had to wait while you visited in the lounge, I would venture to say you are delightful conversationalists."

Lunch at the hotel was a buffet, and each found something to their liking. Seated again at the table, Lip-Service started the conversation. "I hope you are serious-minded people. So much talk now is just mindless dribble or discourse on ultimately unimportant topics."

"I agree with you, Lip-Service," responded Faithful. "We are headed to Celestial City. Our Father in Heaven is our favorite topic, and there is no subject more worthy of our time."

"Exactly. You all seem to be people of conviction. There are so many biblical themes to evaluate! Interesting and amazing subjects, including miracles, signs, wonders, mysteries, and histories.

"With so much variety, there is no need for any other source material. We can discourse on the eventual dissatisfaction with earthly things and the corresponding ultimate satisfaction with heavenly things, or the need for spiritual rebirth. We can contrast the need for Jesus's righteousness with the insufficiency of our works! We can look at what Scripture says about repentance, prayer, and suffering, plus the promises and consolations of the Gospel. We can contrast false teachers and false teachings with what is true."

"Amen," Dependable responded.

"In the end, it's all quite simple. The need for faith, being saved by grace, the futility of living solely by the law for righteousness—they are all right there in the book if one just spends enough time reading and studying it," Lip-Service offered.

Faithful politely interrupted him. "Not exactly. Scripture contains all of those truths, but people often take passages out of context and misapply them. One requires the Holy Spirit's guidance for proper discernment."[265]

"Well, of course. All knowledge comes through the Holy Spirit's revelation of Scripture. Everything comes through grace, not works," Lip-Service quickly agreed. "There are many verses I could quote you on that topic."

"Mr. Lip-Service, where should we start our conversation?" Joyful asked.

"We can talk about anything! We can discuss heavenly or earthly things, right behavior versus right belief, sacred things or common things, past or present or future, foreign or domestic affairs. As long as our conversation is good for us, it will be good."

"If you will please excuse me, I'm going to get some more food for that next conversation. Faithful, you look like you could use a refresh also," Christian said. Under the guise of refilling their plates, they could have a private conversation, while Lip-Service continued talking to the rest of his audience.

"I'm so glad we've met Lip-Service, Christian. He'll be a brilliant companion on this journey. Is he a friend of yours?"

"I did not recognize him at first, but I know of him, and he is not as he appears. That's why I invited you to this buffet conference," Christian responded as they picked through both sides of the long buffet. "He lives in the Drivel Apartments right by the church, so you might have seen him there. He is a verbal chameleon, using the right words to fit into any setting. In church, he uses church words, as he does here. If you sit by him at a football game, you would assume he either played or was an experienced armchair quarterback. He knows enough to fit in, but only repeats what others say. He does not understand the game. Pull up next to him in a bar and, I'm told, it would shock you to learn he had ever set foot in a church. He uses his church words at church, his bar talk when he's out drinking with his friends, and his game jargon when watching sports. All evidence points to a corrupt heart."

"Wow. He had me fooled. I was so excited to meet someone else who would be a worthy companion for us, I allowed it to cloud my judgment," Faithful replied shyly.

"It's so much easier to say the right thing than to do it,"[266] Christian continued. "He uses all the right words, but you don't see the results in his life.[267] In a person of conviction, all of his church words would be words of truth. Even when I wasn't pursuing Jesus, I recognized that the way he lived his life apart from church was inconsistent with what he said at church.[268]

"This man is also untrustworthy in his business dealings. It just so happened that I interviewed one of his prior employees who wanted to come work for my company. I asked why he would leave when Lip-Service's business seemed to thrive. He shared that the growth was deceptive and that Lip-Service sought profit and advantage at any cost. At the first sign of a conscionable action with a client, or any sign of mercy, he would berate an employee for being weak. He has most probably led many away from the truth with his smooth and true-sounding words."

"Thank you, Christian. I feel ashamed about being so easily led astray."

"If I wasn't already familiar with him, he would have fooled me just as easily, Faithful. I would have misconstrued negative reports about him as the Enemy's scheme to undermine the fellowship of the church. Before my discussion with his former employee, I remember being confused as to why others whom I respected seemed to avoid him. I don't say any of this to slander his character, but to point out that you and I both need to grow in discernment and wisdom as we desire to protect one another and our families from those who would deceive us."[269]

"This is rich material for me to share with Dependable before we pray tonight. You point to us as being more mature in our faith, but our loving protector has used you to teach me this great wisdom.[270] You remind me to test one's words against the fruits of their life."[271]

"In Lip-Service, I see much of my own history," Christian continued, looking at the floor. "I said all the right things, but my life didn't reflect any belief in those words. I pursued selfish desires, not visiting those in prison, providing assistance to orphans, mentoring young men, husbands, and fathers, volunteering to support our children's school or extracurricular activities, or helping those in our community who were in a hard place.[272] I was convinced I was a good person because I went to church regularly and said and did all the right church things. A lyric in a song sticks with me on this point: 'Sitting in a church building doesn't make you a Christian any more than sitting in a garage will make you a car with an engine.'[273] On judgment day, we will each be judged, and those who idly profess without belief will be judged on their works,[274] to eternal destruction."

"Lip-Service sounds like he wants to fit in everywhere without making any commitments. From what you describe, it seems he wants to be respected in church without making any sacrifices, to be the modern day Everyman."[275]

"Based on what I know, you understand Lip-Service correctly, and yet you also describe me before we set out on this journey. My heart breaks for Lip-Service. While works don't save, they are evidence of salvation. We perform the works God calls us to because of our great love and respect for him. Likewise, a husband who loves his wife properly serves her with joy, not out of duty, and a child who loves their parents seeks to please them because of the love he or she freely receives, not in striving to earn that love."[276]

Crossing over to the other side of the buffet to further ensure their conversation would be private, Faithful asked Christian, "So, as this man seems ready to join us, how should we separate from him? I fear his theology will be a distraction, or even a danger."[277]

"I wouldn't put it quite that way, for we do not know when or if God will turn his heart," Christian admonished his friend. "As a conversationalist, we must ensure the conversation is intentional, discussing the Gospel, pressing on hollow words. Let's pray that the Holy Spirit will work in his heart, so that we will gain a comrade."

After they returned to the table, Faithful waited for a natural break in the conversation. "How did God present his saving grace to you, Lip-Service?"

"This is an important topic! I love talking about power. God's grace in our hearts gives us the power to speak out against sin. That's the first point . . ."

"Wait, let's stay here for a minute," Faithful stopped him. "Speaking out against sin is easy. The sex trade is a terrible sin, and there is so much momentum against it that one can readily join in that cause. But must one hate the sin first? For example, can one rightfully speak out against the sex trade and yet privately still engage in the pornography and lust that drive it? I think one must hate a sin before he can conquer it. Would you agree?"

"Good point, friend Faithful, though I fear you may be trying to embarrass me by twisting my words. I am a gracious man and we are new friends, so I will assume that I misinterpret your motive. To continue, one has to know about the Gospel."

"Apologies again for my interruption, sir. That is a new topic. Are you trying to avoid answering my first question? Not that you are incorrect, for the Gospel is the first and most important topic. However, having knowledge of the Gospel is a very different thing from declaring Jesus as Lord of your life and believing that the Father raised him from the dead.[278] The father of lies also knows Scripture—better than we do. I hope you would agree that knowing and doing are two different things.[279] Please continue."

"There you go again, disagreeing over semantics. I'm not sure I like how this conversation is going. If you are just setting me up to disagree with me, I don't want to make my next point."

"In that case, would you allow me to share some of what the Holy Spirit has taught me through Scripture?" Faithful asked Lip-Service.

"Freedom of speech is a vital prerogative," Lip-Service declared. "So, of course, you may continue. I value diversity of thought."

"After the Holy Spirit convicts one of sin and a person repents, he extends grace to that person's soul. This includes the sin of unbelief. It is impossible to find grace without first accepting Jesus's death and resurrection as the sufficient source of the forgiveness that allows for this grace,[280] which leads to great sorrow for one's sin, which leads to greater love for him who saves us. I will give you an example from my own life.

"I am a regenerate sinner. The grace granted me to believe and trust in the work of Jesus, through no work or merit of my own,[281] has transformed my life. As a result, I long for Jesus more than anything else.[282]

I have increasing joy, contentment, and peace directly proportionate to the degree of my faith in the Savior. My desire to know him more deeply and serve his purposes with greater dedication reflects the depth of my confidence in him, which the Holy Spirit increases in me. Like all believers. I must continually remind myself, as encouraged by the Holy Spirit,[283] that this is only through a work of grace, because my sinful nature wants to have a part in deserving it. Is your experience similar? Would you agree? If so, I have another proposition for you."

"Who am I to object to such a thorough presentation?" Lip-Service said with an air of condescension. "But what is your other suggestion?"

"Would you say you agree to my last statement, or do you just not object? If you agree, would you say your life reflects this belief? Would people who know you agree? You have nothing to prove to me. I am not your judge. The man who justifies himself is not justified, but the one whom God justifies is, and that justification is only through the salvific offering Jesus makes through taking our sins to the cross, followed by his death-conquering resurrection."

Fidgeting and avoiding eye contact during the whole of the preceding conversation, Lip-Service regained his composure and responded dismissively. "You have your own experience of God. Who are you to tell me what I should believe?[284] I was looking forward to a friendly conversation, not condemnation."

"Correct, Lip-Service. It is not for me to tell you what you believe, nor am I trying to do so. I seek to clarify what you believe. As one who speaks much of Scripture, you must remember it says we are to use it to reprimand, correct, and train.[285] My goal has been to determine if you are one who puts his confidence in God's inspired Word or one who uses Scripture selectively to support his own perspective."

"You offend me with your harshness. Tolerance is the greatest of all virtues, and if you love me the way a Christian should, you would affirm all of my beliefs as equally right and good.[286] I fear, however, that you are a hateful, narrow-minded bigot who refuses to see that all the different right and noble patterns of belief have equal merit. I will have no more to do with you or any of your intolerant friends. Goodbye."[287]

After he stormed off, Looks-Good challenged, "Mr. Faithful, might you have been a little harsh? I mean, he was just trying to enjoy some friendly conversation."

Christian put his arm around his son, leaning in towards him. "Looks-Good, our Savior calls us to share the truth in love. You heard in Mr. Faithful's tone nothing but loving correction, but for those who are dead in their sins, regardless of their lofty words, the truth of Scripture is foolishness."[288]

Turning to address his friend, Christian continued. "Faithful, I was praying for the Holy Spirit to speak through you, and I do believe you spoke the truth in love.[289] Those whom God has called will listen to it, while those whom he has not will not.[290] If Lip-Service had not left us, because he seemed in no way inclined to change his heart, at some point we would have had to separate from him."[291]

"Thank you for encouraging me. God calls us to be faithful to proclamation, acknowledging that the outcome is up to him alone,[292] but I still mourn those who hear the truth and reject it. I'm not happy that Lip-Service left us, though I also realize that his salvation is not up to me and that I cannot argue him into faith. I pray that the Holy Spirit will ultimately draw him to the Savior."

"Most people shy away from these hard, but critically important, conversations. God does not want our empty words nor does he want us to worship him for our own edification.[293] Too often we love people to Hell, avoiding these difficult discussions and, in doing so, implicitly condone beliefs that lead to death. Some even support sinful beliefs and lifestyles explicitly, the fear of lost relationships or rejection by society keeping them from promoting life-saving truth. My heart breaks for those who know so much about Scripture without knowing the Author. I commit to pray that the Holy Spirit will use the words Lip-Service speaks idly now to penetrate his soul and turn his heart to commit his life to the Giver of Life," Christian replied.

The seven of them continued discussing their conversation with Lip-Service over dessert, and then all returned to their rooms to sleep, realizing they had been at "lunch" until well after dark.

* * *

At breakfast, they compared notes on their travels and started to discuss plans for their onward journey when a mutual friend joined them.

"Peace be with you, those whom I love so!"

"Good-Guide, welcome! Please join us. Thank you for the kindness you show to me and my family, and how dedicated you are to guiding us in what is truly good," Christian responded.

After great food and pleasant, God-honoring conversation, they adjourned to the seating around the fireplace to continue their fellowship.

Showing Good-Guide to a seat where they could all see and hear him, Faithful addressed their guest. "I hope you can stay with us for a while. You always have the right words at the right time."

"Before I offer counsel, please update me on your travels."

Each shared facets of the difficulties and trials they had overcome plus the joys and successes they had enjoyed, the attentive hotel staff keeping their drinks replenished.

"I am thankful that you have found victory over these trials, and that you have persevered despite your own weakness.[294] You sowed seed with Lip-Service and Flexible that others may one day reap, and Our Lord blessed you to see him use the Bible you shared with Civility to affect change in his heart. The time is coming when the sower and the reaper will rejoice together.[295]

"You each pursue a crown that will never wear out or lose its luster.[296] Protect it that no one takes it from you.[297]

"Your battle with Apollyon and his gang was noble, Pilgrims, and you honored your Father in Heaven in defending his name.

"Be wary of the allure the pleasures of this world offer with their corrupting influences. Each of you, ask God to show you the depths of your soul, to understand your lusts and desires.[298] Your hearts will lie to you, and contain more evil than you realize.[299] Confess your sins regularly to each other to avoid allowing the enemy a foothold in your lives.[300] Set your focus on reaching Celestial City and all Heaven will support you."[301]

Christiana was the first to respond. "Thank you for your continued help, Good-Guide. What can we expect for the balance of our journey?"

"Those who seek Celestial City will endure many hardships[302] on the way. In the cities and towns you have yet to pass through, your faith will be challenged and the evil one will continue his attempts to lead you away from your destination.

"Loss and death can come unexpectedly on your journey. If one of you is lost to death, they will arrive in Celestial City first, where the King has a crown of life waiting for them.[303] Though death would be emotionally and physically painful for those who remain, be comforted knowing that the follower of Jesus who dies avoids the pains and challenges that others will continue to endure on the road.

"If you find what I expect you will in this next town, leave with honor, committing your souls to the loving protector, continuing to do good, remembering whose you are."[304]

"Wow. That's kind of scary. Thank you for preparing us, for encouraging us and sharing your wisdom with us," Self-Disciplined said, hugging Good-Guide, which they all did in turn, Looks-Good less robustly.

After Good-Guide departed, they ate a hearty lunch, took a brief rest, packed their vehicles, checked out of the inn, and resumed their journey. Faithful and Christian took the SUV with Self-Disciplined and Looks-Good, while all the ladies enjoyed their time to visit in Dependable's car.

CHAPTER SEVENTEEN

Vanity

The natural beauty of the hills,[305] forests, streams, and meadows was increasingly punctuated by graphic electronic billboards advertising any desire in which one could wish to indulge, some pornographic. Nearing the town of Vanity, rainbow flags became ubiquitous, dominating the landscape, and prominent on most signs.

Vanity had an atmosphere of ageless celebration, but at present it seemed to be magnified beyond its normal scope. A giant rainbow banner over the road into town read "Pride of Vanity" with "Annual Pride Festival" in smaller print.

The SUV arrived first to Proud to Be . . . Bed and Breakfast. Faithful told Christian and his sons, "This place was highly recommended by Internet travel sites, receiving especially high marks for attentive hosts, good food, and warm hospitality. They had rooms available, so I booked it for us. Given that banner we drove under entering town, I'm not quite sure what to expect."

After his disclaimer, he prayed, "Lord, please prepare us for what lies ahead in this town. Give us boldness, wisdom, and grace to represent you with integrity and honor."

They gathered their bags and entered the inn.

"Welcome! I'm Mr. False-Teacher. My husband and I are happy you are here. Our goal is to make your stay comfortable. You will see more of me because running the B&B is my job, whereas my husband is the pastor at God's Church for Your Happiness.[306] The church regularly increases his salary because of the generous donations he generates,[307] which we then share with our guests through reasonable rates. The income from the church also allows me to pursue my true calling—a social butterfly.

"You are here during the absolute best time of the year. The town's annual Pride Festival is a destination for people from all over. Someone upstairs must like you because our rooms are booked a year in advance for the festival month. This is the first festival cancellation we've had that I can remember in the entirety of the time we have run our little inn. You have three rooms reserved. I assume one of them is for you, Mr. and Mr. Pilgrim, and then one for each of your boys here, including room for new friends they make at the festival? You will be model guests."

"Thank you for your warm welcome, Mr. False-Teacher. This is my good friend, Faithful, and these are my sons, Self-Disciplined and Looks-Good. Christiana, my wife, our daughter, Joyful, plus Faithful's wife, Dependable, will arrive soon. So each couple has a room with a queen-sized bed, and the third, with the bunk beds and the small adjoining bedroom, is for my children."

"Well, it's clear you are open-minded and should enjoy your time in Vanity. Of course, we support all gender expressions and relationships in our B&B and in our faith, which is why my husband's church is so popular. Our place of worship, under his wise and prudent guidance, avoids those outdated and misinterpreted parts of the Bible[308] that could offend someone or be mistaken to disapprove of some expressions of love and devotion. We focus on God's unconditional love for all with no hatred, his blessing on all relationships, and his utmost desire for one's happiness in any way one chooses to seek it.

"Here are your keys. In your rooms, you will find restaurant suggestions, a map marked with places we recommended to our guests, and a festival brochure. At eight o'clock each morning, we serve a family-style breakfast, because we are all one extended family. I will show your wives and daughter to your rooms when they arrive."

After a sumptuous dinner, they retired to the beautifully appointed living area with its blue, yellow, and white color scheme and large-paned windows. They arrived in time to enjoy a beautiful sunset. The only decoration on the expanse of wall shared with the dining room was an enlarged copy of the *Beautiful Home* magazine pictorial spread on the B&B in a wide, ornate, gold-leafed frame.

* * *

In the morning, heeding Good-Guide's advice to prepare for challenges in the town, all were up early, reading their Bibles and praying[309] in their rooms or enjoying the beautiful morning on the wrap-around covered porch.

At breakfast, they met the other guests.

"Good morning! My name is Tolerant, and this is my partner, All-Loving. Our stupid parents named us Biased and Deceived, but those are such outdated names. We gave each other more modern, loving names when we moved in together," Biased announced.

A rugged, handsome man in his forties, Biased exuded charm and authority, while Deceived appeared to be an attractive woman in her twenties who needed a shave.

"We come here every year for the parade and related events. Vanity refreshes and revives us. Our town is so backwards and parochial that we cannot express our true selves without being judged and hated there," Deceived[310] complained. "Even our families hate us. Oh, they say that they love us, but we know they are lying. Christians, they call themselves, but they tell us they are sad for us, that we aren't living in a way that pleases

God. They say that they want a full life for us. They just want us to fit into their little myopic, conservative bubble. Pure hate speech. Not like you. Your presence here shows that you support all expressions of love."

"I'm so sorry you do not feel loved by your families. Could there be a chance that they do love you, but disagree with the decisions you have made? Might they genuinely believe that there is a greater joy available to you and truly desire that for you?" Christiana asked. "As a mother, I pray to love my children enough to correct them when they make decisions that are unhealthy for them, but also that they never doubt my devotion to them."

"If your families truly are Christ followers, as you indicate, they cannot hate you. They may disagree, but they must love you. It is impossible to commit one's life to the Savior and not love others, regardless of their beliefs. We are all made in the image of God and are therefore worthy of great love. Disagreement is not the same as hatred," Christian added.

"You are just like the rest of them," Biased now joined in, red-faced and loud. "Close-minded. We come here to get away from people like you, to be surrounded by others who are tolerant of and loving towards everyone, like us."

"Everyone who agrees with you, you mean," Joyful countered. "Mom and Dad have said nothing to elicit your wrath. They tried to encourage you to accept love from your families, even though they disagree with your choices, yet you attack them as though they were your enemies. You don't even know them. That doesn't sound tolerant or loving at all. Quite the contrary."

"Society will prove that you are on the wrong side of history," Biased continued. "The way you talk about choices is condescending, like we aren't perfect, just the way we are, that our minds could somehow believe something that we want is not true or healthy. Who are you to judge us?

"We are brave to celebrate our identity. All of our real friends say so. Everyone knows that outdated old 'hate manual' that you Christians read poisons your minds. Thoughtless people like you don't even want to update it to keep up with the times.[311] That book says that those who aren't for us are against us.[312] If you don't agree with us and wholeheartedly embrace our expression of love as good and right and wholesome, you are our enemies. Your Bible says so!"

Mr. False-Teacher listened to this conversation from the kitchen, texting his friend on the city council to alert him that his new guests were troublemakers who should be monitored.

"Would you not agree that it would be disingenuous and dishonest of us to call good that which we do not believe to be so, to speak of that which we believe to be false as true? We would not ask that of you. Our disagreement is no reason not to love you. The reason we, and your families, share what we believe is out of love, not hatred," Faithful entreated. "Jesus loves us each so much that he left Heaven to live a perfectly sinless life, which is impossible for us, and died the death that each of us deserves to die, after which he was restored to life to conquer death forever. As sinners ourselves, we would be hypocrites to hate others whose sins are different. But as redeemed sinners with hope for an eternal life of bliss with our Savior, we love you and want that for you also, but it requires a change of belief, as it did for each of us."

"Liar. Calling us sinners is clear evidence of your hatred. Let's go, All-Loving, we can't stay in this hate-filled environment. The False-Teachers need to get a better filter on their reservation system to avoid these vile, cruel people."

Before the wall stopped shaking from the slammed door, Looks-Good accused the others. "What's with you all? Why do you have to debate everyone? Can't you just leave well enough alone? Those people aren't hurting anyone, and they look like well-off contributors to society.

I know we believe ours is the best path in life, but they are happy enough. Why rock the boat?"

"Son, we are called to give a reason for the hope that is within us,[313] and to speak that truth in love,[314] which is what we tried to do," Christian replied. "We don't know when God might stir a heart to seek him. Contrary to what Biased and Deceived believe, not addressing their sin is unkind and unloving. Too many, misunderstanding kindness, love those close to them into hell by not helping them see the truth."

Looks-Good listened to his dad's response without comment, looking out the window, disengaged.

* * *

Christian, Faithful, Looks-Good, and Self-Disciplined set out to explore the town. The ladies said they wanted to rest. The town had something to satisfy any and every craving.[315] There were food booths with enticing visual and olfactory displays, massage booths with more "intimate" options advertised, rides to thrill, and rides to provide close physical contact in low light. People visiting the fair represented all visible combinations of sexual expression. It was a place where anything was socially permissible, where activities and lifestyles most distant from the commands of Scripture appeared most revered.

An older man had been following the four of them and joined them at a table when they stopped for a drink.

"Hello. How are you? I'm Watcher, and I've lived in this town for a long time. I saw you leave your B&B, and you looked a little bewildered. Is there anything in particular you want? If you can dream it, we can provide it. That's why people come here. So that I can honor the identity you choose, by what pronouns do you wish to be addressed?"

"Thank you for your kindness. I prefer his/him. How long has this town been here?" Looks-Good asked.

This is the oldest known town in the world. Let me share the history:

The town's founders, Beelzebub[316] and Apollyon,[317] saw so many repressed, unhappy people on the path to Celestial City that, in their kindness and wisdom, they built this town in the direct path to that destination. With no alternative routes, they ensured misguided people blindly following the guidance of religious crackpots could not miss the opportunity to find joy and satisfaction in who they have decided God intended them to be. Each person I have met who stayed here tells us they has[318] been in forced denial of who they is. Residents and long-term guests are grateful that our founders provided this place where each can choose what they wants. Anyone who is loving and kind can purchase a home or condo and stay here forever. With the ability to satisfy every desire and endless entertainment, there's no reason to go anywhere else.

The Prince of Celestial City was a famous guest of this town about two thousand years ago. Beelzebub himself was their host and offered them the position of permanent mayor if they would show our founder the honor they deserved.[319] What a simple request. Mr. B, as we call them, showed them every street and country represented here, but that pea-brained, inflexible Prince wouldn't even consider it. They took nothing offered to them, which shows just how ungrateful they is.

Now, you folks stand out a bit here with those uptight, holier-than-thou clothes you are wearing. No one in your party shows nearly enough skin for a warm day like today, and it's always warm here. Dressed like that, you will draw unwanted attention, and should expect to be heckled as fools.[320] I can take you to a nice clothing store where you can find appropriate clothing to better show off your beautiful physiques.

I was also eavesdropping on your conversation. It's part of my job. You don't need to use your church talk in Vanity. People are free to say whatever they want. There's no such thing as that archaic concept of "foul language" here,[321] because, unlike your churches, we are open-minded and love all people.

Also, unbind those wallets of yours. As I mentioned, you can find anything you want here. Live a little!

Christian responded. "Thank you for your kindness. We are only passing through town, and do not need to purchase anything here because what we value is waiting for us in Celestial City.[322] What you describe as free-spirited and open is the evil one's deception. Would you allow us to share what we believe?"

"Are you crazy? You want me to give you a chance to brainwash me as you have your poor children here? No thank you!" Watcher turned and left the four of them to wander through the town, though he remained within earshot, wincing every time they responded to a comment or question with what he would call "intolerant Bible hate speech," making notes on his smart phone and recording their conversations when he could do so without notice.

Looks-Good stopped at a snack stand and bought a drink while the others continued walking. Soon thereafter, several merchants began shouting at Christian and Faithful. As more people joined in the verbal assaults, the police eventually arrested the two of them for disturbing the peace and using hate speech, leaving Self-Disciplined to fend for himself. Looks-Good remained near enough to see what transpired but far enough away to avoid association.

At the police station, the men were questioned together, Christian first. His interrogator asked why they were in Vanity. "Officer, as we told the person who arrested us, we are only passing through town. We have no agenda. We have not provoked anyone. Are we not allowed to respond when asked why we seek Celestial City? We defended ourselves with Scripture when accused of something we know to be false,[323] but we did not initiate any of those conversations."

The chief of police entered the interrogation room. "We are loving people here. I don't want to hold you if I don't have to. If you will simply change your attitude and celebrate Vanity while you enjoy the opportunities it offers to you, apologize to those you offended, and praise our brave citizens who choose to express their love differently than you do, I would have no reason to hold you. You would be free to go on your way." Faithful replied for them both. "We cannot call a lie truth."

"Then you have tied my hands. Don't say I didn't try to help you," the chief replied.

They were subsequently charged with hate speech and taken to an ancient jail cell on the street level, immediately adjacent to the sidewalk, near the town square. The wall on the sidewalk side of the cell was constructed of floor-to-ceiling heavy bars about six inches apart, otherwise open to the street.

Some passersby mocked them mercilessly, while others threw all sorts of disgusting things at them.[324] Pedestrians passed by increasingly farther away from the cell because of the increasing stench. Still able to maintain a sense of humor, Christian mentioned to his friend, "Well, at least now we understand the origin of the term 'rotting in jail.' It sure smells like we are doing that."

A trial was arranged for that afternoon. Looks-Good went to tell his mom, sister, and Dependable what happened so that they could attend the trial. None of them were permitted to visit the men in the cell.

When the time came for the trial, Looks-Good said to his mom and siblings, "You go on ahead. I need some time alone to process what I've seen. I'll catch up in a little while."

After they left, he wrote the following note and placed it on the pillow of his parents' bed:

Proud to Be...

BED AND BREAKFAST

Vanity

Dear Mom & Dad, Joyful, and Self-Disciplined,

I love you all and hope you enjoy the rest of your journey. I have always been a good person, said and done the right things, and never done anything too bad. I think I've earned the right to live a little. For nineteen years, I have missed out on so much because I've tried to live like the rest of you. I'm going to stay here for a while to learn who I am before I join you further down the road. I will find someone here to sell me one of those certificates the rest of you have.

You don't need to worry about me. I've already made some friends who have agreed to let me stay with them as long as I want.

Love,
Looks-Good

He never rejoined them on their journey.

CHAPTER EIGHTEEN

Escape from Vanity

People hurled all manner of profanity at them in their cramped, foul, open-air prison, falsely accusing them of myriad crimes and abuses. Christian and Faithful did not respond to the taunts, threats, and accusations, following the model their Savior established two millennia before.[325]

To encourage Christian, Faithful said just above a whisper, "We suffer far less than our High Priest did before his blameless death, which provided us with eternal life. This has given us the opportunity to understand what Saint Peter meant when he expressed joy in being found worthy to suffer for the Savior."[326]

A guard soon came and transferred them to an interior cell with a shower. "Give me your clothes and each of you bathe. It's time for your trial and we don't want your stench to offend the judge. Here are towels. You will find shampoo and soap in the corner. I'll be back when your clothes have been cleaned and pressed. We want to make sure we present you at your holiest," he said taunted them, the other guards and prisoners laughing.

Guards led them to their sham trial, which was presided over by Judge Hate-Good. As with the trial their Savior endured, the prosecution produced many false witnesses,[327] but, unlike his trial, this prosecution team secured false testimony as well. The court's social media feed documented the paid and coached witnesses for those who could not fit into the packed courtroom.

Many of Vanity's upstanding and honorable residents and visitors came forward voluntarily to testify to the heinous, hateful behavior with which these men abused our town, its citizens, and its guests.

Some noted the unprovoked condemnation by these two when they referred to brave expressions of love as "not pleasing to God," contrary to the wise teaching of Pastor False-Teacher's excellent position papers and sermons on God's love for and approval of all relationships. Other wounded neighbors described how these men provoked them by saying their good, respectable actions were "contrary to God's plan for humanity's thriving," even calling some of them "sinners" right to their faces! Some were so hurt by this hate speech that they could barely testify, even under oath.

This author has never before seen so much hate expressed in one place! Had there not been a short recess for lunch, I'm not sure I could have endured it much longer. The town fortunately had the foresight to fill the vending machines outside the courtroom with anti-anxiety medications that less sophisticated towns sell only by prescription. They refilled them after the break.

Throughout the trial, many noted that these liars sometimes tried to mask their hatred with language like "a better way," even going as far as spewing such vile deceit as "we share these truths with you because of how much we love you." They have no idea what love is! The tears in the courtroom were evidence of the hurt feelings these people had caused. The testimony of our town's esteemed citizens reopened those wounds in the recounting of their horrible words and actions, which violated the highest value espoused by Vanity and encapsulated in its laws—tolerance.

Town officials expressed concern that such malicious rhetoric further undermined the high principles of open-mindedness and freedom of expression upon which the town was founded, accusing the two people of trying to destroy our community. A few testimonies were especially noteworthy, and I will quote these from the court record.

First, this was the testimony of our esteemed Envy.

"Judge, these are vile humans, though I use the term 'human' loosely in their case. I have known them for many years. They disregard those who hold different beliefs than they do, claiming that those beliefs are 'contrary to the principles of faith and holiness,' like their perversion is the only right way. I've been to their church and heard that person, Faithful, teach others how to corrupt the minds of good people who might believe differently, calling it a desire to 'save the lost,' as if we were the ones lost! They[328] has taught that our high and noble principles of tolerance and personal happiness are false and would lead to some future horrible punishment. So, not only does they speak about the good, free, and healthy lifestyles we enjoy with nothing but disdain and hatred, but goes further to condemn us as individuals. I can continue if needed, but I pray this is enough to convict them because, if I have to continue, I may become sick."

After his testimony, the courtroom exploded in angry shouts. It took Judge Hate-Good a full five minutes to calm the room down. I feared his desk would break under the repeated hammering of his gavel. Soon, extra officers were brought in to keep the gallery calm and protect these horrible people, though I don't understand why they should be protected.

Another testimony worthy of specific note is from a poor visitor to our city who came to enjoy the festivities, but their vacation was ruined by the abuse they received from the two accused.

"Sir, my name is Deluded. I just came here for a good time. I don't know these people at all, and based on the way they treated me, I have no desire to know them. What I do know is that the opinions the one who calls themself Faithful so vehemently expressed are hateful. When we spoke on the day in question, they said that my religion, our religion, was false and would lead us to ultimate destruction. They said that the way we lived did not please their God, which shows beyond doubt they doesn't know the true god, who wouldn't condemn anything that makes us happy. What more evidence would anyone need? This devil is so full of hate and unwilling to keep their vile thoughts to themself, trying to poison the minds of adults and children alike with their exclusionary drivel, like they is somehow better than us."

The last testimony I quote is from Suck-Up, a senior member of Vanity's town council.

"Your greatness, I have known this person, Faithful, for a long time, and he—to use the personal pronoun they has selected for themself today—has spoken that which ought not be spoken for all of that time! Often he has contradicted our most honorable leader, Beelzebub, and most recently, verbally attacked my fine peers on the city council who sac-

rificially serve this city. He had the audacity to call out some of our council members by name in his rants! He has condemned the values of Mx.[329] Fleshly-Desires, Ms. Luxury, Mrs. Self-Love, and Mr. Never-Enough as contrary to long life and health.

"I must ask Your Worthiness to consider what would happen if this person's primitive lies poisoned the mind of one of our illustrious leaders and they was persuaded to follow these lies? That could devastate this town and undermine our ability to stay on the right side of history. Christian has even spoken of you as an unworthy judge, and you heard it for yourself that they does not respect the authority of this court."

Judge Hate-Good, showing his nobility in the face of such disrespect, with kindness and mercy, offered the men an opportunity to respond, wherein the person Faithful responded in a mean way that sealed his fate. I am confident that our worthy judge will protect our town family from further abuse with a harsh sentence, as would be appropriate.

Please note that, for this reporting, I have corrected the offensive hate speech offered by the defense in order to protect the reader's sensitivities. It is enough to note their disrespectful assignment of a title like 'Mr.,' 'Mrs.,' or even the disgusting 'Miss' when discussing an individual based on their misconceived perceptions of a person's outward appearance, rather than their true identity as each has chosen. This caused great hurt and disruption in the courtroom.

Faithful's response, not recorded by the court, was as follows:

Judge Hate-Good, we did not seek conflict as accused. We replied to questions with the truth revealed by the Spirit of the Eternal Father as set forth in his Word. People accused us of trying to make them believe something. Anyone who believes these truths and chooses to leave their prior life behind, who turns to follow the path to Celestial City to find eternal life with true and lasting joy, chooses to do so because the Spirit of our High Priest turns the hearer's heart to that truth. I am an obedient servant to my Lord, who shares his truth, with no power to make anyone do anything.

The reason I speak contrary to what is taught here is out of my deep love for all people, which is genuine, not contrived as I am accused. My desire for many to join me in a beautiful eternity in the Savior's presence is genuine. Beelzebub, as the founder and senior official in this town, and as the sworn enemy of my Lord, has no authority over me.

In answer to Envy, what I stated was that the laws and customs of this place stand in opposition to the laws God has presented in his Holy Word, which I believe to be the only good, true, and helpful source for our ultimate contentment and union with our creator. If I misrepresent these truths as presented in Scripture, I welcome correction.

Deluded's accusations are not wholly accurate. I have been consistent in saying that worshiping the true God requires a faith which comes from the Holy Spirit. If God does not draw a person to himself, he or she cannot know him. Thus, offering anything to God as worship that does not reflect his character as he presents it in the Bible is worship of a false god.

As for the final accusation, the witness of Suck-Up, I said that the mayor of this town and the council members in their current state will not find their way to Heaven, and are leading the inhabitants of this town to an eternity in Hell. I speak such not out of anger or hatred but because I hope to persuade some to seek the truth. I pray for this town to repent and turn to find eternal joy.

The Judge asked Faithful and Christian to stand as he announced their judgment, "Sirs, your outspoken views will cause nothing but hateful division in this town, and thus I cannot in good conscience allow you to remain in this city. I sentence you to . . ."

The loud report of a gunshot cut short the judge's pronouncement. Faithful collapsed, killed instantly. The room erupted in cheers and chants of "death to all who would deny us our desires."

In the ensuing chaos, Christian escaped through a side door, while Self-Disciplined rushed his mother, sister, and Faithful's widow through the back door. All of them made it back to the B&B. They found Looks-Good's note and barely glanced over it while they rushed to pack the vehicles, paid for their rooms, and left town, just before a friend of Mr. False-Teacher called with a request to stop them.

Before his friends could find their way out of the courtroom, Faithful was welcomed at the gate of Celestial City, restored to perfect health. There, he received a hero's welcome[330] and a beautiful crown.[331] He was presented to his great High Priest, where Faithful removed his crown and set it at his Savior's feet.[332]

CHAPTER NINETEEN

A New Ally

In his rush to leave, Christian had packed everything and everyone into the SUV, leaving him driving Faithful's car alone. A man walking along the road caught his attention. Christian pulled alongside, rolled down his window, and addressed him. "I'm sorry to disturb you, but I felt a nudge to stop and talk to you."[333]

"I saw you in the courtroom. I'm sorry for the loss of your friend. My name is Hopeful. Seeing the way you and your friend conducted yourselves at the trial challenged me. Your friend gave his life to support the precious truth of God's Word. If you are going to Celestial City, and if you will have me, may I join you?"

"Friend, you are welcome. Our Lord, in his perfect sovereign plan, chose to take my brother in the Lord Faithful to be with him. It was too soon for me, but how quickly he has provided me you for a new companion,[334] for which I am grateful."

Hopeful joined Christian in the car. "Your friend's witness at the trial convicted me of my implicit acquiescence in things I knew to be wrong. Faithful's loss will not be without fruit. There are others in town who, like me, have remained silent for too long, though they believe what the Scripture teaches as true. They will seek those willing to hear and many more will pursue the Lord of Celestial City."[335]

"Hopeful, I trust the Lord's will in all things, even those I do not understand. For example, it is hard for me to believe that good could result from the sudden loss of my close friend, though intellectually I know it will. I needed your encouraging words. Thank you.

"On a less spiritual note, I have not eaten since we were imprisoned, and in my haste packing, I put all the food in the SUV," Christian told his new companion. "Do you mind if we look for a place to eat in the next town?"

"Of course! In you, I believe I get to see an example of what Jesus must have meant when he told his disciples at the well in Samaria, 'I have food to eat that you do not know about,'"[336] Hopeful responded.

"He was fed on the Word of his Father, though I do believe he has miraculously sustained me through my ordeal," Christian responded. "That said, I am hungry now! That place looks good, and it's not crowded, so let's eat there."

After they parked and got out of the vehicles, Christiana addressed her husband. "Christian, we need some time to talk about what happened in Vanity. Can we sit outside and talk before we go into the restaurant? I know you are probably famished, so I brought you one of those amazing apples from along the stream to tide you over until we eat."

They sat in a garden area outside of the restaurant used for overflow waiting.

"In the rush, I didn't even have time to grieve either Looks-Good's departure or Faithful's murder," she wept. "I feel like we failed Looks-Good. We raised him to act justly and honorably rather than believe rightly, so we are at least partly responsible for this. He is technically old enough to make his own decisions, but I never thought he would leave the family so abruptly. I don't know if I can forgive myself."

Holding his wife as she cried, Christian tried to comfort her. "I miss them too. I already feel the hole in my heart they have left, and pray that the comfort our Lord promises us will gradually fill that hole.[337]

"We made mistakes, but our God is sovereign over our mistakes. We erred in the way we directed our children when they were younger[338] and when we were not following Jesus as we do today, but we cannot circumvent God's plans, nor can we determine our children's salvation. You and I were raised to be good church people rather than seeking our Lord alone, yet God in his kindness and out of his grace chose to draw us to himself, and I praise him that he has chosen Joyful and Self-Disciplined to complete the journey to Celestial City with us. That all said, I join you in lamenting Looks-Good's decision to pursue his sinful desires. What we can do is pray."

After all had closed their eyes and bowed their heads, Christian continued, "Holy Spirit, we pray you will change Looks-Good's heart and draw him to know you. We pray that one day we will see him in Celestial City. I pray you will comfort Christiana and me in the loss of our son, and Joyful and Self-Disciplined in the loss of their brother. Further, Lord, please comfort us in the loss of our friend Faithful, and, in particular, Dependable in the loss of her husband."

"Thank you, Christian," Dependable sobbed. "It's all so fresh that I haven't fully felt the loss yet, but I know it will come. I am comforted knowing Faithful will be waiting in Celestial City, completely whole and enjoying the presence of our Lord."

CHAPTER TWENTY

Debate

The restaurant was full. Christian added his party to the waitlist and returned, as others started to fill the overflow waiting area.

"Where are you headed?" Christian asked the man who sat down beside him.

"Why, to Celestial City, of course. My name is Midas. I'm from Free-Speech.[339] I might be able to help you fellow travelers make your trip more comfortable. I can turn a profit anywhere."

"I am familiar with Free-Speech. If I remember correctly, it's a town of gated neighborhoods and grand estates, correct?" Christian asked.

"That's the place. Many of my wealthy family members live there, and always have. My great-great-great-grandfather was the patriarch of the Free-Speech family, from whom the town took its name. He was an endearing man whom people naturally trusted, and he leveraged that trust to create great wealth. Everyone there knows at least a few of my family members. For example, there is Two-Faced, who has the gift of seeing a situation from both sides; Anything-Goes, who can find profit in any situation, like our patriarch; Double-Tongued, my uncle, who is the pastor of Free-Speech Church. He crafts his messages to avoid any offense. In the rare event he offends someone, especially in preaching, he can backtrack without sounding indecisive. What a gift!

"Most of my skill, however, my grandfather taught me, who built a private-hire chauffeur service for those who will not stoop to a common taxi. There are a few in my family, fortunately few, who live with relatives because they are stupid with their wealth. They shamefully squander their well-earned income on useless missionaries, or they give away money to build orphanages and other ridiculous 'needs' from which they will never profit. We try not to talk about them. I'm rather ashamed to reveal that side of the family, but I find it surprisingly easy to be open with your family. May I share more? It might be helpful to you."

"Please do," Hopeful invited.

"One of my great uncles read about this tithe thing in that old book you hold there, where you give away ten percent of your money for religious things. He was an incredibly successful investment banker and took that tithing nonsense to an extreme. Rather than giving away ten percent, he only kept ten percent! Unbelievable, I know. He gave away ninety percent of what he earned! Because of his incredible success, his life was still comfortable, so he didn't bring too much shame on our family, but what a waste! He should have lived like a king. I'm sure those greedy missionaries and other lost causes never appreciated his sacrifice for them."

Self-Disciplined whispered to his mom, "I would have liked to have met his great uncle! What a generous man."

"You have an interesting family heritage. Are you married?" Joyful asked.

"Oh yes, I married very well. Confidence is my wife's maiden name. She and her family befriend the wealthy and the servant class and all in between. What a boon for the business! This gift also suits us well in the way we practice our faith. We are much more accommodating than those narrow-minded sorts. As my uncle taught us, we make certain that we never cause offense. We are willing to 'go with the flow,' and follow the way the good people in the town interpret religion as it evolves. One must keep up with the times, of course. We know when to wear our religion on our sleeves and when to keep it to ourselves. A confrontational, offensive mindset has a negative effect on one's ability to profit.

"The hostess is waving at me, so my table must be ready. Would you like to join us?"

"Midas, we place our faith in what we learn from the Holy Bible as written, so I'm afraid our views would offend you. Thank you for sharing your family history with us."

After Midas sat down at his table, he was joined by several friends: Hoarder, Greed, and Miser. Christian and his party were seated at the table next to them.

* * *

"Midas, my friend, so good to see you again," Hoarder started. "We were just reminiscing about our school days back in Coveting, remembering our teacher, Mr. Dissatisfied. Looks like we've all benefited from him teaching us how to profit in any and every situation, especially how to use religion to shift wealth from the foolish to the wise. It is easy to take advantage of religious people if you can just earn their trust."

He then leaned in and whispered to Midas, "Who was that I saw you talking to in the waiting area?"

Midas didn't seem to mind his new acquaintances overhearing him.

"Some people going our way, but it sounds like their path to Celestial City won't be as lucrative as ours. They seem to be haughty Christians who need to be enlightened by those of us who interpret religion correctly. They only believe what is written in that out-of-date guidebook—the Bible. Silly, really. We all worship the same god, only in different ways."[340]

"Midas, if you know, I would like to learn more about how their faulty, probably judgement, approach to religion differs from our enlightened view."

"I'm happy you asked, Miser. The misguided teachings of that sort of people fascinates me. I've heard these people talk about Jesus's sayings where he talks about selling everything to buy one pearl[341] or someone who liquidates all he has to buy a field because of the treasure it holds[342] as if it was actually sage advice. I don't know where people get these crazy notions. There are better ways to negotiate; to get what one wants without losing anything. Somehow, these people figure that zero-sum, flawed negotiation techniques can lead to gain from sacrifice, even self-induced poverty. Like God could possibly want that.[343] How could anyone call God 'good' if he, or she, expected such foolishness? I am thankful for our enlightenment, that we know that true religion results in ever-growing prosperity and the accolades of one's friends and acquaintances. I feel sorry for those poor, misguided people."

"You are on the right track there, Midas," Hoarder agreed. "Only a fool would give up what he has for such hollow promises. That's the loser's game Mr. Dissatisfied taught us to avoid so many years ago, the misguided notion that one should sacrifice one thing to gain another. What about those teachings about being wise as serpents, making hay when the sun shines, and the bees lying dormant all winter and only making honey in nice weather?[344] These crazy people seem to believe that a hard life makes them holy. Sheesh! A good God would not create good things if he didn't want us to enjoy them!

"Look at Job. God only tested him for a little while and then gave him even more. Or consider Abraham, or David, or Solomon, and their great wealth. Solomon was one of the wealthiest men of all time. He even wrote a book in their Bible about the good life, describing how he indulged in everything he could possibly want. God wants us to live the good life as a testament to him."[345]

"Well said, Hoarder," Greed commended him. "It's so clear that both Scripture and reason are on our side. With each other, it would be a waste of our time to even discuss the foolish notion of sacrifice and the risk to one's safety it represents, but to help our new friends see where they have gone astray, I propose we debate them. They need our wisdom. We can help correct their erroneous beliefs."

Midas turned his chair towards the Pilgrims' table to discuss their thoughts. "Would you be willing to engage in a friendly debate? I'd like to compare our worldviews, and I think we may be able to help correct some of your erroneous thinking."

"That could make for an interesting lunch!" Hopeful said. "Christian, would you please represent us?"

Christian nodded affirmation.

Both parties turned their chairs so that they were in one large circle around their tables. Midas set the stage. "Let's assume that some hard-working person wanted to gain the wealth he deserves, and he chose to leverage these silly rules you people believe you have to follow, turning them to his advantage? He didn't believe them, of course, but created the appearance that he did. Do the ends justify the means? Can he fake religion and maintain his honor?"

Greed spoke for his table.

Let's start with a pastor. He often starts life poor. However, if he is clever and tailors his message to those who have the most to donate to his church, and thus to his own well-being, he will grow in popularity with the right people, where he can leverage his fame to write books and generate additional income. He uses religion to achieve the good life that God intends for him to live, and would be wise to follow the path of many before him in this endeavor, with the following stipulations:

First, he cannot break any laws that would cause him to go to jail. This would lose him the gain God intended for him, as religious people would not trust him. Of course, what is not illegal is permissible.

Second, as long as his gain comes from his hard work and study, such that he becomes a better man, the gain has to be aligned with the mind of God.

Third, as he meets the needs of his church, he must become increasingly winsome and outwardly unselfish and generous, and thus becomes a better pastor and role model.

In summary, this pastor would reap the rewards of his work and calling. We should not use words like covetous in our discussion, but realize he enjoys the natural result of his dedication as he takes advantage of the opportunities God presents to him. This is an example from ministry, but it could apply to any line of work.

I offer a second example. Let's consider a tradesman, like a plumber, or a welder, or a handyman. Say this person barely makes enough money to pay the bills, and sometimes cannot pay them at all. He buys a nice set of clothes to fit in with a big church in a wealthy part of town, and signs up to be a greeter to extend his network, as he looks for a godly, wealthy wife and good, rich clients. It seems to me that people assume religious people are hardworking and honest. He puts a little fish and an innocuous Bible verse on his business card and in his advertising. This improves his brand and enhances his reputation.

He is right to leverage his religiosity for increased wealth. This is honorable and good, and here's why:

First, to become religious is a virtue. A person doesn't have to believe all of that silly stuff, it's the appearance that's important. Religious people don't do bad things because it would undermine the benefits of being religious in the first place! That makes this approach to life honorable and good.

Second, it is not against the law to marry well or to seek better prospects. It is good to do so, and the increased status from both enhances one's honor.

Third, because the gain comes from his being religious, and religion is good, then his wealth comes from being good. So, we have a good tradesman, who either finds a good, wealthy wife, good, rich customers, or both! He makes a lot of money, all from finding religion, which is good. Thus, if one becomes religious, he should expect wealth to follow. I'd argue that if such a man did not benefit in this way, his religion must not be true. A good God would never let his people be poor, because he is not poor, and aren't we made in his image?

"Well done, Greed! Truer words could not have been spoken," Miser said as he shook his hand, nodding like a bobble head. All of his peers congratulated him.

"Christian, I pose the same question to you," Miser continued. "If one's goal is wealth and comfort, is religion a good means to attain those gifts? I'm curious to see if you share our views or, if not, how yours differ."

"Thank you for the opportunity. We do have quite different views," Christian responded. "Hopeful, please correct my teaching if necessary."[346] Midas and his friends started squirming in their seats and lost their smiles soon after he started his rebuttal.

Ends rarely, if ever, justify the means if they are not aligned from the beginning.

I disagree with your premise that wealth should be one's primary goal. While wealth in and of itself is in no way sinful or evil,[347] and can be used for great good, Scripture says it is easier for a camel to go through the eye of a needle than for a rich man to enter heaven.[348] Glorifying God in our work[349] and encouraging others to place their faith in him should be our primary goals. Wealth and pride can become such distractions that they keep someone from seeking heaven. Riches can lead someone to see God only for what he has, not for who he is.

You seem to be men who value religion, so please let me share a few examples from the Bible that present a different view.

Jesus miraculously fed five thousand men who came to hear him preach. They did not come for food, but were so focused on his teaching they wouldn't leave to return home to eat. Jesus saw they were hungry and fed them.[350] This happened another time with four thousand.

They did not expect to receive food when they came to listen to him—only to feed on his Word. If they had come in anticipation of a free meal, they would have been no better than any other hypocrite who acted deceitfully in search of personal gain.

There is an example similar to your first one, Greed. A man named Simon was a magician who wanted to buy the Holy Spirit so that he could earn more from his magic, which the apostle Peter condemned.[351]

A different story might offer a contrast to your second example. Hamor and Shechem were not Jewish, but they desired wealth through trade and marriage into a wealthy

Jewish family. They thought these rich Jews would welcome them if they circumcised themselves and would then allow Sechem, Hamor's son, to marry Jacob's only daughter, whom he had previously raped. His actual desire for the marriage was to cover his impetuosity and disdain for the Jews so that they could continue trading. In the end, Hamor, Shechem, and their entire household were all killed.[352]

My next example is the Jewish religious leaders in the time of the Bible, called Pharisees. They would put on a show of long prayers to separate a widow from her wealth. Jesus condemned this behavior.[353]

My final example is Judas, who was a follower of Jesus, one of his inner circle, who initially went out to proclaim salvation through him. Yet, it seems he used his access to Jesus for his own financial gain. At least partly because of his desire for additional wealth, he betrayed Jesus.[354]

You propose deception as the path to prosperity, though you use gentler language. While man may value that approach in the way you present it, God does not.[355] Any man who would abuse religion to gain the world would just as readily eschew that religion if he believed the gain would be greater without it. What good is it to gain the world in the name of faith only to lose one's soul in the process?[356] If I read your body language correctly, you do not share my views. I fear you seek worldly goods that will not last into eternity.[357] If what you believed is not true, would you want to know it?[358]

"Our beliefs serve us quite well, thank you," Midas retorted. "We live well and do not have enemies. We wish you well, and I'm sure we will see you further down the road."

"I pray we will all find our way to Celestial City," Hopeful replied.

Everyone turned their chairs back to their tables. The Pilgrims and their guests completed their meals and departed to continue their journey. Standing to the side of the door, Christian invited his friends and family: "Let's stop and pray for them right now, but out of sight, so that we don't create the appearance of praying 'at' them.[359]

"Holy Spirit, you can change hearts. Please turn the hearts of Midas, Hoarder, Greed, and Miser to the one who is true. We can speak to them about your truth, but only you can convince them of it. Please do that. In the name of Jesus, Amen."

As they walked back to their cars, they passed in front of the window where Midas and his friends were sitting.

"You must have touched a nerve, Dad," Joyful said. "They do not look like they are doing as well with their beliefs as they said they were! Their conversation looks pretty heated."

As they walked towards the car, Christian told his family and Dependable, "If men cannot bear the truth spoken by other men, how will they stand before Jesus at the final judgment when he can read their hearts, not swayed by winsome words? If men cannot respond to words spoken through those of us who are like jars of clay,[360] how will they respond when rebuked by flames of a devouring fire?"[361]

That question hanging over them, they continued. For this leg of their journey, the guys were in the SUV and the gals in Dependable's car.

CHAPTER TWENTY-ONE

The Allure of Riches

The verdant, bucolic scenery they enjoyed as they traveled from the restaurant was unspoiled by advertisements. The travelers passed quaint towns that completed the pastoral setting. A rare advertisement jarring the landscape grabbed their attention:

The weathered-wood building at the entrance to the mine provided a welcome invitation.

"Dad, can we get out? I need to stretch and that mine looks cool. Can we go see the mine? What can it hurt?" Self-Disciplined asked. "Joyful might find another shopping opportunity ahead." Fortunately for him, she was in the other vehicle.

"Why not? I bet we all need the stretch."

As they all approached the building, a man dressed in clean, pressed miner's garb stepped out to meet them.

"Welcome, travelers. My name is Demas[362] and I care for this mine. Come in and sit down. I'll tell you a little about the history of this special place."

He offered the six of them drinks as they sat down on the rustic but comfortable furniture. "Miners extracted gold from this mine for decades. Many of them grew wildly rich. Eventually, the owners decided they had enough money to live out their lives in luxury and provide for their families well into the future. They turned it over to me to steward for travelers who might want money to continue their journeys to Celestial City in greater comfort, or so they need not worry about their provision. Many, or most, did not plan on the trip being as long as it is, nor did they anticipate the many opportunities for diversion along the way. It's fortuitous that the good Lord above put this mine here."

"Old mines are often dangerous, and we need no more money. From what I know of human nature, plus the warnings in Scripture,[363] the allure of great wealth at this point in the journey could deter one from the path to Celestial City, rather than provide support in arriving there.[364] How many of those who found gold went back to Vanity?" Christian asked.

Demas stood up to his full height before leaning closer to Christian and responding, "This mine is not dangerous unless one is careless." He completely ignored the second question.

"Thank you for your invitation, but we will return to the road to Celestial City. Before we go, though, I'd like to talk to you about your name. I think I recognize some of your ancestry in it. For example, there was Gehazi[365] I read about in the book of Kings in the Bible. Or Judas, one of those closest to Jesus yet who betrayed him for just thirty pieces of silver,[366] the value of a field.[367] Are they in your family tree?"

Demas replied in a more agreeable tone, "They are. None of us has a sinless family lineage. I do hope you make it to Celestial City, but I'll be here to help you if you need it."

As they left the building, an expensive sedan pulled up and parked in a reserved spot right next to the porch where they were standing.

Four familiar people got out.

Midas addressed Christian and Hopeful, laughing. "Well, if it isn't our misguided friends, so heavenly minded that they are no earthly good.[368] What a surprise to find you here, the way you look down on the good things in life. This was one of our planned stops along the way, a final opportunity to enrich ourselves and make the balance of the journey as comfortable as possible. We still expect to enjoy upgrades along the way and can never have enough. Providence placed this mine here to bless those who seek Him and who are wise enough to take care of themselves on the journey."

They must have called ahead, for while Midas was still talking to Christian's group, Demas brought out overalls, picks, lamps, and other mining tools.

The travelers watched Midas and his friends enter the mine as they pulled out of the parking lot. But they missed what happened next.

Midas found a rich vein. As he and his friends dug out the gold, their section of the mine collapsed, killing all four of them. Dust escaped through openings in the landscape, evidence of prior collapses caused by antiquated and sometimes rotten support infrastructure.

They joined with many others who gave up their lives in that mine, never reaching the eternal promises of Celestial City. The desire for comfort overwhelmed the drive to reach their heavenly home.

* * *

Within binocular sight from the building at the mine, Joyful noticed a sculpture of a beautiful woman in a fine dress, not far off the road, standing on an ancient stone base protected by a large circular structure with Roman columns and a Byzantine domed roof—ancient architecture devoid of wear or damage.

"Mom, can we stop, please?" Joyful asked. "I want to see that statue up close."

Christiana flashed her lights to get her husband's attention and motioned that they would pull over onto the wide shoulder. As they all got out, Joyful was the first to the statue.

"What is this material? We've seen so many statues in museums and parks, but I've never seen that stuff."

"Odd. It looks like powdered salt," Self-Disciplined responded. He looked around and continued, "The sign over there reads, simply: 'Lot's Wife.'"[369]

Dependable heard Self-Disciplined just as she was walking up to the statue. "This is humbling. Too bad that statue wasn't on the road before the mine rather than after it! We could easily have fallen into the same trap Lot's wife did. I don't know about the rest of you, but the possibilities for wealth offered by that gold mine enticed me more than I like to admit, and I'm so thankful for Christian's faithfulness and leadership." The others nodded, embarrassed.

"I wanted to argue with you at the mine, Christian. I like to believe I don't desire wealth, and thought a little more in our pockets might be prudent, uncertain of what lies ahead of us," Hopeful confessed. "This reminder of Lot's wife convicts me of my sin of greed, which I have not shared with you. It also reflects the underlying sin that too often I do not trust God to meet my needs.[370]

"My sin is not that different from Lot's wife's. When we left the mine, it drew my heart back to it. Praise God that he used you to rescue us, as he used Lot to rescue his family."

"Praise God that the Holy Spirit led me, because I was closer to succumbing to the same temptation than I want to admit," Christian lamented.

"We all need reminders like this," Christian continued. "But it's more than a reminder—it's a caution. Demas must be blind to the reminder provided by this statue, though he should be able to see it from his house. Unless he lacks all curiosity or never leaves the mine, he must have visited here at some point. My guess is, his misguided stewardship consumes him. He may understand Jesus died for his sins, yet be drawn to the comfort of a past life, and genuinely believe he is helping others achieve the ease he remembers.

"Lot's wife's story was similar. An angel of the Lord rescued her from destruction, yet she couldn't let go of her past. I wonder if she looked back not simply out of curiosity, but longing for what she gave up. Lot had been successful in the city they left, and he led them away from the comforts which that lifestyle provided—towards an uncertain future. My assumption is that her confidence remained tied up with Lot's provision and not in the Lord who saved her. So, as she walked away, she wasn't ready to leave her safe, comfortable life. This is part of the meaning of the phrase, 'a man cannot serve two masters.'"[371]

Christiana, who had been at Christian's side, hugged him more closely. "Christian, I am thankful for the wisdom God gives you. I love that I get to be your wife and praise God for the endurance he gave me to carry me through the years while he shaped you more into the image of his son. He gave me a front-row seat to watch him use your small steps of faith and obedience to grow you into the man you are today.

"I'm grateful that he called us on this journey now and not early in our marriage, when we were both so blind to the truth in our self-righteous religiosity. Back then, any of the traps which the evil one has put in our path would have undone us. I would not have had the wherewithal to endure what we have, nor what I have to assume still lies ahead."

CHAPTER 22

Calm Before the Storm

After traveling a few hours, Self-Disciplined asked, "Dad, do you know the name of the river that has been running parallel to us?"

"Perfect timing for your question, son. The sign we just passed gave it two names: 'River of God'[372] and 'River of the Water of Life.'[373] I remember the first from the Old Testament and the second from the New Testament. And it looks like a nice place for a break."

They parked beside a beautiful meadow, the river just beyond it bordered by lush vegetation. Scattered white clouds like tufts of cotton dotted the deep blue sky as their shadows drifted across the grass and flowers in the meadow. The air was pure, and the temperature was warm, but not hot. The leaves on the trees purred in the gentle breeze.

A sign near the river read: "The water from this river requires no purification. The fruit on the trees and berries on the shrubs are edible. Many of the leaves have medicinal properties. All are for your use and pleasure. Please take some with you when you depart."

Joyful cupped her hand to drink from the stream, after which she squealed loudly enough to be heard over the cascading water, "This water tastes incredible! I thought water was just water. I love this place!"

"A lot better than your diet soda, isn't it?" her brother teased. "And this fruit is the best I've ever eaten! Only a few bites in, and I'm not as hungry."

"At home you would have eaten the whole tree," Joyful shot back at him.

"And still been hungry! Never have I been full with so little!" Self-Disciplined answered. "All those days and nights camping and hiking in Scouts tell me this is a safe place for us to rest. After that incredible food, I'm ready to take a nap. This soft grass makes for a comfortable bed. The natural sounds created by this breeze and the flowing water are immensely better than my white-noise machine in Pleasantown. The twenty-third Psalm says, 'He makes me lie down in green pastures. He leads me beside still waters. He restores my soul. He leads me in paths of righteousness for his name's sake.'[374] This must be the place where this psalmist wrote that."

"Even in this great peace, I miss Looks-Good. Can we please pray for him?" Christiana pleaded.

"Of course. Lord, please lead someone to our son to speak to him words of correction that he will accept," Christian prayed. "Please draw him to you. We pray we will see him one day in Celestial City."

Though only early in the afternoon, they all lay down. The burbling brook, purring leaves, gentle breeze, and warm air lulled them into a restful, peaceful sleep.

* * *

The bright morning sun woke them. Each gave thanks for rejuvenating sleep. They hiked and enjoyed the peace and provision they found in the meadow and surrounds for the day, then enjoyed another night of rejuvenating slumber; rest they would need for their onward journey.

The following day, waking with increased vigor, they filled their water bottles at the river and packed fruit in their coolers. Self-Disciplined knew which plants had medicinal value and took some leaves.

"Thank you, Lord, for well-needed rest," Christian offered after they packed the vehicles and were about to get in. "You all look as rested as I feel. It's time to continue our journey."

The Pilgrims climbed into The Chariot while the others took the car.

* * *

The road had deteriorated, increasingly filled with potholes, dips and curves. Several of the passengers became carsick. The road then split. To the left, it looked new, smooth, and well-maintained. The arrow pointing to the left read: "Easy By-Path." The road to the right, which looked like it would be as uncomfortable as the road they had been traveling, read: "Narrow Path." They stopped to confer, as they had been without cell phone coverage for days.

"The road we are traveling is making us carsick and irritable," Christian said. "The left road looks far smoother, runs parallel as far as I can see, and is only a slight deviation. I think we will veer left."

"But Dad, Good-Guide said to stay on the narrow path,"[375] Self-Disciplined reminded him. "Last time we tried something different, we had a pretty rough outcome."

"Thank you for that reminder, son. This road looks new, so I'm sure Good-Guide has not seen it since he came this way. And it's only a slight deviation.

"Here comes a car from that smooth road. We can ask them."

Christian waved down the other car. The driver called out to him, "Hello, I'm Misplaced-Confidence, and this is my wife, Easy-Going. How can we help you?"

"Good day to you both. My name is Christian. I'm traveling with my family and our friends. Does this path lead to Celestial City?"

"It seems to. We started down Narrow Path, which should be named Awful Path, so we backtracked and took the good road. As far as we traveled it seems to lead to the same place and parallels the rotten road. We realized we had left something when we stopped for a snack and were heading back to get it. If you can wait a little while, you can follow us."

They were soon back and the Pilgrims and their fellow travelers fell in behind them. The road was so level and smooth that it lulled the passengers to sleep while the drivers fought to stay awake.

Misplaced-Confidence drove much faster and was soon out of sight. Attempting a turn too fast, no guardrail to stop him, he drove off a high, steep cliff. Both people in the car died instantly upon impact. Because the car did not explode, or even smoke, when Christian and the others drove past the spot where the car left the road, there was no evidence of the accident.

Her eyes darting around the windows, Christina asked, "Honey, where is the river?"

The Narrow Path was no longer visible. They had lost their guide and their reference. As the road was too narrow to turn around, they could only continue forward, still with no cell service to provide their location.

A violent storm blew up without warning. Thunder woke everyone with a start. The white-knuckled drivers were laser focused on navigating the wind, blinding rain, and storm-induced darkness on a slick road with steep drop offs and no guard rails.

A wide spot in the road under a large tree broke the rain, allowing the drivers to pull alongside each other and talk without exiting their vehicles.

"So much for that gentle, peaceful road we took! This is awful. Misplaced-Confidence seemed so genuine and well-informed," Christian lamented. "He must really know this road as fast as he was going. They are so far ahead of us I haven't seen them for miles."

The drivers, Christian and Hopeful, could barely hear Self-Discipline from The Chariot's passenger seat, his voice cracking as he spoke. "Dad, I didn't think this was a good idea. I wanted to honor you both as my father[376] and as a wise man of God, but it really bothered me that we ignored Good-Guide's directions. I bet he provided the 'nudge' I sensed, and I should have pushed you more. Would you have been mad at me?"

The storm abated and became a gentle rain.

"Son, I hope I would not have gotten angry, but I still may not have listened. Paul taught those of us who are older to be open to the teaching of those who are younger.[377] I still have much to learn.

"Up ahead is a blue sign that seems to indicate lodging, and the large building not too far off the road looks interesting. Let's go see if we can get out of this rain, get some supper, and find comfortable beds."

CHAPTER TWENTY-THREE

Death's Door

"Dad, this looks so cool! It's some old castle. We have never stayed in an actual castle before!" Joyful cried out.

"Lodging to befit Princess Joyful," her brother said in his most regal voice.

Christian drove through the main entrance, where a burly, middle-aged man met them. Before they could gather their luggage, he took them to a large room in the basement without offering them any greeting or information. The room appeared to be an old dungeon.

"What an amazing experience! This must be one of those reenactment places where they make the experience just like ancient times," Self-Disciplined said as the others looked around, soaking in the ambiance.

The door groaned on its hinges as their host closed and locked it from the outside.

"Hmmm. That's a little unnerving, even if it is just part of the adventure. Seems like it would be a fire hazard if they lock all the rooms from the outside," Christiana fretted.

For the next three days, they were trapped with no food or water.

"Family and friends, I pray you can forgive me one day. I seem to be on a run of poor choices and have failed you yet again. This was a big one. We're in this place with nothing and no way of escape," Christian groaned. "There is no way out. This is certainly not just some kind of immersive experience, as I also thought at first. It seems to be something far more nefarious.

"I like to believe I wanted a smooth, easy path for you, but realize it was mainly for myself. Self-Disciplined, you questioned my decision with deference and respect, yet I ignored the insights God had given you because I fell back on my old ways, stubbornly relying on my own wisdom. Now, here we are, stuck, hungry, with no idea who these people are or their plans for us. It's like we're living out a horror movie."

The layout of the castle and grounds hid its true purpose—it was the hub of a drug cartel. Many violent men and women worked there in the manufacturing and distribution of illegal narcotics. On the evening of the third day, several large men entered the dungeon carrying baseball bats. One spoke to them.

"You are not our first guests. And, like most, you will not leave."

As he finished speaking, they fell upon the traveling party and beat them mercilessly before leaving them for dead. Not one of them cried out during their beatings, like lambs led to the slaughter.[378]

The following morning, their captor visited his prisoners. "My name is Hopeless. How you all survived the beatings my men gave you last night is beyond me. Most do not. I am not heartless or without mercy. I simply cannot allow any of you to leave here. You know my face and what happens at this location, which must remain a secret. My business has been safe here for years because I do not allow unexpected visitors to depart.

"I brought you a gift to end your pain."

Hopeless laid a loaded high-caliber handgun with an extra full clip on the table beside him, near the door. "Before you think that there are any other options, I want to be clear. None of you will leave here alive. Each evening will be like yesterday, and your days will continue as they have since you arrived until you perish. That is, unless one of you has the strength of character to offer kindness to those you love, ending their lives and your own quickly."

He locked the door behind him and left them to their decisions.

Christian evaluated his options aloud. "He's probably right. I remember in the Bible Job even sought his own end rather than live the horrible life he had been living.[379] This is no way for us to die, slowly and painfully. God certainly could not intend this for us."

He moved towards the table with the handgun as he continued, "I accept my responsibility to resolve this problem."

"Christian, you definitely made a poor choice, but so did some of our Lord's disciples[380] who were with him every day," Christiana responded. "You mention Job, but remember, God restored him after his test. Even if he hadn't, taking matters into one's own hands says that we don't trust the plans that our Father in Heaven has for our lives. Do we believe he has control over all situations or not?"

"Dad, also remember the command not to commit murder.[381] There are not any caveats to it; it includes killing oneself as well. I don't know how, but God will use this time of trial for our good and his glory," Joyful added with a new lisp.

"Suicide has the added complexity that you are willfully killing not just your own body but your soul as well. That's just not an option," Dependable added, the sound of her voice muffled by a broken jaw.

Hopeful joined the conversation through the gaps where teeth used to be. "We don't know how God will use this time. I did not share the Gospel with any of our captors. Maybe God will use us to bring his redemption to these men. But, in any case, we cannot end our lives in a manner contrary to how we have lived them. We must remain firm in our trust in our Lord while we seek a way of escape should our captors' hearts be hardened to our Lord's truth."

"Let's pray that God will sustain us, and give us words of life and truth to share with our captors." Self-Disciplined led the group in prayer, though unable to kneel or even sit upright.

When Hopeless returned later that afternoon and found them praying rather than dead, he broke into a rage.

Hopeful tried to share the truth of the Gospel with him, though Hopeless's fist silenced the evangelism.[382] "Shut up with that religious nonsense. No one leaves my house alive unless they are on my business. Decide for yourselves how long you want to keep suffering, you fools!" He continued describing in great detail the various gruesome ways their torturers had killed those who preceded them.

In as kind a voice as such a monster can speak, Hopeless continued, "Please receive my kindness and mercy. End your lives quickly and painlessly. I must protect my business. It's nothing personal. To further show my compassion, my men will not visit you tonight so that you have the energy to do what is right."

He left, locking the door behind him.

"Remember what the Jews did at the Masada?[383] They killed themselves rather than become slaves, and history revered them for doing so. Is this really that different?" Christian asked.

"Let's review your journey," Hopeful started. "You eventually made it safely to Narrow Gate. After God trained you and gave you time to prepare, you battled Apollyon and his Pit Devils and shortly thereafter survived your trip through the Valley of the Shadow of Death. You endured your trial in Vanity and escaped. This is another kind of trial. Don't let your fears lead your decisions.[384] God does not promise us ease during our journey, but he does promise us a certain end if we endure with his help."[385]

With that, they agreed to pray through the night, either to find a way out or to honor God with what was left of their lives.

* * *

Before dawn the next morning, Christian woke the group. The others had to pay close attention to follow his rapid speech. "Oh my goodness. What a fool I've been, and not just for leading us to this place! In a dream, the Lord reminded me that I have had our way of escape with me all along. When I first came to faith, my mother gave me a key and I always wear it on a chain around my neck. She named the key 'Promise,' to remind me that God promises to sustain us during times of doubt and despair.[386] I never thought of it as an actual key that might open an actual lock! Let's see if it fits!"

With that, he tried the key in the lock, to find the lock opened smoothly.

"That was easy enough, but this door is so loud it will wake the entire household, so be prepared to move as fast as your injuries allow."

To their surprise, the door to their cell opened easily and silently, allowing them to crawl to the top of the dungeon's stone staircase unheard. The hinges on the door into the hall, however, were not as quiet and awakened their jailers. Initially frozen by fear, the prisoners realized none of their captors could move.[387] They were free to limp and crawl into their vehicles, which remained where they had left them, untouched, the keys still in the ignition. Before anyone in the house regained the ability to move, the travelers were well on their way.

They backtracked to where the road split, with no pursuers.

Christian got out of the car at the split, raised his hands to heaven, and announced, "God, I praise you that you are a God of second chances, and that you prevented our captors from pursuing us."

They added a warning to the Easy By-Path sign before continuing.

"Stay on Narrow Path. The easy road leads to destruction."[388]

CHAPTER TWENTY-FOUR

Satisfaction Mountain Park

Narrow Path climbed until they came to a campground with large canvas wall tents. At the parking lot entrance, engraved in beautiful gold script on the polished face of a granite boulder, they read:

As he tumbled out of the SUV, Christian fell to his knees as he prayed aloud, "Thank you, Lord. In the presence of those you have sent with me, I confess to you my failure to trust you, my desire to control our plans, and my repeated rejection of Good-Guide's direction. Thank you for your faithfulness to follow through on your promise to keep us on your path. Please grant me obedience and faith to continue in your way. Please give us rest and healing."

Shepherds tended their sheep in the mountains, orchardists picked fruit from fully laden trees, and farmers tended flourishing livestock in verdant fields. It looked like they were entering a Grandma Moses farm painting.

The staff member at the front desk welcomed them. "This is a working farm. The shepherds, farmers, and orchardists love you. The Lord of Celestial City placed them here to care for you. Our first stop will be the infirmary, where the medical team will attend to your wounds before you rest."

Their injuries treated, they were escorted or wheeled to their respective lodgings. From the outside, these appeared to be simple, off-white, heavy canvas tents—otherwise unexceptional, except for their large size. However, upon opening the flap, each found inside luxurious accommodations commensurate with a fine hotel: a whirlpool bath, a beautiful glove-leather sofa and oversized chairs, a large bed with fine pressed linens, and a large wooden desk. The lighting was warm and bright, yet not harsh. A crystal decanter of cold spring water sat on a richly carved coffee table with a tray of glasses.

Self-Disciplined and Joyful burst into their parents' tent with renewed energy shortly after Christian and Christiana had entered it themselves.

"Yours is as fancy as ours! Try the water. It's even better than the water back in that stream with all the fruit trees," Joyful exclaimed.

"This sure beats those wall tents at Scout summer camp, and I don't miss the spiders or mosquitos either," Self-Disciplined reminisced.

The satiating fruit they had picked next to the river, still fresh, had been delivered to their tents along with their luggage. The fruit sustained them as they rested until a late supper.

They walked together to the dining room for their first proper meal in many days. Their injuries healed at a miraculous rate.

"Good evening. I'm David and I'll be serving you. Here is some fresh bread to get you started. Everything we serve is from this property. Our cooks use produce exclusively from our gardens, plus dairy and meats from animals raised here, which have eaten nothing but what grows in the park and drunk the same fresh, cool water we serve our guests and enjoy ourselves.

"When I'm not waiting tables, I'm a shepherd by trade. You are now in Immanuel's Land. Everything here belongs to the Lord of Celestial City, which you can see from the top of Welcome Peak. All who come here are those whom the Lord has chosen for himself,[389] and I remind you that our High Priest laid down his life for you.[390] There are fewer false travelers this close to the city. Only those called by name turn in here.[391]

"I watched your travels. From where I tend my flock, I can see both Narrow Path and Easy By-Path. You chose the easy way first. Most people who take that path are those the Lord has not called and either die after careening into the ravine like the couple you followed or succumb to Hopeless's designs. You are safe here. The Lord of Celestial City reminds us to care for strangers.[392] You will find regenerative rest and refreshment here."

"I had no idea Misplaced-Confidence and Easy-Going had crashed and died!" Christian gasped.

"What can we expect on the road ahead?" Dependable asked.

"Those whom God has called to know him will reach their destination, but those who have not entered through Narrow Gate will not find their way into the city,"[393] David replied before departing to let them enjoy their food.

They enjoyed a healthy meal perfectly prepared to each person's preference, with delicious fruits and vegetables picked fresh and ripened on the plant along with meats impeccably aged with no additives.

After several courses, as they finished eating, David returned to their table.

"I hope you enjoyed your meal," he said with a genuine interest beyond that of typical hired staff.

"We were just telling each other that this is the best meal we have ever eaten in our lives, and not just because it was the first we had eaten in what seems like forever," Joyful gushed. "Praise God that he healed our jaws and restored our missing teeth before dinner! I don't know how to describe the flavors. This beats the best Thanksgiving dinner hands down! It was like the first time I had ever eaten real food! I am full, yet without feeling fat like I usually would after a big meal."

"If it helps, you still look a bit fat," her brother dug at her. "Just kidding, you've never looked better."

"Your delight blesses me," David beamed. "Even your childish banter tells me your injuries to your bodies and minds are healing.

"Tonight you will debrief the trauma you experienced at Hopeless's estate with our staff, who will be available for as long as you each need. The Holy Spirit's presence is especially vivid here. I pray you will each find peaceful rest when you finish. Good night."

As David departed, six people arrived. They looked like they walked in straight from the sheepfold, though with none of that "sheepy" smell. God used their giftedness to shepherd these weary travelers through processing the gruesome abuse Hopeless inflicted on them.

A few worked with their debriefers until the early morning hours and fell asleep not long before the sun came up, while others returned to their tents after only a brief discussion. Each slept soundly and woke up with the sun fully rested regardless of hours slept, all far more alive than one would expect less than twenty-four hours after escaping their near-death experience in the castle. Their damaged bodies, including cracked and broken bones, were almost healed.

* * *

After a delectable breakfast, the guests joined several farmers in a large sitting area, comfortable without pretense.

"I'm in awe," Christiana announced as everyone settled into their seats. "I was awake until three or four o'clock this morning with my debriefer, and woke up with the sun only a couple of hours later, but I feel both physically rested and healed of my emotional trauma. It's not like I don't know that it happened, but I'm not burdened by the memory. Does everyone else agree?" All nodded.

"As we have come to expect! Good morning, my name is Experience. Your restored health is what all who come here find. You met David last night. Knowledge, Discernment, Sincerity, and I are all shepherds, as were those you talked to last night. During your stay, we will discuss the trials and tribulations of your journeys, including mistakes made and lessons learned, which you will find lead you to praising God for how he has sustained you.

"But first, we will tell you about this property, which is far more than the serene camping area you have enjoyed so far."

Knowledge started by describing Error Hill. "The bodies of Hymenaeus and Alexander, men whom the apostle Paul used as examples with Timothy, are at the bottom of a cliff on the other side of that hill, a constant reminder of what happens to those who teach contrary to the truth of the Bible.[394] Also, if you look in the far distance in that direction, you can see those people wandering among tombs. That land belongs to Hopeless, and those are some of his victims whom he did not kill.

Instead, he gouged out their eyes and left them to live among the tombs to display his power and control. They pursued the same destination you seek, but were not called by name and wandered out of the way of understanding. They are now to remain among the dead."[395]

"Let's take a walk," Discernment invited. "I have something else to show you."

They arrived at an opening in the side of a hill, similar to a mine shaft. Inside, at a distance, they could see the glow from a lake of fire.[396]

"This is the passage to Hell. Many have walked this way who, it seemed, had been on the same path you all are traveling, and some for a long while. Those who entered here include those who sold out their birthrights to satisfy immediate desires, including Esau;[397] those who appeared to walk closely with our Lord yet did not trust him to save them, who sold him out in the end, including Judas;[398] those who disingenuously committed to their community of believers, then lied and abandoned their commitments, like Ananias and his wife Sapphira;[399] those who believe only in their good works, whom the savior has never known;[400] those who personify unrepentant evil in this life, including Adolph Hitler; and ultimately all who remain far from God, who never call on our Lord for salvation."

The walk back to the campground gave each time to think about what they had seen and heard. "How do we avoid those fates?" Self-Disciplined asked Sincerity.

"You must focus solely on the one who saves, and rely on him alone for your strength to continue. This comes through prayer and seeking answers in Scripture. These will sustain you on your onward journey. Foremost, however, you can rest assured, knowing that he promises not to lose any of his own."[401]

The shepherds then walked them to the top of Clear View Hill, where Knowledge showed them the gate of Celestial City through binoculars, as well as the road that would lead them there.

* * *

They stayed several more days, mornings spent sharing their experiences with their hosts, what God had taught them through their successes and failures. During their afternoons, the shepherds taught them about the farm and shared Scripture with them as they freely roamed the grounds. When they were fully restored and healed from their emotional and physical wounds, they prepared to continue their journey. The shepherds loaded their vehicles with food and water.

After they said their goodbyes, David left them with a warning. "Flatterer lives near the place where you will stop next, and there is a hotel called The Enchanted Inn. Do not listen to him, or stay there. I pray safe travels for the remainder of your journey."

CHAPTER TWENTY-FIVE

Another Decision, Another Mistake

The drive on a well-paved road through gentle rolling hills was such a change from most of the travel to this point. They approached a small town, announcing itself with a sign: "Welcome to Self-Deception."

"Dad, does this town have a cute place for lunch?" Joyful asked.

"You mean one of those overpriced places you and Mom like, where you are as hungry after you eat as you were before, all salads and fruit drinks?" Self-Disciplined worried.

"Calm down there, Self-Disciplined," their father responded. "I gave up on getting a cell signal, so I can't check. We'll just go into town and find a compromise."

Not far into town, they arrived at a diner. "This looks like it could be our only option, so it seems the town has decided for us," Christiana smiled. They were seated without a wait.

"Hello, I'm Ignorance and I'll be your server. As you can see, we aren't crowded today, so take your time."

Dependable thanked him. "Are you from here?"

"Nope. I'm headed to Celestial City, just working to save up some travel money."

"We heard there are still challenges between here and there. Have you talked to other travelers, or met any returning? Do you have your certificate, your proof of redemption?" Joyful asked.

"Many said there were challenges to get here, but I have not spoken to any heading back. I don't have a certificate, but I'm not worried. I know what God expects. I pay my bills, pray, donate my ten percent to the church, and give money to people living on the streets. I'm a good person and I do good things. God will overlook mere details when I remind him of all the good I've done."[402]

"How are you so certain? The Bible says that unless someone comes through the gate that was opened for him, he deceives himself about being on the right path,"[403] Self-Disciplined responded. "It sounds like you pursue Celestial City on your own terms. The Bible describes a person who attempts to enter Heaven that way as a thief or a robber."[404]

"We love each other best when we live and let live. You follow your faith your way and I'll follow mine my way. What's most important is that we have a faith. The rest is semantics. That gate you talk about, I know about it, but it's a long way from where I grew up. It would be a waste of time to go that far out of the way when we are already this close. Everyone from my part of the country goes the same way."

When Ignorance had gone to get their drinks, Christiana shared her concern with Dependable. "I'm afraid there may be more hope for a fool than for our waiter.[405] What I find particularly sad is that in his own perceived wisdom, he shows himself foolish."[406]

"Sad he is not on the right path. He's not bad on the eyes," Joyful chimed in.

"Joyful, you're a mess," her brother teased her.

When he returned with their drinks, Christian asked him, "Can you sit with us for a story? I would like to tell you about a man named Enough-Faith."

"I have time and enjoy stories."

"A group of brothers named Faint Heart, Mistrust, and Guilt found Enough-Faith alone in an empty street, stole his money, and beat him unconscious. They left him when other people appeared on the road. When Enough-Faith regained consciousness, he continued towards Celestial City, but he had to beg for his food and lodging for the remainder of his journey."

"Did the robbers take everything?" Joyful asked her dad, but looked at Ignorance.

"That's where it gets interesting," Christian continued. "His most valuable asset was his certificate for entrance to the city, but as this was nontransferable, it had no value to them. However, he also had several valuable jewels that the robbers didn't find. Though there were opportunities along the way to sell them and make his trip more comfortable, he would not do so, and this proved him quite wise. The King of Celestial City awarded them to him for the life he had lived."

"Esau sold his birthright for a meal.[407] Why didn't Enough-Faith sell one or two of his jewels to fund his journey?" Hopeful questioned.

"Esau's story is not a good reference," Christian continued. "There is no evidence in Scripture of Esau having faith. He lived for the moment only. Enough-Faith, to the contrary, prized his jewels because of the giver. He knew these jewels would not buy him access to Celestial City, but he could offer them to the Lord there in thanksgiving. Though his faith was small, it was sufficient because he placed it in our Savior, and thus he could not sell cheaply that which was bought for him so dearly. It was worth the struggles of this world to carry his exceptional gifts into the next.

"We must presume that these robberies are not uncommon on the king's highway. Remember that we do not travel alone. Our entourage is better than the best military convoy. Our trust must be in God to protect us, then we can rejoice as David did in the Valley of the Shadow of Death,[408] and be as resolute as Moses when he said he would rather give up the promised land than to go one step without God.[409] We can progress without fear, with God before us, though thousands come against us.[410]

"God has carried us here, and I trust he will continue to deliver us to his promised end."

Ignorance's demeanor changed. He would not engage in any further meaningful discussion, and kept their conversation to food and drink needs and paying the check. He did not even give Joyful extra attention any longer. The travelers finished their meals and walked to their cars.

* * *

"Oh no. Look up the road," Christian groaned. "It splits, again. I'm not sure you all can survive another one of my poor decisions!"

A man approached them from the restaurant, also heading towards his car. "Not sure which path to take? Going to Celestial City, yes?"

"I thought so. You appear to be the kind of people who should be headed that way, the way you carry yourselves so confidently and present such a kind demeanor. Where else would people of your strong moral character possibly be going? I could also overhear a little of your conversation in the café. You sound wise and thoughtful as well. If anyone deserved to reach that destination, it would definitely be you good people. I'm heading that way myself. Just follow me."

Without any deliberation, they got into their vehicles and followed him.

An hour or so down the road, Christian said to Christiana, "I've messed up again! I'm not sure how, but it seems I lost the man we were following. I'm going to go talk to Hopeful."

He stopped in the road and got out of the SUV to confer with his friend.

"I get us into mess after mess. I've lost the kindly man we were following. Look behind us. The road is much rougher and narrower than I realized. We can't back up. I guess we go forward and pray for a way out?"

Hopeful responded kindly, "I'm not sure we have any other options. Full steam ahead!"

They continued forward until a car blocked their way. As they pulled up, a man emerged from the car who immediately inspired their trust.

"You followed a man who seemed helpful and played on your lofty thoughts of yourselves. Am I correct?"

Christian, head hung low, his voice almost inaudible, replied simply, "Yes."

"You are not the first to be deceived by Flatterer, the false teacher. He looks so kind and helpful, like an angel of light.[411] The Lord of Celestial City sent me to you. Follow me. I will set you back on the correct path. Where did you stay overnight?"

"With the shepherds," replied Joyful.

"Did they not provide you good instruction and directions? Did they not warn you about Flatterer?"

"They did. David warned us specifically about Flatterer—by name. I had all the best intentions to heed their guidance, but this man was so helpful and seemed like he knew us,"[412] Christian answered.

"Let's sit under that tree," their Guide directed. "There will not be any more traffic on this road today."

When seated, he chastised them,[413] then offered them comfort. "I am sure you are embarrassed at being taken in by Flatterer and do not want correction from a stranger. As many as our Lord loves, he rebukes and chastens.[414] Stay focused on what he has taught you and reminds you. Repent of placing confidence in your own wisdom, ignoring what you learn from Scripture.[415] The directions the shepherds gave you are correct. Follow them. There is a place to turn around ahead, and I will lead you back to the correct road and start you down the proper path."

CHAPTER TWENTY-SIX

Not Dissuaded

"Lord, please, no more splits!" Christian begged under his breath as he drove safely past the split. A gorgeous, classic sports car approached from the opposite direction, barely squeezing in beside them. The car's license plate read: "My Way."

A convertible with the top down, the driver called to Christian and Hopeful when they lowered their windows.

"Would I be correct to assume you seek Celestial City? Mount Zion? If so, how far have you come?"

Hopeful spoke from the second car, "We met along the way and came different distances, but have been traveling for many weeks."

The driver of the other car roared with laughter before Hopeful finished his answer. "What a waste of money, time, and energy. You've all blown months of your lives on this ridiculous quest of yours."

From the back seat of The Chariot, Joyful asked, "Why do you laugh at us? Is there some reason we might not be allowed in when we get there?"

"Get there? That's just it. There is no 'there.' You've been chasing after the wind, on a fool's errand, a wild goose chase."

"You are correct that the place we seek is not of this world, but the world to come. Maybe what we seek is not what is but what will be," Christian interjected. "By the way, my name is Christian. This is my family, and these are friends we've made along the way."

"Forgive me for not introducing myself. My name is Atheist. I set out for that same mythical place, but I am no closer today than when I left my home twenty years ago!"

"But so many people encouraged us that such a place does exist and is on this path. Scripture points the believer to it as well." Christiana joined in, leaning across Christian from the passenger seat.

"Why do you think I have spent this long looking? My friends encouraged me also, and I found vigorous support for such a place in Scripture and elsewhere, but if anyone could find it, it would be me. I wanted the ease and peace it offered, those streets of gold and the beautiful landscape. What I sought most was its health benefits—living forever with no sickness! Too many of my friends died after long bouts of cancer and other diseases, and I sure didn't want that.

"I searched in vain.[416] Eventually I came to my senses and am man enough to admit my mistake. Both the place and the Lord who is supposed to rule there are pure fiction, so I am going back to the things I left where I can be comfortable and leave this foolish search.[417] I'm sorry you all wasted so much time already. Take my advice. Cut your losses, turn around, and go home. I'm done with this empty pursuit for good." Atheist drove off, his tires screeching, leaving black streaks on the road.

Hopeful squeezed in alongside the Pilgrims' SUV, and Christian asked, "While I know without a doubt we are on the right path, and we even saw Mount Zion with the shepherds, does anyone find any credibility in what this man has said?"

"He seeks what he cannot find," Dependable answered. "His unbelief has blinded him to the goal.[418] Celestial City is not hidden *per se*, but the ruler keeps those like Atheist from finding it. We committed to this way in faith[419] before we saw our destination, and this will carry us. We seek the Lord of the city, not the place itself. He sought the place and not the Lord. I'm surprised that I am reminding you of this, as I expected you to remind me! Remember what we read, 'If you stop listening to correction, my son, you will stray from the words of knowledge.'[420] We will continue on, and not be enticed back and destroyed. We must keep our faith and be saved."[421]

"Thank you, my friend, for your loving reminder. This is one of the benefits of traveling in community. It's also important to ensure our goals remain aligned. The hopes and dreams of this world are not all that have kept Atheist from finding Celestial City. The one who rules this world actively engages people to keep them, to keep us, from God.[422] Scripture reminds us that there is no lie in the Bible.[423] Because we seek the Lord of the place, and because he has drawn us, we will find it."[424]

"I wish he hadn't driven off so quickly. We didn't get to share the Gospel with him. He knows the Bible, but not the Author, which grieves me," Self-Disciplined lamented.

They drove until they came to the parking lot for The Enchanted Inn. Hopeful waved Christian into the lot and got out of the car to talk to him.

"I can barely keep my eyes open and I'm afraid I might veer off the road. Why don't we stay here for the night? It looks comfortable and safe."

"Remember what the shepherds told us about this place?" Christian asked him. "We may enjoy a restful sleep here, but never wake up. I am not about to disregard their advice again!" Then he requested their passengers' aid: "Please help Hopeful and me stay awake, to be watchful and alert, so we can arrive safely at our next stop."

"Yes, please! I see the practical wisdom of our Lord sending his disciples out in pairs.[425] On my own I would have given in to my sleepiness from that big lunch and endangered everyone with me!"

"Honey, why don't we drive on further and look for a place away from here where we can stop, get some fresh air, take a walk, and talk some to awaken our minds and our bodies," Christiana suggested to her husband.

They found a rest stop with ample open space and an area with picnic tables and benches. After a refreshing walk in the clean air, they sat down to rest and enjoy the cool breeze under a cloud-dappled sky.

"Now that our lungs are full of fresh air, I think we should sing 'Tune My Heart to Sing Thy Grace' to remind us not only what we've been through but to carry us to our destination," Joyful recommended.

"Excellent suggestion, Joyful. Please lead us," her mother responded.

They joined together and sang *a cappella,* led by Joyful, her full voice restored with no vestige of the lisp from Hopeless's castle remaining.

> *Come, Thou Fount of every blessing*
> *Tune my heart to sing Thy grace.*
> *Streams of mercy, never ceasing,*
> *Call for songs of loudest praise.*
> *Teach me some melodious sonnet*
> *Sung by flaming tongues above.*
> *Praise the mount, I'm fixed upon it*
> *Mount of Thy redeeming love.*
>
> *Here I raise my Ebenezer,*
> *Here by Thy great help I've come.*
> *And I hope, by Thy good pleasure,*
> *Safely to arrive at home.*
> *Jesus sought me when a stranger,*
> *Wandering from the fold of God.*
> *He to rescue me from danger*
> *Interposed His precious blood.*[426]

Christiana thanked her daughter. "What a brilliant suggestion, Joyful. That is certainly just what I needed, and what I think everyone needed.

The singing has further filled our lungs with this sweet air and our minds with the encouragement to continue."

"Thank you, Joyful. That was a beautiful, fitting reminder for all of us," her dad seconded. "Let's have a picnic for supper and enjoy this place a while longer."

"Not bad, sis."

Testimony

As they finished their picnic, Christian asked, "Hopeful, would you encourage us and share the story of how you came to pursue our Lord?"

"I pray my story may encourage someone and am happy to share. Thank you for asking!"

Before I started following Jesus, I pursued everything the world offered. The phrase "live life to its fullest" defined mine. I attended, or hosted, parties day and night, fueled by alcohol and drugs. I relied on illegal drugs to keep me awake or put me to sleep, to make me wild or calm me down. I progressed from a user to a dealer to a distributor. With my connections and the wealth my lifestyle generated, I purchased lavish houses and expensive cars. I had intimate relations with many women and some men who either were or wanted to be part of my world. Nothing was out of my reach as I tried to satisfy my increasing and ever-changing desires. I never contracted any diseases, by God's grace alone, because I did nothing to protect myself or my partners. I encouraged and paid for many abortions. That's how I ended up in Vanity—it readily offered everything I thought I needed to make me happy. It also shortened the distri-

bution chain because most of my customers were there. I'm thankful Hopeless did not recognize me in his castle, as he used to be one of my primary suppliers.

"But God . . . " has become one of my favorite phrases in the Bible.

But God . . . Earlier in my life, while I still lived in Pleasantown, he sent me Faithful. It was years ago that my friend shared the truth of Scripture with me, though I did not understand it as truth then, of course. Something about him compelled me to listen, which I now recognize as the Spirit of God, whom we know as Good-Guide. So even though I thought Faithful was an idiot, I still met him for coffee now and again because at least he was a kind, loving idiot.

Something he said one time rattled my world view. I don't even remember the words, and recall that I wasn't yet ready to concede the possibility of anything beyond what my immediate, carnal indulgences offered me. But over time, through the patience of my friend, Faithful, the Holy Spirit convinced me that my life would lead to death. Not dying of old age or disease, but a living death.[427] And then I saw in or heard from the Bible where it said something about God punishing the disobedient.[428] That unsettled me, at least a little.

Soon, however, my old life fully consumed me again, and I moved to Vanity.

Even there, God patiently pursued. I had no clue. It began intellectually. The things I learned from those who followed God started to make sense, so in my great wisdom (he grinned sheepishly), I determined there might be something to that religious stuff. I condescended to give the Lord some of my attention. I was an even greater fool then than I am now!

The truth he has since shown me is that he, in his grace alone, awakened my mind to who he is and what he has sufficiently accomplished on my behalf. I did nothing to earn or deserve this. He stirred my heart to attract my attention.[429] At one point, in my pride, I thought I was clever to understand that God's plan might be better than mine. He kindly and gently showed me my error, while affirming that I must still decide to follow him.

Though my beliefs started to align with Scripture, my desires and behaviors changed at a snail's pace. I didn't want to leave the comforts I worked so hard to earn and enjoyed so much. How could I leave the people I considered my friends, though now I see they only befriended me for the drugs and other decadence I provided?

I wanted God on my terms. The life of comfort I created held a tight grip on me. I wanted his benefits with no change to my lifestyle, to dictate to him the conditions of our relationship.

My great grandfather was a famous evangelist who led many to faith, so I figured his goodness flowed into me in spite of myself. God showed me that, just as my own works cannot justify me,[430] neither do I have any inherited goodness credited to me.[431]

Yet God kept pursuing me[432] in so many subtle ways. When I reflect on this period in my life, I now understand what the Bible means when it refers to God's still, small voice; he used it when I would likely have missed his voice booming from heaven.[433]

Let me share some examples of his perseverance.

First, occasionally, I would meet a godly man or woman in Vanity—yes, a few existed there—and God would speak to me through them.

Second, when I walked by the one church in town faithful to God's Word, I heard Scripture through the open window, which I had never noticed before, despite passing by often.

Occasionally my heart would bend towards someone who became sick, often because of the drugs I had sold or given them. At times I would see a hearse pass and it would bring to mind my own mortality, if even for a moment.

More frequently, I pondered what might happen to me if there were a real Heaven and a real Hell, and what if the path I was on led to Hell?

I soothed my doubts and fears as I always had—with drugs, alcohol, and sex. But God kept pursuing me, even when I ran to a life he hated. His love literally overwhelmed me.[434] What kind of God pursues a lost cause like me?

I decided I needed to do better. I started going to church, read the Bible Faithful gave me, and prayed. I even tried to share my newfound faith with my old friends. They pulled away from me because they said I wasn't as fun anymore and they didn't like my God talk. But I didn't want to talk about anything else![435] It was new and different and I knew something they didn't.

I alienated my old friends and rejected all the people at church who reached out to me because I felt unworthy. The result? I was lonely and empty—God was not sufficient for me yet. Though fear initially made me open to him, God showed me the truth that my own righteousness is nothing more than a filthy rag.[436] In my confusion and desperation, I would go back to my old life for a few days at a time to soothe my loneliness. I lived a yo-yo life.

I could . . . not . . . stop . . . sinning! I thought God's job was to fix that after I joined his team. Throughout the day, I failed often as I succumbed to the sins I tried so hard to avoid. As I raced towards rock bottom, I decided I had nothing to lose and asked a man from the church to meet with me. Today I would say he mentored me, but I didn't have that vocabulary then. I don't even remember his name, but he said something that resonated with me when I continued to struggle with sin after I confessed and tried to be better, only to fail again and again. He told me I had to be as righteous as a man who had never sinned if I would be saved. That, I certainly wasn't. But, if someone lived and never sinned, and then died and rose again to conquer death, the Father would credit that life to me. He would see that life when he looked at me, not my own.

If only![437]

The good news he shared with me, which we all live now but was foreign to me then, was that such a man did live, and he did die, and he was raised, and I could be clean! Jesus Christ lived the life impossible for me to live and died the death I deserved to die. He would make me clean—truly and forever clean—if I placed my faith in what he did, not in what I tried to do.

I gave my life to him.

Or I thought I did.

Things were great for a while, but then my thoughts attacked me, aided by the evil one. I had strayed so far, I reasoned, that it made no sense for Jesus to save me, just like that. I convinced myself that a few words wouldn't overcome all I did.[438] No way it could be that easy. I decided I must still owe him something. Sure, a change of heart might work for a good person like Faithful, but I had gone too far and done too much wrong.

I shared this with that same man from church, who read with me the story of the creditor forgiving debts. The Holy Spirit showed me that, though my sins were great, God's forgiveness was greater and faith alone in the work of his son was sufficient to save me.[439] My mentor recommended I spend a day fasting and praying for Jesus to reveal himself to me.[440] Amazing how hunger can focus prayer! He recommended I approach God simply, asking him to be merciful to me though a sinner, to implore him to change my heart to know and believe in Jesus Christ, and to seek his righteousness only.[441]

I prayed a simple prayer, over and over: 'Lord, I ask you in your great grace to save me through the death and resurrection of your son Jesus Christ.' I can't tell you how many times I begged God to reveal his son to me such that I couldn't let go of him. Now I realize I had it backwards, and it was him who would not let go of me![442]

Now I realize I didn't have to beg, but it's all I knew and God kindly responded. I might have been asleep and dreaming, or possibly awake and seeing, but I saw a radiant man dressed all in white, who had to be Jesus. His look pierced through my eyes into my soul, and he said, "Believe in me, and I will save you."[443]

I answered that I was too great a sinner to be saved, to which he responded, "My grace is sufficient for you, and my power is perfected in your weakness."[444]

And yet I had more questions. I asked him how I might place my faith in him permanently. I would start well but finish poorly—call me Mr. Wishy-Washy. Just look at my history!

He replied, "I came into the world to save sinners.[445] I died for your sins and rose to be your righteousness."[446] Overwhelmed by the peace I felt when he spoke to me, with no condemnation for my sins against him,[447] but only love for who I was in him, I had contentment for the first time in my life. I hated my old life, and what I did grieved me, but guilt no longer consumed me.

I found joy in a life focused on God and seeking his will for me. My old friends often reminded me of all the fun things we used to enjoy together that were 'forbidden' to me now that I had become "religious," to use their words. They couldn't understand that my life was full, that I was more content with my new life than I had ever been with the old one.

Rather than avoiding people at church, I began to look there for new friends. God encouraged me as I shared my story. I came to find out that many of the people I had previously avoided because of their righteous living had stories similar to mine! I found true fellowship and full satisfaction in that city so generally devoid of both. Then God used Faithful's death to connect me with you and seek new, deeper fellowship and inspire a greater commitment to follow my Savior.

"Hopeful, thank you for sharing your story, and for being so honest and transparent in doing so," Christiana said as she hugged him.

"I can't express how thankful I am for what God has done in me, and, I hope, through me," Hopeful replied.

"Lord, thank you for the work you have done in Hopeful's life," Christian prayed. "Thank you for the life you allowed him to live, to understand so clearly that what you offer us is so much greater than what the world can offer. Thank you for bringing him into our family."

Their conversation ended well after dark. Self-Disciplined got sleeping bags out of the SUV and they all spent the night where they were.

CHAPTER TWENTY-EIGHT

Ignorance

The next morning, another car pulled into the parking area. Ignorance got out and greeted his former customers.

"It's good to see you again, Ignorance. How are you with God today?" Dependable charged right in.

"We're good. God and Heaven often occupy my thoughts and I desire them."

"Unfortunately, Ignorance, there are many who esteem God, and even imagine Heaven, yet never get there. There's a verse in the Bible which says, 'The soul of the sluggard craves and gets nothing, while the soul of the diligent is richly supplied.'[448] You crave the effects of God but are not diligent in desiring the person of God."

"But I want them. I would leave everything to gain them."

"Leaving the known comforts of home for the promise of Heaven can be so difficult that some will not make the better choice," Christiana joined in. "What has changed your mind to leave everything to gain God?"

"My heart convinced me."

"Your heart is likely to deceive you,[449] Ignorance," Christian admonished as he took the lead in the conversation with Ignorance. "Scripture says, 'The one who trusts in his heart is a fool.'"[450]

"Makes sense for someone with an evil heart, but my heart is good."

"What makes you think your heart is good?"

"Because thoughts of Heaven comfort me."

"Your heart may deceive you to hope for an outcome which you have no basis to expect. The enemy of God is a great deceiver, using men's hearts to convince them of things that are almost true, and feel good, in order to keep them from what is actually true and actually good," Chrisitan continued.

"Seriously though, my heart and my life all agree. My heart shows me so!"

"What if your heart told you I was a murderer and adulterer? That wouldn't make me one, and those who know me would defend my character. More importantly, however, the one we seek in Celestial City knows all, including the thoughts on which we do not act. He determines the final judgment," Christian challenged.

"But doesn't a good heart lead to good thoughts, and from there, to a good life? Isn't a good life evidence of following God?"

"You list the order accurately, but I fear you misunderstand the source. God changes a person's heart—he is the only one who can. Only a God-changed heart can lead to correct, good thoughts. Only submission to our loving Savior, accepting his death on one's behalf, and confidence in his resurrection leads to a truly good life. No one's heart is innately good."

"You just said the same thing I did but with more words. I give up. What are good thoughts, then?"

"May I pick up the discussion here?" Hopeful asked, and Christian conceded.

"Ignorant, we are not trying to trap or confuse you. We love you and want you to join us in Celestial City.

"The specifics here are important. Good thoughts are only those which agree with the truth from the Bible. Let me first reiterate the common state of man. It is the foundation of your misunderstanding. No one is righteous in oneself, and no one does good on their own volition.[451] Without God, all of man's thoughts are sinful,[452] which is partly what is deceiving you, because you describe thoughts which are good in and of themselves. Truth is, truly good thoughts can only come from God, even for the non-believer. Evil intentions, however, are instinctive and start in childhood."[453]

"No way my heart could be bad. I'm a good person!"

"That statement is why I argue that you have never had a genuinely good thought," Hopeful continued. "You depend on something evil by its inherent nature to be naturally good, but the Son of God is the one who passes judgment on our hearts.[454] Because of sin, you cannot see yourself as you really are until God removes your spiritual blindness.

"I reiterate that our thoughts can only be truly good when they are consistent with God's Word. On our own, they cannot be right. The enemy wants to deceive you in this, because it keeps you from seeking the truth that will allow you to turn to God, which is this: in Christ alone one finds righteousness. He is the only source of the good heart you desire, and it requires a non-surgical transplant. Once we find our self-defined righteousness repugnant, we can start towards right thoughts; when we ask God to reveal to us our sins and we confess them as he shows them to us."[455]

"I'm not perfect, and I know Jesus is the one who justifies."

"You are perfectly correct, and that is valuable knowledge, though I doubt you understand what it means. I have heard nothing in this conversation where you express a need for justification through Jesus. You speak rightly that he is our source of justification, but it's not given to anyone without asking. The righteousness of God and your own righteousness cannot coexist," Hopeful responded.

"Seriously, I get it! Christ's death for sinners justifies me, and he graciously accepts me because I follow all the rules in the Bible! Because I say these right things, Jesus makes the good deeds I do, especially the religious ones, acceptable to the Father."

"Wow! That's an interesting interpretation! Except that it is contrary to Scripture," Hopeful continued to pursue Ignorant's heart with love and sound doctrine. "This faith you describe is false, taking Christ's justification and applying it to you as though it's yours to take on your terms. Your works cannot justify you,[456] regardless of how good they seem.

"I am sad, Ignorance. The justification you describe cannot and will not save you. All the sacrifices you make as you strive for a life of goodness have you on a path to the same destruction as an unrepentant thief or rapist. The soul of the justified runs to Jesus for righteousness. We have none of our own.

"Our works come out of salvation, in recognition of what Jesus does for us. They do not purchase it. We are presented as spotless by the spotlessness of Jesus, our Presenter, not because of our own good cleaning."[457]

"Nonsense, Hopeful. How could God just give us this salvation and expect nothing from us? That's contrary to everything I've been taught as a child about helping my neighbor and working hard and making good choices. If I had known I could just run to Jesus for my salvation, I would have had a lot more fun in my life!"

"I struggled with that as well. The truth of God's Word is foolishness to the world,[458] and this is part of that truth. You will remain far from God unless the Holy Spirit convicts you of your error, and miss saving faith in Christ, the only source of righteousness. On your own merits, you will lose true love for him, his Word, his ways, and his people.

"In one respect, we are both right. We do have to do something. We must repent and believe. But the gift we receive is free. You are also right that you would have had much more fun had you known this before, and peace and trust to go with it—but probably not what you would consider fun in your broken state."

"Your faith sounds like it might be good for you, but I'll keep mine. It works for me. I'm sure yours works for you. I'll catch up to you in Celestial City."

"Ignorance, you break my heart," Christiana said as she wiped tears from her eyes. "You work so hard to be good and, on your current path, you will not join us. The principle that all good things lead to the same place is one of the enemy's clever lies. I'll leave you with a few parting truths to consider and pray that you will turn and seek the only one who can give you what you seek. No one can come to Jesus unless the Father reveals him.[459]

"I pray the Holy Spirit will change your heart and awaken you to your own sinfulness. Then you will behold the beauty of the free gift of grace offered to you."[460]

"You all wear me out. You just don't get it. I'm going to stay here and rest for a while. Go on ahead. I'll see you there." Ignorance turned his back to them and walked away.

* * *

Back on the road, Christian lamented to his wife, "What saddens me most for Ignorance is his confidence in his inherent goodness and faith in his good works to save him.[461] He makes sacrifices and pursues actions which will not lead him to Celestial City. He loses the joys of this world and gains nothing in return."

"Dad, it wasn't that long ago that we were like Ignorance," Self-Disciplined reminded. "There were so many people like him back in Pleasantown, including us. And that was just our town! Those thoughts must be pretty widespread."

"You are right, Self-Disciplined. The Bible reminds us the god of this world blinds people to what is true.[462] How about the rest of you?

Was Ignorance never taught the path to salvation, or was he taught, but rejected it for his own world view?"

"Dad, Self-Disciplined and I haven't been around as long as you and Mom, but I remember reading that everyone has some knowledge of God,[463] yet most are ignorant of the truth. So, while you and Hopeful did a great job trying to share it with Mr. Ignorance, I doubt he is capable of understanding it right now and, as a result, continues to convince himself he has earned salvation on his own merits."

"Do you think he ever fears his salvation is not genuine?" Self-Disciplined asked. "I agree with Joyful. Don't look at me like that, we do agree with each other sometimes!

"It sounds like Mr. Ignorance has convinced himself he is good enough and will earn his way in through his good deeds. But we read in God's Word, 'The fear of the Lord is the beginning of knowledge; fools despise wisdom and instruction.'[464] I see Mr. Ignorance in this verse. He is more afraid of how people think of him than God's wrath.

"Genuine fear of the Lord is not the fear of loss but conviction that our sin separates us from God. That fear drives one to run to Jesus for the only salvation that creates a right relationship with the Father. It makes people pursue God and his Word, as sanctification makes them increasingly reflect the life of Jesus."[465]

"Well, out of the mouth of babes! Where did you get all that, little brother?" Joyful needled him. "Just messing with you. Pretty astute for a youngster."

"You're only two years older than me! I do read, you know."

"I praise God for the wisdom he has given both of you. I wish I had been as wise at your age," Christian praised his children before he continued.

"People like Ignorance are always uncertain of their salvation and worry about it, regardless of their bravado. This must be the case because in their minds, salvation relies on their works and begs the question, 'Have I done enough?' The answer is always 'no,' because God requires us to be perfect.[466] Perfection is impossible, of course. We know it is through our faith in Jesus—that he was crucified and has risen—that his perfection is attributed to us.[467]

"Ignorance and those like him misunderstand. Their uncertainty is exacerbated by the evil one's desire to rob them of joy, which causes them to fight harder to conquer their sin on their own. They worry fear will spoil their faith, though their faith is spoiled already because they base it on their ability. Some people bent this way consider overcoming fear a badge of honor, but the absence of fear for this person is acquiescence to the lie of their sufficient self-righteousness."

"Truly said, Christian," Christiana encouraged him. "It's been such a joy to grow with you. For most of our marriage, we were more similar to Ignorance than we were different. We tried to help each other better ourselves to be worthy, and affirmed each other in the lie that we achieved righteousness through our works. And we taught that to our children in word and deed. Before the Holy Spirit changed our hearts, we also lacked hope for right belief."

"Sorry to break up this great discussion, but we have been on the road for a pretty long time. It looks like there's a rest stop up ahead and I really need to use the facilities. I forgot to go at the last stop and I've had a lot of water. Could we please stop?" Self-Disciplined begged.

"I need to stop, too," Joyful squirmed. "Thanks, little brother."

"A nice place to sit. Facilities look clean. Good call, Self-Disciplined," his mom agreed.

CHAPTER TWENTY-NINE

Backslider's Story

"Whew. Thank you for stopping, Dad. I feel better," Self-Disciplined breathed a sigh of relief.

"Let's take a walk and get some exercise, then meet back here," Christian suggested.

When they had returned and all were comfortably seated, Christiana turned to Dependable. "In the SUV, we were discussing how the fear of the Lord differs from the fear someone like Ignorance has, and it made me think of Backslider. I think I remember some similarities in his story. He lived in our neighborhood when our children were young, but moved away. Didn't he move near you?"

"Close. He moved to a different suburb of Pleasantown named Graceless, next to my hometown of Honesty, but we attended the same church before we joined your church. His ministry blessed our church, including classes he taught, like how the fear of sin is God's kind way of turning one to himself. God used him to plant the seed for us to set out on this journey."

"Interesting! There must be more to that story, if you are willing to share," Christiana encouraged her.

"Yes. He came to our house to talk to Faithful when he had doubts. He shared with my husband that he feared expressing his doubts publicly would undermine his teaching and people's confidence in him.

"At some point, he befriended a man called Self-Reliant and eventually stopped teaching classes at church. After a while, he stopped coming over to visit and ignored Faithful's counsel. Then he stopped attending church."

Joyful's eyes widened as she gasped, "What happened?"

"Faithful and I asked that same question. We talked about it with our pastor and looked for answers in Scripture. If you will endure a lengthy monologue, I'll share the whole story."

"Please do! I'm sure we will all learn something important," Christiana answered.

I will start with his theology as he shared it with us and as we perceived it change, then go through some specifics we saw in his personal life. I only share this by way of instruction, not to judge him or gossip.

Though he seemed to be awakened to the ways of faith, he pursued God out of his strength. He attended a conference on Hell, and said, "it scared me into religion," to use his words.

That is what he was chasing—religion, not Jesus. When he had convinced himself that he was in God's good graces because he was diligently religious, he was ripe to be plucked by the evil one. He did much good for the church, and built his classes on a solid biblical foundation. Backslider's life reminds us that not all who do the right things are saved for eternity with God. Jesus even noted this in his Sermon on the Mount, that not all who call him Lord will spend eternity with him.[468]

Because Backslider did not place his faith in Christ alone, he was subject to the fears that ultimately overcame him. His status in the church afforded him associations with others who had high standing in the town. Once he had convinced himself of his goodness, he didn't need to fear Hell. His new well-meaning but lost friends played a large part in fostering this lie.

He started to interpret Scripture to support his politically correct beliefs, and avoided any statement or action that would jeopardize his position as a wise teacher in the eyes of believers and non-believers alike, or rob him of the comforts that his self-defined goodness earned him in town. Scripture speaks to this in Proverbs: 'The fear of man lays a snare.'[469]

As time passed, he assured himself that his interpretation of God's Word surpassed the simple teaching of the church. He found the church's focus on confronting sin a distraction from the work necessary for salvation. What initially turned him towards faith, the beauty and purity of salvation by grace alone through faith alone in Christ alone, became a stumbling block to his sense of earned righteousness and entitlement to Heaven gained by his merits. With no fear of Hell, he was free to pursue faith on his own terms, and in so doing, walked away from his hope of salvation.

His decline was so gradual that we were blind to it until it was too late. I regret that we were not more diligent to pursue him with the truth of God's Word. It's not a valid excuse, nor intended to be, but part of our lack of awareness was the long period over which this change gradually occurred. It was years.

The evil one is also patient as he sets snares. He plays for keeps and cleverly bides his time.

To recount changes we noticed in Backslider's behavior that led us to believe the progression I just shared:

First, Backslider's conversation trended more towards what he did and not what God did for him, in him, and through him. He still peppered his speech with church words like "blessed" and "led by God" and "as God's Word says." In retrospect, we realized it was so subtle we missed the shift.

Then he attended morning prayer in our home less often. When he did attend, he shared progressively less of his struggle with sin and dependence on God, though he still helped others work through their challenges. When he missed prayer, his excuses seemed reasonable, so, again, we missed the signs.

As we looked back to understand the transition, we realized that time with his new friend, Self-Reliant, took priority over time with his friends from church, and this is when the changes began to occur.

One summer, he announced he would not teach his signature class, "You and the Bible," in the coming fall in order to rest and refresh the curriculum he had taught for several years to keep it from becoming stale. That rationale sounded healthy and logical.

Because he usually taught during the service, we rarely saw him on Sundays, so when he began to attend church less frequently, we did not notice his absence until he was not there at all.

My husband and Backslider were good friends, and they still spent time together during his gradual withdrawal. Faithful recalled that during their conversations, his friend was increasingly focused on the character flaws or hypocrisy that he identified in other people at church or in ministry around town.[470] Faithful tried to correct him gently,[471] but Backslider was unwavering.

Honesty and Graceless were small towns quite close to each other, so we would see him around town more and more often with people whose lives seemed far from God. When Faithful shared his concerns about the company his friend kept, Backslider just passed it off as God blessing him with new friends to help him evaluate different perspectives so that he could expand and strengthen his relationships[472] and be a better friend to people. Sounded like a good plan.

Backslider strove to maintain his persona as an upright and faithful churchgoer, but Faithful ultimately noticed inconsistencies in what his friend said and did and the image he strove to portray, possibly reflecting a dual life. My husband worried that his righteousness was a facade, masking a deep desire for carnal living and sinful passions. When he confronted him from time to time, Backslider always had a plausible answer, and would convince him it was just a misunderstanding or that he had chosen his words poorly in their conversation. "Don't you worry about me. All is well," was his all-too-frequent answer.

We started seeing him around town with women who flaunted their promiscuity. At one of his visits to our home, Faithful confronted him in love, yet directly, and honored him by doing so privately in our home office. Backslider became defensive and left abruptly. It turned out to be his last visit to our home, despite repeated invitations.

He stopped attending church altogether and would not return calls from us or any other of his prior friends from church. He avoided places we frequented. We knew him from the time we thought he was a man firmly on the path to Heaven to the time he was speeding down the highway to Hell—and we missed the turn. We prayed together every night that God would convict him of his errors so that he would turn back to the truth, right up to the night before Faithful was imprisoned, and I will continue to do so until my days end.

The group emptied a tissue box during her story.

"Thank you for that summary, Dependable. I cannot keep from crying during stories like Backslider's," Christiana said.

"Yes, thank you for sharing that with us. It has to be hard sharing experiences that remind you of your husband, yet you did so with grace and honored his memory. I can only imagine how you and Faithful must have felt watching Backslider's fall first-hand, yet helpless to stop it. I'm pretty sure I would have missed it as well. That story is all too common, and it is disheartening. My heart hurts for you both. I also miss Faithful," Christian replied as he wept.

Joyful prayed, "Lord, please turn Backslider's heart to you. You promise us in your Word that you will welcome any who repent and return to you.[473] We pray for a repentant heart for him. Amen."

CHAPTER THIRTY

End of the Road

They sat in silent reflection until Christian broke the silence. "It's time we continue our journey, but it looks like this is the end of the road—literally! From here, we will have to walk. Everyone, grab your backpack and water. Leave the keys and everything else in the vehicles. Even this close, there are likely those not ready for or called to Celestial City who will benefit from them. Let's burn the ships."[474]

As they walked, Self-Disciplined asked, "Dad, what's happening here? We've only been walking a little while, but it's uphill and I have more energy than when we started. Maybe there's something with the air?"

"I feel like I could walk forever! The birds' melodic songs harmonize more beautifully than any symphony, and there are more flowers than I've ever seen, both in variety and abundance," Joyful rejoiced.

"Joyful, this place was made for your gifts," Self-Disciplined grinned, putting his arm around his sister as she leaned her head on his shoulder.

"I love your *joie de vivre*, Joyful," her mother commented. "The sign says 'Beulahland.'[475] Based on the time, the sun should be setting now, but the shadows aren't getting any longer, nor is it getting cooler. I wonder if there is perpetual sunlight and perfect weather here?"

Everyone was too distracted by the sights and sounds and smells to respond, nor did she seem to notice the lack of an answer.

After some time enjoying their new surroundings, Dependable wondered out loud, "Could our troubles be over? We could see this place from other spots along the road, which I found incredibly encouraging through the dangers we faced. But those places are not visible from here."

Joyful responded with her usual exuberance, "Self-Disciplined, you said you thought we had only been walking a little while, but that perception must reflect some sort of renewed energy, as you said, because I can't even see where we started. I just looked at my watch and we have been walking for hours! We must be near Celestial City because I recognize some of those sounds I thought were birds as human voices harmonizing with nature. While still as beautiful as the lark's song, I can now distinguish some of the words. What I hear is: 'Behold, the Lord has proclaimed to the end of the earth; behold, your salvation comes; behold, his reward is with him, and his recompense before him. And they shall be called The Holy People, The Redeemed of the Lord; and you shall be called Sought Out, A City Not Forsaken.'"[476]

Cresting the top of the mountain they climbed, Hopeful joined in the excited conversation. "Those must be the walls of the city! They look like they are made of pure gold, embedded with huge pearls and precious stones. From this height I can see behind the walls, and the streets appear to be paved with gold."[477]

"Oh my goodness," Joyful exclaimed, beaming, "the sight of the city is almost blinding in the sunlight. Combine that with the sweetness of the air, the song of the voices harmonizing with the music of the birds, plus the natural beauty around us, and it should overwhelm my senses, but it doesn't. I'm not even remotely tired, but can we stop for a little while to soak this all in? Prior to now, I did not know how to follow that passage from the Psalms where it says, 'Be still, and know that I am God,'[478] but now it's all I want to do. I'm okay if we want to continue, but for the first time in my life I really just want to be still."[479]

That thought must have resonated with everyone else, for they all just stopped and stood silently. After an indeterminate amount of time had passed, they continued walking, passing through orchards, vineyards, and gardens. The land was increasingly more cultivated as they progressed. They entered one of the gardens, where the gardener spoke to the group.

"Welcome. Before you is one of the King's properties that I oversee. He had these planted for his own delight and to provide nourishment for travelers to Celestial City. You are free to eat and drink anything you find here. When you are ready, please proceed to that grove of trees over there, where you will find the ground more comfortable than the best mattress. Though I doubt you are tired, you still require sleep on this side of the wall. All travelers find rest here, even those not invited to the city."[480]

Joyful was first to the orchard and took a bite from a piece of fruit she picked. "Oh… my… gosh! This is the… best… food I have ever tasted, in the most beautiful place I have ever been!"

The group looked like bobble heads nodding so vigorously, elation beaming from every face.

"From the hill, it looks like Celestial City promises even greater beauty than this, but, for now, I am so thankful for this place that the King of that city has provided for rest before entering."

They removed their small packs and settled into the comfort of their grassy beds. In the grove of trees, the rustling leaves combined with the celestial song lulled each into a deep, restful sleep within minutes.

CHAPTER THIRTY-ONE

Test of Faith

All were awake, bright eyed, furrowed brows smooth for the first time during their long journey. Several of them sang or whistled.

Christian spoke to them. "That is what I call rest! Assuming my watch still works, it's only five o'clock, but my sleep replenished my energy beyond what I've ever experienced. It gives a new meaning to that saying 'Short but Sweet.'

"Our senses must have adapted to the majesty of this place, as none of us is squinting any longer. I agree with Joyful; we could not have enjoyed this environment at the beginning of our travels. It would have overpowered us.

"But this is not our final destination, so time to move."

Before they were ready to leave, two men arrived. They looked like living statues gleaming in gold-leaf raiment; their faces radiated light.

"Because you have grown in trust and faith through your journey, you are no longer afraid of us. Please tell us about your travels."[481]

They sat down and each shared a component of their shared or unique experiences through their different lenses and interpretations. The conversation lasted several hours, but there was no sense of time passing.

At the conclusion of their discussion, one of the men declared, "You must undergo two more trials, even in this place, before you can enter the city. Though we will walk with you, you must overcome these challenges in your own faith."

"Behind us is your first obstacle," the other said. "At the bottom of this mountain, you can see a river. There are no bridges or boats provided by the Lord of the city and no way to circumvent it. You must go through the river to reach the city gates. Only three people entered the city without going through the river or the gate—Elijah,[482] Enoch,[483] and the original builder, Jesus.[484] And they will be the only three until the last days, when the final trumpet sounds."[485]

"Is the river deep throughout, or might there be a shallower place to wade across?" Christian asked anxiously.

"The water varies in depth according to the faith the wader has in the Lord."

They descended the hill and entered the water together. Christian immediately started sinking, then panicked.

"The water is deep! I'm going to drown. To be so close and yet to drown in sight of the gates makes this my saddest day."

"Dad, do not be afraid. Our feet are on solid ground on the bottom," Joyful and Self-Disciplined encouraged him almost in unison. "Ahead of us there are men at the gate, ready to welcome us."

"But it's deeper here and I continue to sink. I'm afraid my sins have caught up to me at last and prove me unworthy. Family, Hopeful, Dependable, it is you that those men wait to welcome. I am lost," Christian cried in despair.

"Christian, your own strength will not save you. You know on whom to call," Christiana lovingly challenged him.

Calm but firm, Joyful and Self-Disciplined called to their father. "Dad, Jesus is the one who makes you whole. Trust him alone.[486] There is now no condemnation for him who is in Christ Jesus!"[487]

Christian lifted his head and shouted, "Jesus, please rescue me! I believe, help my unbelief![488]

He turned to his family and continued in excitement, "I see him again! Thank you! He reminds me he will be with me as I pass through the waters, and that the rivers I cross will not consume me.[489] I allowed my fears to overwhelm me, contrary to the peace we have experienced since arriving here. The thought of not entering the land of plenty with all of you was crushing me. My feet are on solid ground now."[490]

As they climbed out on the other side, the men who had been with them when they entered the water met them. "We are ministering angels, sent by the King to minister to those who are heirs of salvation. We will attend you to the gate. Welcome."

Christian fell to his knees and wept tears of joy and relief.

CHAPTER THIRTY-TWO

Celestial City

The Pilgrims, Dependable, and Hopeful entered the river in the clothing given to them just after their salvation, beautiful but worn. They emerged on the other side clothed in spotless, shining white robes.

They immediately met their second challenge. The climb from the river to the gate was steep and long, the city at the top hidden by clouds.

Dependable spoke as she entered the clouds about three-fourths of the way to the top. "Before we left home, to climb to this point would have required several breaks. If I could have made it this far, I would have been so breathless from the effort and the altitude that there is no way I could carry on a conversation. Yet, here I am, here we are, talking as if we were out for a gentle stroll through the orchards where we rested in Beulahland."

The ministering angels tried to describe the inexpressible glory and beauty of Celestial City, inhabited by angels and the spirits of the redeemed,[491] wearing white robes in paradise, fed by the tree of life and its never-fading fruits, in the presence of the King for all eternity.[492]

"You will never again experience the challenges you endured during your journey. Christian, we watched the wrong paths you followed. The King has forgiven you for these. Here there are no wrong turns, nor sickness, sorrow, or death. All the former things have passed away. You will join Abraham, Isaac, Jacob, and all the prophets of old, the people whom

God rescued from evil to join him, each walking in the righteousness of the Father through the work of his Son.[493]

"Perfect rest from your labor awaits you. Joy is exchanged for your sorrows. You will enjoy the fruit of your prayers, tears, and sufferings for the King. Each of you will be given gold crowns to wear until you are presented to the King of the land, where you will eagerly lay them at his feet.[494] You will know the King as he truly is,[495] and enjoy endless days singing his praises along with all who are there.[496] Inside the gates, you are now forever beyond the reach of the enemy and his lies."

As they neared the closed gate, a company of the heavenly greeted them and their hosts introduced them. "These loved our Lord when they were in the world and left everything behind for his holy name. He sent us to shepherd them through the final stages of their journey, that they might behold the face of their Redeemer."

When they finished speaking, the crowd cheered, shouting, "Blessed are those invited to the Lamb's marriage feast."[497]

Several of the King's trumpeters, gleaming in white, came out to announce their entrance into Heaven with beautiful music, so that all the heavens echoed with the sound.

The city seemed to empty to welcome them, crowding around on all sides. As they walked, the music, the joy in the faces of their welcomers, and the shouts of homecoming increased, while the bells within the walls rang out. The overwhelming joy expressed in each of their faces left them temporarily speechless. In this euphoric state they reached the gate,[498] over which was written in jeweled script:

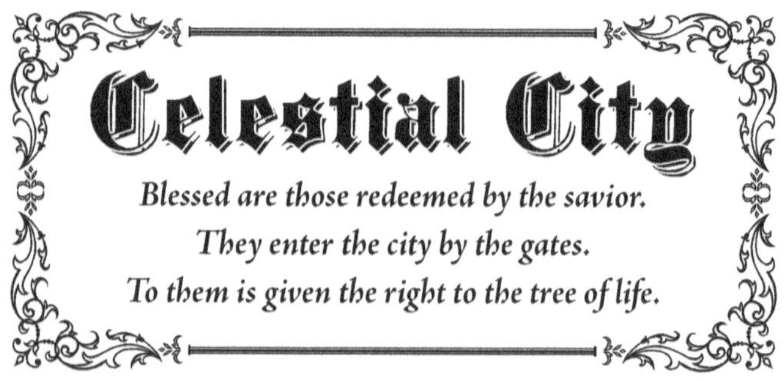

Civility and Faithful, with many of the ancient patriarchs, including Moses, Enoch, and Elijah, watched their entrance from the wall over the gate. The ministering angels announced, "These exiles left their homes in Pleasantown, which we know as Condemned City, traveling in the love they have for the King of Celestial City."

Each offered their sealed envelope to be delivered to the King for review. Upon opening and reading them, the King sent back word to open the gate with these words: "Welcome those righteous who kept the truth and remained faithful."[499]

As Christian, Christiana, Joyful, Self-Disciplined, Hopeful, and Dependable entered the gates, they were transformed; their clothing shone like gold. Each received the promised crowns to the sound of bells tolling their entrance to the city. The crowd shouted in unison, "Welcome!"

They then heard the voice of the King of that city, clear and close, "Enter into the joy of your Lord!"[500]

The travelers joined all present in exclaiming, "Blessing and honor and glory and power to the one seated on the throne, and to the Lamb, forever and ever!"[501]

"This … is … awesome! In the truest sense of the word!" Joyful and Self-Disciplined cheered.

Joyful continued, "The streets are literally paved with gold and the city shines like the sun,[502] just like it says in the Bible—even the crowns and the angels. The Bible always started with 'fear not' when an angel showed up, but here there is no fear!"

"We are home," Christian said through joyful tears, his shoulders relaxed for the first time since leaving Pleasantown, and likely many years prior to that. "Lord, we praise you for bringing us safely to your kingdom."

After the crowd reentered the city, the gates were closed and bolted behind them, thus ending the Pilgrims', Dependable's, and Hopeful's trials. They began their eternity in the presence and service of the Savior.

CHAPTER THIRTY-THREE

Not Welcome

Ignorance reached the river a few days behind the last group. False-Hope helped him reach the far bank in a boat he kept hidden in the reeds. Ignorance thus avoided the faith and risk required of those who had crossed before him.

He struggled up the hill, taking several breaks and falling often. When at long last he reached the closed gate, he was alone. His voice mocked the text as he read it aloud with no audience to hear, "'Blessed are those who are redeemed by the savior? They enter the city by the gates? To them is given the right to the tree of life?' Sounds a bit convoluted. What happened to simply, 'Welcome to Celestial City. Congratulations! You've earned it.'"

He swung the metal knocker like a battering ram and danced back and forth like he was waiting for someone overdue.

In time, guards peered over the wall and asked him, "Who are you? How did you get here? What do you want?"

Ignorance replied confidently, a shocked look on his face, "What do you mean? I've read about the King of this place, and know all about him. I've done the good things his book says to do.[503] So open the gate and give me what is mine."

"Where are your documents?"

He replied with growing impatience, "What documents? I told you, I did what I was supposed to do, so just open the gates. Why do you make me wait?"

The guards reported the situation to the King, who not only refused Ignorance admission, but sent angels to bind him and take him to the opening on the side of the hill in Satisfaction Mountain Park. There they handed him over to those at that entrance, who conducted him in to eternal absence from God and the never-ending suffering of Hell.[504]

CHAPTER THIRTY-FOUR

Awakened Challenge

I awoke in a cold sweat, understanding for the first time through my dream that there is a path to Hell from the very gates of Heaven. The truth of what Jesus said in the Bible was indelibly imprinted on my mind, "Not everyone who says to me, 'Lord, Lord,' will enter the kingdom of Heaven, but the one who does the will of my Father who is in Heaven. On that day, many will say to me, 'Lord, Lord, did we not prophesy in your name, and cast out demons in your name, and do many mighty works in your name?' And then will I declare to them, 'I never knew you; depart from me, you workers of lawlessness.'"[505]

I have shared my dream. Interpret it as you will. Agree or disagree, but do so based on what you find in the Bible, not relying on your thoughts alone.

My dream expounds elements of Scripture as God chose to reveal them to me. Allow him to lead you into revelation of who he is through his Holy Word, to know him and his Son, Jesus, crucified and risen.

The Holy Spirit, through Scripture, reveals the key to salvation and how to live a holy life. He transforms those who believe to better reflect the Savior. Store up the words in the dream I have told if they lead you to believe and act upon the truth of the Bible. Discard any that are superfluous or lead you away from it.

Questions for Personal or Group Reflection

Whether answered individually or in a group study, the purpose of the following questions is to help the reader(s) apply the triumphs or challenges in each chapter to one's own life. I encourage you to use Scripture to support your answers. The Bible references in the footnotes will provide you with a good place to start.

Chapter 1—Pleasantown

- Cultural norms often conflict with what the Bible teaches. Have you tried to defend the truth of Scripture when your friends sided with culture? If so, how did it go? What might you do differently next time? If not, what keeps you from sharing this truth and how can you overcome that obstacle?

- Which motivates your behavior more often—fear of something (loss, punishment, repercussions) or hope for something (praise, reward, gain)? How has that affected your relationships, leadership in your family, or your workplace? How would you like to be different and how will you pursue that change?

- This story is told from the perspective of a dream. How can you discern if your dreams, thoughts, or ideas are from God? What Scripture confirms your answer?

Chapter 2—Challenged

- Christian says, "Friends, you know I am a peacemaker, and not prone to cause a controversy." Is it possible to be a peacemaker[506] and still confront false teaching? Provide examples of how you have done so or would do so.

- Do you agree with Christian when he says that he has not been a good friend to Obstinate and Flexible because he has not tried to correct them when their views differed from the Bible? Why or why not?

- Christian seems confident that Celestial City (Heaven) exists. Do you think the Bible references a literal Heaven, or is it more figurative? Support your answer with Scripture.

Chapter 3—Flexible's Journey

- Self-Disciplined uses Scripture to support his claim that the Bible is true. Is this "circular logic" a valid way to support the truth claim of Scripture? Why or why not? (Consider reading chapter 4 in Wayne Grudem's *Systematic Theology*[507] to help you answer this question.)

- Have you read something in Scripture that you thought might not be true? What was it? How did you reconcile your belief with what you read? If you have doubts about the truthfulness of Scripture, with whom can you discuss those concerns?

- The footnotes include this quote from G. K. Chesterton: "The Christian ideal has not been tried and found wanting. It has been found difficult; and left untried."[508] Put this quote into your own words. Why do you agree or disagree?

Chapter 4—Tempted

- Christiana and Joyful are drawn to quaint shops and cafés on their journey. It could have been a bookshop or outdoors superstore drawing in the whole family. Is there anything wrong with that? Could there be? If so, how does one know when he or she has crossed that line?

- Pastor Ear Tickler teaches that we should ignore sin and focus only on the gifts God offers us. If you followed this advice, how would following such advice affect your faith and growth into the image of Christ? What do you find in the Bible on this topic?

- Self-Disciplined references suffering as a blessing. How can that be? Give examples from your own life and Scripture.

Chapter 5—Not Narrow Gate

- People often post their "best face" on social media, like Pastor Legality did. How can you use social media to more honestly reflect your life and in a way that glorifies God?

- What is the difference between godly obedience and legalism? How do you fulfill your desire to obey God and his commands without falling into legalism?

- Good-Guide is rather harsh with Christian because he loves him. When is it loving and kind to share the truth you know will be hard to hear? Share a time when you have done this, how, and the results, or discuss how you would.

Chapter 6—Narrow Gate

- If you had the opportunity to sit across from Jesus in the flesh today, how would you feel towards him? Confident? Overwhelmed? Afraid? Something else? Why?

- Christian's voice at the door was feeble and weak, yet Interpreter still opened the door and welcomed him. How does this relate to your experience as a Christian? How do you feel knowing that God answers your requests even if you express them weakly and without confidence?

- Interpreter says he turns no one away, and then qualifies his statement to refer to those whom Good-Guide sends. Why did he qualify his statement? Support your answer with Scripture.

Chapter 7—House of Visions

- Has reading the Bible frustrated you because it did not make sense? Have you read it and found surprising clarity? Most people experience both. What methods could you use or have you used to help you understand the more difficult passages? (If you need help, talk to a more spiritually mature Christian friend or your pastor.)

- This chapter is told through stories and pictures, a common approach when Jesus teaches. Why did Jesus teach in parables rather than just saying things plainly? (The disciples had the same question!) Support your answer with Scripture.

- Which room interested you most? Why?

Chapter 8—Relief

- After a long life of deceiving and hurting people, can someone just start following Jesus and receive his forgiveness like Civility did? If someone receives complete mercy, is justice denied? How can justice and mercy coexist? Support your answer with Scripture.

- If someone deceived you, hurt you physically or emotionally, stole from you, or did so to someone you love, and, afterward, started following Jesus, would you receive them with joy as a fellow brother or sister in Christ? What would you want to see in their life to help you do so? Would you be angry if he or she had not suffered first? If your answers are not what you want them to be, how can you grow so that you would answer differently?

- When you first became a Christian and asked Jesus to remove the burden of your sin, did you experience the relief the Pilgrims and Civility felt? Describe what you remember about that time.

Chapter 9—Rebuffed

- What do you think it means to be lazy with respect to faith? Have you been lazy in your faith? Who in your life can help you find or renew zeal for God and his Word?

- The character Tradition implies that logic and tradition are as valid as Scripture in guiding one's beliefs and behavior. Some depict Scripture, tradition, and reason as the three legs of a stool. Do each of these merit the same weight? Why or why not? Support your answer from the Bible.

- Why do you think Tradition and Hypocrisy lack packs heavy with the weight of their sins? Does this imply they have no sins to forgive? Explain your answer.

Chapter 10—Three Choices

- Tradition, Hypocrisy, and their drivers placed their confidence in their own wisdom. Have you done the same? Explain. If not, do you know others who have? Describe what happened (without naming names if discussing as a group).

- Share a time in your life when you ignored what you knew to be the right decision based on Scripture or ignored the nudges of the Holy Spirit, because your thoughts made more sense to you. What happened?

- The Bible commends godly rest as a way to honor God and enjoy his blessings.[509] However, the Pilgrims' sleep is described as a sinful choice. What is the difference between sinful sleep and godly rest?

Chapter 11—Lodge Beautiful

- Can you remember a time when you had or lacked spiritual boldness in the face of a trial? Describe the situation and the outcome. How can you prepare yourself to respond with spiritual boldness?

- Is it possible to live your life so that you never make a sinful mistake? Use Scripture to explain your answer.

- What should you do when you feel trapped in your inability to stop sinning? What Scripture verses guide you in your response?

Chapter 12—Museum at Lodge Beautiful

- Watchful tells the travelers that the Lord has many ways of protecting his own. How have you experienced God's protection? Use specific examples.

- What is the *Lamb's Book of Life*? Is your name written in it? How can you be sure? Support your answer with Scripture.

- Do you think it surprised the Pilgrims to find enemies on the road to Celestial City, and that they would need armor and weapons?

As a Christian today, what enemies do you face and how do you prepare for those battles?

Chapter 13—Battle in the Valley

- Satan (represented by Apollyon in this chapter) is a liar by nature, but can be smooth and convincing in order to try to separate us from God. What lies do you believe that are keeping you from being closer to God?
- Satan loves to remind us of past (or current) sins in an attempt to make us feel unworthy of God's love and forgiveness, and wants us to believe that our sins are unforgivable. Use Scripture to refute this.
- When Apollyon accuses him of sin, Christian not only agrees, but implies that he is more of a sinner than his enemy realizes. How does this disarm Apollyon's attack?

Chapter 14—New Valley, New Dangers

- Describe a time in your life when you were afraid and God conquered your fear.
- When they were anxious and afraid, the Pilgrims turned to prayer. What does the Bible say about prayer in these situations, and what is the promised outcome?
- What do you think the Valley of the Shadow of Death represents in the life of a Christian? Have you ever walked through this valley? Describe your experience.

Chapter 15—Companions

- Is there someone you hold in high esteem as a faithful follower of Jesus? What impresses you about this person? How would learning of their failures and sins affect you?

- Self-Disciplined says, "The law is good to condemn, but not to save." Is he correct? Support your answer with Scripture.

- The lives of the Pilgrims are in some ways similar to those of Faithful and Dependable, but there are also significant differences. What elements of the Christian life should be common to believers and what components can differ? How do these similarities and differences encourage or challenge you?

Chapter 16—Lip Service

- How would you confront a friend, in a loving but firm way, who claims to be a Christian but whose life reflects none of the fruits of the Spirit?[510] What would you say to them? Have you ever done so? If so, describe the outcome.

- The Pilgrims failed to convince Lip-Service and Flexible of the truth of Scripture. Good-Guide, however, sees this not as failure, but as "sowing seed." People do not always respond immediately—or seemingly ever[511]—to the seeds of truth that the believer sows, only to sprout and grow later. How does this affect your view of evangelism, sharing God's Word? How do you know when to stay and when to walk away? How could you separate from a person like Lip-Service while leaving the door open to future conversations?

- What are your greatest temptations? Comfort? Self-sufficiency? Control? Lust? Something else? How do you fight temptation? What does Scripture say about confessing to others? Do you confess regularly to another person?

Chapter 17—Vanity

- Christiana tries to comfort Deceived and help him understand that his parents love him. How can you show love to someone who lives in unrepentant sin without condoning their sin?
- Deceived mentions that his church is careful to avoid controversial teachings to ensure everyone feels welcome. Is this biblical? Support your answer with Scripture.
- Biased accuses Christian of being "on the wrong side of history." Can scriptural truth become outdated? Should changing social norms influence your view of what the Bible says is true? Explain your answer.

Chapter 18—Escape from Vanity

- The reporter for the court stated that Faithful and Christian "have no idea what love is." Why do you think he or she says this? Is it true?
- Faithful references Peter's quote about finding it a joy to suffer for his savior. Can one really do that? Could you? Explain your answer or describe your experience.
- What are some things the Bible tells us about heaven? What about heaven entices you?

Chapter 19—A New Ally

- Have you lost someone close to you or experienced deep disappointment? How did you process this loss? Did your faith help you?
- It's easy to say we trust in God's better plans, but it can be hard to live that way in the face of significant loss or disappointment. What verses can you use to comfort and encourage yourself or others?
- What inspired Hopeful to join the Pilgrims and Dependable on their journey to Celestial City? Does this change your thoughts about Faithful and his sacrifice? In what way?

Chapter 20—Debate

- Christian references Matthew 19:24 about how difficult it is for a rich man to reach heaven. Do you agree it is hard for a rich person to follow Jesus faithfully? Why or why not?
- Greed argues that the goal of work is predominantly wealth creation, and that it should apply to any kind of job. What does Scripture say about how to approach work?
- Is it wrong for a follower of Jesus to acquire wealth? Support your answer with Scripture.

Chapter 21—The Allure of Riches

- 1 Timothy 6:10 is often misquoted as "money is the root of all evil." What is the correct language? What does that mean to you?
- While money can distract someone from following Jesus, it can also be a helpful aid in ministry, providing for the needs of families and individuals, the church, and its missions. What are some warning signs that money might be pulling you or someone you love away from Christ?

- What would hold you back from answering "yes" to anything God would ask of you? What comforts do you not want to give up?

Chapter 22—Calm Before the Storm

- Describe a time when you have felt God providing you supernatural rest. If you have not experienced this, what do you think it would be like? Pray through Psalm 23. (If praying through Scripture is unfamiliar to you, Episode 999 of the *Desiring God* podcast[512] may be helpful to you.)
- Self-Disciplined tried to question his dad respectfully, but Christian ignored him. What keeps you from listening to the counsel of those younger than or junior to you?[513] Does your demeanor make it hard for someone to question you? How can you become more inviting to suggestions?
- What does Scripture say about obeying those in authority? How can you respectfully question a parent or leader without violating the commands of Scripture?

Chapter 23—Death's Door

- Some believe a Christian should not suffer, even going so far as to say that suffering is evidence of distance from God. What does Scripture say about the probability of suffering in the life of a true follower of Jesus? (The Gospel Coalition website offers a good overview of the Theology of Suffering.[514])

- Hopeless offers the travelers the means to commit murder/suicide to end their suffering. This is not fundamentally different from assisted suicide, which is gaining acceptance as a "loving option" in some countries. How have you or could you comfort someone with a terminal illness? (For additional information, see Todd Billings's article in *Christianity Today*.[515])

- Hopeless tries to share the Gospel with his captor. Have you been in a situation where sharing the Gospel might seem crazy or even dangerous? What did you do? What would you do?

Chapter 24—Satisfaction Mountain Park

- Though not using the Word, this chapter addresses the question of election: do we choose God, or does he choose us? If the latter, does our choice then actually matter? Support your answer with Scripture. (Consider reading chapter 32 in Wayne Grudem's *Systematic Theology*.[516])

- Election (also called predestination) is a controversial topic for many people. How do you address difficult topics in your conversations? What do you think the most loving approach is and why?

- David shows his guests several examples of people who seemed to be on the path to Celestial City (following Jesus), yet who failed to reach their destination, warning the Pilgrims and their companions against error. If the true follower of Jesus is predestined for eternity with God, why must he or she be concerned about things that draw one away from the correct path? What does this mean for the life of the Christian?

Chapter 25—Another Decision, Another Mistake

- Ignorance believes he will enter heaven based on his merits. Followers of Jesus do good works in response to the grace he has given us. Share examples of good works you did before and after your salvation. How do they differ, both in practice and intent? Use Scripture to contrast this position with Ignorance's view.
- Some struggle with understanding a loving God who punishes and rebukes. Use Scripture to show that it is loving for God to do so. As a parent or a child, has your experience with discipline (offering it or receiving it) differed from the Biblical model? If so, how?
- How can you tell if your sense of guilt is the Holy Spirit convicting you or Satan condemning you? Read and discuss Olan Stubbs's article, "Conviction vs. Condemnation" in *Campus Ministry Today*.[517]

Chapter 26—Not Dissuaded

- What is your hope for heaven? Why do you want to go there? Why do you think Atheist was so discouraged?

- The Bible describes Heaven's awe-inspiring physical attributes, but what does it say will be the best thing about it? Use Scripture to defend your answer.

- Community is vital for Christians. When Atheist causes Christian to doubt his quest, Dependable reminds her friend of the truth. Who is walking with you on your Christian journey, to encourage and remind you of Scripture's truth? Who do you encourage and challenge? If you don't have someone walking with you, or someone with whom you are walking, ask God to reveal that person or those people to you.

Chapter 27—Testimony

- Hopeful talks about a "life of death." What does that mean? Has God rescued you or someone you know from such a life? Share that story.

- Regeneration[518] is the moment when God gives a person a new spiritual life, which results in a change in that person's nature, producing the fruits of the spirit.[519] Where do you see evidence of regeneration in the story of Hopeful?

- Hopeful shared the story of his Christian journey with the Pilgrims. Have you shared the story of your walk with Christ with others? If not, do so. Write out your story this week.

Chapter 28—Ignorance

- Share a time when your emotions tempted you to disobey God's Word, knowing such action would be wrong. If you disobeyed, what was the outcome? If you did not, what helped you remain faithful? How can you bolster your resistance to this or other temptation in the future? (Note, if you are more of a "thinker" than a "feeler," replace "emotions" with "thoughts" in this question.)

- Some societies are increasingly trending towards a "follow your heart" mindset. How would you lovingly use Scripture to confront a friend who holds this view?

- Christian says, "True fear will drive one to run to Jesus for the only salvation that can create a right relationship with God." Have you ever feared that you are not saved? If so, how did you address that fear? If not, what is the basis for your confidence?

Chapter 29—Backslider's Story

- Have you ever mentored or discipled someone and been encouraged in their progress and apparent devotion, only for them to abandon your teaching and walk away from faith? If so, describe what happened and how it affected you. How did you know when to stop investing in this person? If you have not, imagine how it would affect you.

- What process do you find in Scripture for providing correction? Describe how you would implement or have implemented this process.

- Though Scripture tells us that we cannot lose our salvation,[520] the ultimate proof that we have committed our life to Jesus is that we remain faithful to him until our earthly life ends. How can you guard against walking away from God as Backslider did?

Chapter 30—End of the Road

- Joyful references Psalm 46:10a, "Be still, and know that I am God." What does that mean?
- How do you balance being still before the Lord with doing the work he has called you to do? Is it possible to work diligently and be still? Why or why not?
- Hopeful describes heaven in almost unrealistic terms. Does the Bible support his view? Use specific Scripture to support your answer.

Chapter 31—Final Challenges

- The river the travelers have to cross represents death. How do you feel knowing that death is a future certainty (unless Jesus returns before then)? Will you be ready? Why or why not?
- Within sight of Celestial City, Christian doubts his salvation. Describe a scenario where you have also doubted your salvation. How were you reassured?
- What verses of Scripture would you share with a believing friend who doubts their salvation? How would you pray with them?

Chapter 32—Celestial City

- Do you believe you are righteous? Why or why not? What does the Bible say about man's righteousness?
- In this chapter, when the angels describe heaven, what excites you? What doesn't? Why?
- Does the description of heaven in this chapter sound like you have imagined it to be? Does it align with what you find in Scripture? Has this chapter and the related Scripture passages changed your thoughts? If so, how?

Chapter 33—Not Welcome

- Do you think Ignorance was treated fairly? Why or why not? What is God's standard of righteousness? Where in Scripture do you find this?

- It can be hard to accept that a "good person" would end up in hell "just because" he or she did not place faith in Jesus for salvation. Does anyone "deserve" entrance into Heaven? Why or why not?

- In your own words, how can a person know for certain he or she will be welcomed into heaven?

Chapter 34—Awakened Challenge

- When you teach, mentor, or counsel others, do you encourage them to determine their own conclusions as the dreamer does? Why or why not? If you are teaching Scripture rather than your interpretation of Scripture, does it change your answer?

- What image or chapter from the book challenged you? Encouraged you? What do you think God is saying to you in that concept or chapter? Read through the Scripture references in the footnotes for that section and ask God to reveal his truth to you.

- The author continues to speak through his Word to readers today. To enrich your reading and keep you open to God speaking to you through Scripture, ask yourself a few simple questions:[521]
    1. What does the passage say about God, Jesus, or his plan?
    2. What does the passage say about people?
    3. According to the passage, what am I doing well, or what do I need to change?

Changes and Additions

The following is a summary of the structural and name changes from Bunyan's original:

1. Bunyan had two volumes, one relating to Christian and one for his wife and children. I have omitted the second by including the entire family into this update as often a family comes to faith together, as we also see in Scripture,[522] though I did change the number, ages, and gender mix of the children. I did not intentionally include the scenarios from Book 2 in this translation.

2. The role of women in the church leverages more of their gifts today than it did in the 17th century, so I have introduced couples and more women into the story.

3. Chapter 6 is completely new, and several of the contexts in Chapters 20-22 do not appear in Bunyan's original.

4. Bunyan published his book without chapter breaks; I added breaks to make it more readable and to facilitate study using the included questions.

5. I changed many of the names to resonate more with a 21st-century reader. The following are the names I have chosen and how they correlate to Bunyan's names, in order of appearance. There are many names for God throughout. The list below only identifies people.

The Pilgrim's Progress for the 21st Century	The Pilgrim's Progress
Christian Pilgrim	Christian
Christiana Pilgrim	Christiana
DoWell Family	New to this translation
Good-Guide	Evangelist
Obstinate	Obstinate
Flexible	Pliable
Looks-Good Pilgrim	New to this translation
Joyful Pilgrim	New to this translation
Self-Disciplined Pilgrim	New to this translation
Help	Help
Pastor Ear-Tickler (expanded role)	Worldly Wiseman
Civility	Pastor Ear-Tickler's assistant, new to this translation
Pastor Good-Life	New to this translation
Pastor Legality	Legality
Omitted from this translation	Civility, Legality's son
Good-Will	Good-Will
The Beelzebubs (street gang)	Beelzebub and those with him
Interpreter	Interpreter
Carpe Diem	Passion
Contented	Patience

The Pilgrim's Progress for the 21st Century	The Pilgrim's Progress
Oblivious	Simple
Lazy	Sloth
Presumption	Presumption
Tradition	Formalist
Hypocrisy	Hypocrisy
Fearful	Timorous
Doubtful	Mistrust
Watchful (at Lodge Beautiful)	Watchful (at palace named "Beautiful")
Discretion	Discretion
Prudence	Prudence
Piety	Piety
Charity	Charity
Michael	New to this translation
Apollyon	Apollyon
Pit Devils	New to this translation
Backpackers	Men
Faithful	Faithful
Dependable	New to this translation
Lustful	Wanton
Adam	Adam

The Pilgrim's Progress for the 21st Century	The Pilgrim's Progress
Passion	Lust of the Flesh
Attraction	Lust of the Eyes
Accomplishment	Pride of Life
Discontent	Discontent
Shameless (Shame)	Shame
Lip-Service	Talkative
Mr. & Mr. False-Teacher	New to this translation
Biased / Tolerant	New to this translation
Deceived / All-Loving	New to this translation
Watcher	New to this translation
Beelzebub / Mr. B	Beelzebub
Judge Hate-Good	Judge Hate-good
Envy	Envy
Deluded	Superstition
Suck-Up	Pickthank
Omitted from this translation	Lord Old Man
Mx. Fleshly-Desires	Lord Carnal Delight
Ms. Luxury	Lord Luxurious
Mrs. Self-Love	Lord Desire of Vain Glory
Omitted from this translation	Lord Lechery
Mr. Never-Enough	Sir Having Greedy

The Pilgrim's Progress for the 21st Century	The Pilgrim's Progress
Omitted from this translation	Jury Members by name
Hopeful	Hopeful
Midas	By-Ends
Two-Faced	Lord Turn-About
Omitted from this translation	Lord Time-Server
Free-Speech Family	Lord Fair-Speech
Omitted from this translation	Mr. Smooth-man
Omitted from this translation	Mr. Facing-both-ways
Anything-Goes	Mr. Any-thing
Double-Tongued	Mr. Two-tongues
Confidence	Confidence
Hoarder	Hold-the-World
Greed	Money-Love
Miser	Save-all
Demas	Demas
Misplaced-Confidence	Vain-confidence
Easy-Going	New to this translation
Hopeless	Giant Despair
Omitted from this translation	Diffidence
David	Shepherd
Knowledge	Knowledge

The Pilgrim's Progress for the 21st Century	The Pilgrim's Progress
Experience	Experience
Discernment	Watchful (at Delectable Mountains)
Sincerity	Sincere
Flatterer	Flatterer
Ignorance	Ignorance
Enough-Faith	Little-Faith
Atheist	Atheist
Backslider	Temporary
False-Hope	Vain-hope

Questions, Thoughts, Suggestions, or Corrections?

Is there something you would like to see added, changed, or corrected in a future update? Do you have questions or other thoughts?

Contact David through his website at **www.DHarakalAuthor.org** or send an e-mail to **DHarakalAuthor@gmail.com**.

Please Leave a Review

I hope you've found this book a helpful, challenging, and enjoyable read. Please do me a favor.

Would you consider giving it a rating wherever you bought the book? Online book stores are more likely to promote a book when they feel good about its content, and reader reviews are a great barometer for a book's quality.

Please go to the website where you bought the book, search for my name and the book title or look through your account's purchase history, and leave a review. Please consider adding a picture of you holding the book. That increases the likelihood your review will be accepted!

Thank you in advance,
David Harakal

Endnotes

Unless otherwise noted, all Scripture quotations are taken from *The Holy Bible, English Standard Version*®

Preface

1   Patricia Bauer and Vybarr Cregan-Reid, "The Pilgrim's Progress," *Encyclopedia Britannica*, May 12, 2020, www.britannica. com/ topic/The-Pilgrims-Progress.

2   *American Heritage Dictionary*, s.v. "allegory," accessed March 12, 2022, www.ahdictionary.com.

3   Eph. 6:19 (English Standard Version)

4   *Holy Bible*, English Standard Version, Crossway, 2008.

Chapter 1—Pleasantown

5   Acts 2:17

6   Isa. 64:6

7   "Today, there are Turquoise Tables all across America from California to Maine. In all fifty states and in eleven countries. Turquoise Tables have become a symbol of hospitality, a safe place to sit down and connect over a cup of coffee or glass of sweet tea." (Kristin Schell, "The turquoise table," The Turquoise Table, last modified March 17, 2020, accessed April 8, 2022, theturquoisetable.com/.)

8   Ps. 38:4

9   Acts 16:30-31 answers a similar question.

10   Prov. 26:12; Isa. 5:21; Rom. 12:16

11   Matt. 23:5-7; Luke 11:42-43

12   Rom. 8:5-7

13   Eccles. 2:10-17; Rom. 12:2; Phil. 4:11-14; James 3:17
       (for example)

14   Matt. 16:17

15   Eph. 2:8-9

16   John 14:16,16:13

17   John 10:4

18   Heb. 9:27

19   Ezek. 22:14

20   Matt. 9:36

21   Matt. 3:7

22   Matt. 7:13-14

23   Ps. 119:105; 2 Pet. 1:19

Chapter 2—Challenged

24   Luke 14:26

25   Bennard, George. 1913. "The Old Rugged Cross." Additional
       Scripture references: John 3:16,36; Phil. 2:8

26   Matt. 19:29

27   Jer. 20:10

28   Eccles. 1:14

29   Luke 23:43; Rev. 21:1–3

30   Isa. 55:9

31   1 Cor. 1:18

32   1 Pet. 1:4; Heb. 11:16

33   Luke 9:62; Josh. 24:15b

34   Prov. 26:4 (Used contrary to the scriptural context.)

35   Isa. 5:21

36   Prov. 3:7, 26:16; Isa. 5:21

37   John 8:31-32; Heb. 13:20-21

Chapter 3—Flexible's Journey

38   Acts 17:16-21

39   2 Tim. 3:16-17

40   John 14:26

41   Matt. 12:33-35; Rom. 8:5-8

42   Titus 1:2

43   Isa. 45:17; John 10:27-29

44   Matt. 13:43; 2 Tim. 4:8; Rev. 3:4

45   Isa. 25:8; Rev. 7:16-17, 21:4

46   Isa. 6:2; 1 Thess. 4:16-17; Rev. 5:11

47   Rev. 4:4

48   Rev. 14:1-5

49   John 12:25

50   2 Cor. 5:2-5

51   Rom. 3:24, 5:17, 8:32; Rev. 21:6, 22:17

52   Slough of Despond in the original.

53   Ps. 40:1-3

54   "The Christian ideal has not been tried and found wanting. It has been found difficult; and left untried." [G. K. (Gilbert Keith) Chesterton, *What's Wrong with the World, 7th Edition* (London: Cassell and Company, Limited, 1910), 35.]

55   Matt. 25:31-33

56   1 Pet. 4:10

57   Prov. 16:9

Chapter 4—Tempted

58   This chapter is new to this update of *The Pilgrim's Progress.*

59   2 Tim. 4:3-4

60   2 Cor. 11:3

61   Jer. 23:16

62   John 8:34

63   Ps. 84:11 taken out of context.

64   "god" intentionally lowercase

65   Prov. 14:12

66   Rom. 8:26a

67   1 Thess. 5:19-21

68   2 Tim. 4:3-4

69   "christian" intentionally lower case.

70   Col. 2:8

71   Ps. 119:71; Isa. 53:3; 2 Cor. 1:3-4

72   Rom. 5:3-5

73   Acts 17:11

74   James 1:12

75   2 Tim. 3:16

76   Ps. 19:7-10

77   2 Pet. 2:1-22

78   "A Bible that's falling apart usually belongs to someone who isn't." - Attributed to Charles Spurgeon. (Specific context unknown.)

79   2 Pet. 3:16-17

Chapter 5—Not Narrow Gate

80   Matt. 23:23-28

81   Prov. 16:9

82   Gal. 1:6-7

83   1 Cor. 3:18-20

84   2 Tim. 4:3-4

85   1 Sam. 9:27

86   Heb. 12:25

87   Heb. 10:38

88   Isa. 6:5

89   Heb. 4:14-16

90   Matt. 12:31; Mark 3:28

91   John 20:27

92   John 6:44

93   Jer. 2:13

94   Luke 2:14

95   Luke 10:4

Chapter 6—Narrow Gate

96   1 Cor. 1:18

97   John 10:3-4

98   Ps. 25:4-5

99   Matt. 7:7-8

100   Matt. 8:8

101   Ps. 48:1-2; Heb. 12:22-24

102   Lev. 19:33-34

103   Matt. 12:24

104   John 6:39

105   Ps. 2:11

106   Rev. 3:8

107   Rom. 5:3-5

108   Matt. 7:13b

109   John 6:37; 2 Thess. 2:13-14

110   Matt. 7:13-14

111   John 14:26, 15:26, 16:13-14

Chapter 7—House of Visions

112   Matt. 13:10-17; 1 John 2:20, 27

113   Ps. 119:105

114   Mal. 2:4-7

115   1 Cor. 4:15

116   Gal. 4:19; 1 Thess. 2:7

117   Phil. 2:9-11

118   Dan. 7:22

119   Prov. 14:12

120   Ezek. 36:24-27

121   Rom. 5:20, 7:6; 1 Cor. 15:56; Gal. 3:19

122   John 15:3; Acts 15:9; Rom. 16:25-27; Eph. 5:26

123   James 5:8

124   1 Tim. 6:10

125   Phil. 1:6; 1 Pet. 1:3-5

126   Matt. 20:16

127   Luke 16:19-31

128   "He is no fool who gives what he cannot keep to gain that which he cannot lose." - Jim Eliott, Christian missionary who was killed by those he was trying to save with the Gospel during Operation Auca, an attempt to evangelize the Huaorani people of Ecuador. (Jim Eliott, October 28, 1949, Journal Entry, quoted by Justin Taylor, in "They Were No Fools: The Martyrdom of Jim Elliot and Four Other Missionaries," thegospelcoalition.org, The Gospel Coalition, January 8, 2016, www.thegospelcoalition.org/blogs/justin-taylor/theywere-no-fools-60-years-ago-today-the-martyrdom-of-jim-elliotand-four-other-missionaries/.)

129   2 Cor. 4:18

130   Gen. 25:29-34; Gal. 5:16-17

131   Eph. 3:20-21

132   John 6:39-40

133   Acts 14:22

134   2 Pet. 1:11

135   Luke 10:20

136   Luke 8:13

137   Rom. 10:9

138   Matt. 12:31-32; Mark 3:28-29

139   Acts 3:19

140   Heb. 6:4-6

141   Luke 19:14

142   Heb. 10:28-29

143   2 Tim. 3:14a

144   Ps. 95:1-3; Isa. 26:21; Dan. 7:10; Mic. 7:16-17; John 5:28-29; 1 Cor. 15:52; 1 Thess. 4:16; 2 Thess. 1:7-8; Jude 1:14; Rev. 20:11-14

145   Dan. 7:9-10; Mal. 3:2-3

146   Mal. 4:1; Matt. 3:12, 13:30

147   Luke 3:17; 1 Thess. 4:16-17

148   Rom. 2:15

149   John 14:26-27

150   John 14:26

151   Ps. 119:36; Eph. 1:16-17

Chapter 8—Relief

152   Isa. 26:1

153   Prov. 28:13

154   Matt. 18:6; Mark 9:42; Luke 17:1-2

155   Eph. 2:1-10

156   Matt. 11:28-30

157   Zech. 12:10

158   Luke 7:47-48; Rom. 8:23-24

159   Zech. 3:4

160   Eph. 1:13

161   Eph. 4:17-18

Chapter 9—Rebuffed

162   1 Pet. 5:8

163   Paraphrased from quote attributed to Napoléon Bonaparte. (Specific context unknown.)

164   Prov. 6:10-11

165   John 10:1

166   In contrast to Ps. 19:7-8

167   Prov. 1:7; Col. 2:3

168   Gal. 2:16

Chapter 10—Three Choices

169   Isa. 49:10

170   1 Cor. 2:14

171 Prov. 6:6-11

172 Attributed to Will Rogers (1879-1935), an American cowboy turned actor known for his "humor and folksy observations." (Specific source unknown.) ("Learn About Will," Will Rogers Memorial Museum & Birthplace Ranch, 2016. www.willrogers.com/learn-about-will.)

173 In contrast to Eph. 1:11-14

174 1 Thess. 5:7-8; Rev. 2:4-5

175 1 Thess. 5:6-7

Chapter 11—Lodge Beautiful

176 Mark 8:34-37

177 "The will of God will not take us where the grace of God cannot sustain us." - Billy Graham (Specific context unknown.)

178 Heb. 12:1-2

179 Gal. 6:10

180 Matt. 17:2

181 Heb. 11:15-16

182 Rom. 7:15

183 Rom. 7:16-19

184 Phil. 4:8

185 Isa. 25:8; Rev. 21:4

186 Gen. 19:14

187 John 12:43

188 1 Sam. 2:8; Ps. 113:7

189   Rev. 7:15-17

Chapter 12—Museum at Lodge Beautiful

190   John 8:58

191   Heb. 11:1-40

192   Luke 15:7

193   Rom. 8:37-39

194   Eph. 1:3-4; Rev. 3:5

195   Rev. 5:1-5

196   Rev. 20:12

197   Isa. 40:31

198   Rev. 19:11-14

199   Dan. 12:1; Rev. 12:7-9

200   World War 1 (1914-1918)

201   Eph. 6:10-18

202   Exod. 4:2-5

203   Judg. 4:1-24

204   Judg. 6:36-40

205   "GOAD—(Heb. malmad, only in Judg. 3:31), an instrument used by ploughmen for guiding their oxen." [M. G. Easton, Illustrated Bible Dictionary and Treasury of Biblical History, Biography, Geography, Doctrine, and Literature (New York: Harper & Brothers Publishers, 1893), 292].

206   Judg. 3:31

207   1 Sam. 17:1-58

208   Judg. 15:14-16

209   Rev. 19:11-16

210   Isa. 43:5-7

211   Eph. 1:3-6

212   Eph. 6:11

213   Deut. 20:1-4

Chapter 13—Battle in the Valley

214   Deut. 20:4

215   Rev. 9:11

216   Matt. 24:24

217   Rom. 6:21-23

218   John 8:44

219   Gen. 3:1 as an example of Satan attempting to sow doubt.

220   Jim Elliot, ibid.

221   Matt. 5:10-12

222   Acts 10:43; 1 Thess. 5:23-24; 1 John 1:8-9

223   Mic. 7:7-8

224   Rom. 8:37

225   James 4:7

226   Isa. 40:28-31

227   Dan. 12:1

228   Rev. 22:2b

Chapter 14—New Valley, New Dangers

229   Num. 13:25-33

230   Job 10:18-22

231   Ps. 69:14-15

232   Eph. 6:18

233   John 14:26

234   Ps. 23:4

235   Phil. 4:6

236   John 16:33

237   Phil. 4:7

238   Amos 5:8

239   Job 12:22

240   Ps. 23:4

Chapter 15—Companions

241   2 Cor. 3:18

242   Col. 1:28-29

243   2 Pet. 2:22

244   1 Cor. 10:12-13

245   1 John 2:15-17

246   1 Tim. 6:12

247   Heb. 12:1-3

248   Eph. 4:22-24

249   John 14:26

250   Gal. 2:19-21

251   Rom. 8:2-11

252   Prov. 2:1-15

253   Eph. 5:25

254   1 Cor. 1:18-19

255   Ps. 51:17

256   1 Cor. 1:26-31, 3:18-20

257   Luke 16:15

258   Prov. 15:1; James 1:19-20

259   1 Pet. 3:15

260   Matt. 6:19-21

261   Phil. 3:7-11

262   Phil. 3:8-9

263   Isa. 6:9-10

264   John 6:37-40

Chapter 16—Lip Service

265   John 16:13

266   Matt. 23:3

267   1 John 2:3-6

268   Rom. 2:17-24

269   Matt. 24:24

270   Prov. 27:17

271   Matt. 7:15-20; Luke 6:43–45

272   James 1:22-27

273   Broitry, "Pursuit," recorded 2012, track 4 on *Nothin' Special* EP, Spotify.

274   Matt. 7:21-23

275   "*Everyman* is a morality play that first appeared in England early in the sixteenth century" by an unknown author. The main character, Everyman, "is allegorical and represents the choices open to all men." ("Everyman," Encyclopedia.com, updated June 8, 2018, www.encyclopedia.com/literature-and-arts/ literature-English/English-literature-1499/everyman.)

276   Phil. 2:4-8

277   1 Cor. 15:33; 2 Cor. 6:14

278   Rom. 10:9

279   John 13:17

280   John 16:8-11; Rom. 7:24-25

281   Rom. 4:4-5; Gal. 2:16-17

282   Matt. 5:6, 13:44-46

283   John 14:15-17

284   Isa. 5:21

285   2 Tim. 3:16-17

286   Reflects postmodern thinking as it applies to faith and how a Christian should act.

287   1 John 2:19

288   1 Cor. 1:18-21

289   Eph. 4:15

290   1 John 4:6

291   1 Cor. 15:33; 2 Cor. 6:14

292   Ezek. 3:17-19; 1 Cor. 3:6-9

293   Isa. 1:11-13

294   Heb. 12:1-3

295   John 4:36-38; Gal. 6:9

296   1 Cor. 9:24

297   Rev. 3:11-12

298   Ps. 139:23-24

299   Jer. 17:9

300   James 5:16

301   Heb. 12:1-2

302   Acts 14:22; 2 Cor. 1:3-5; 2 Tim. 3:12

303   Rev. 2:10

304   Rom. 8:9; 1 Cor. 6:19-20

Chapter 17—Vanity

305   Most of the content in the chapters about Vanity is new to this
       update of *The Pilgrim's Progress*.

306   Matt. 7:15-16; 2 Pet. 2:1-22

307   Matt. 6:24

308   Contrary to 2 Tim. 3:16

309   Eph. 6:10-18a

310   As their given names reflect their character true to the allegorical
       format, unless they are addressed directly, Tolerant is referred to
       as Biased and All-Loving as Deceived.

311   Nor should one seek to "update Scripture," based on Deut. 4:2, 12:32, Prov. 30:5-6, and Rev. 22:18-19.

312   Faulty view of Luke 9:50 taken out of context. Refer to 1 Tim. 6:3-5 for a more thorough correct view.

313   1 Pet. 3:15

314   Eph. 4:15

315   Eccles. 1:1-2, 2:10-11,17

316   Matt. 12:24

317   Rev. 9:11

318   Intentional pronoun misuse in this sentence aligns with the GLAAD Media Reference 10th Edition (glaad.org/reference). This protocol continues in this and the next two chapters when someone local to Vanity is speaking.

319   Matt. 4:8-9; Luke 4:5-7

320   1 Cor. 2:7-8

321   Contrary to Eph. 4:29

322   Ps. 119:37; Matt. 6:19-21; Phil. 3:19-20

323   1 Pet. 3:15

324   Matt. 5:10-12

Chapter 18—Escape from Vanity

325   Isa. 53:7

326   Acts 5:40-41; 1 Pet. 4:12–19

327   Matt. 26:59

328   This and other grammatical errors in chapters 21 and 22 result from the use of one of the LGBTQ+ preferred personal pro-

nouns with the correct verb tense, contrary to what the written pronoun would imply. In this case, and most of this chapter, the reference is to Faithful alone.

329   "Mx.? Nonbinary teachers embrace gender-neutral honorific," nbcnews.com, NBC News, January 20, 2019, www.nbcnews.com/feature/nbc-out/ms-mr-or-mx-nonbinaryteachers-embrace-gender-neutral-honorific-n960456.

330   Luke 6:22-23; 2 Cor. 4:17-18; 1 Pet. 1:5-7; 2 John 1:7-8

331   James 1:12

332   Rev. 4:10-11

Chapter 19—A New Ally

333   Ps. 32:8

334   Mark 6:7

335   Acts 8:1-4

336   John 4:32

337   2 Cor. 1:3

338   Prov. 22:6

Chapter 20—Debate

339   Prov. 26:25; Eph. 5:6

340   1 Cor. 15:33; Col. 2:4

341   Matt. 13:45-46

342   Matt. 13:44

343   Mark 10:29-30

344 Matt. 10:16, then Prov. 10:5 quoted out of context, followed by a local proverb referenced as though it was a part of Scripture.

345 Eccles. 2:3-10, ignoring verse 11.

346 Mark 10:1

347 Prov. 28:20; Luke 16:10-12

348 Matt. 19:24

349 Col. 3:23

350 John 6:1-15

351 Acts 8:9-23

352 Gen. 34:1-31

353 Luke 20:45-47

354 Matt. 26:14-16, 27:1-5; John 17:12

355 1 Sam. 16:7

356 Mark 8:34-38

357 Matt. 6:19-21

358 When desiring to share the truth of the gospel with someone, this is a good question to ask to determine if the person is open to the truth.

359 Matt. 6:5-6

360 2 Cor. 4:7-11

361 Deut. 4:23-24

Chapter 21—The Allure of Riches

362 2 Tim. 4:10

363   Prov. 11:28; Matt. 6:24; Mark 10:21-22; and 1 Tim. 6:10 are representative verses. There are over 2000 references to money in the bible. (Peter Anderson, "Bible Verses About Money: What Does The Bible Have To Say About Our Financial Lives?," biblemoneymatters.com, Bible Money Matters, October 8, 2021, www.biblemoneymatters.com/bible-versesabout-money-what-does-the-bible-have-to-say-about-ourfinancial-lives/.)

364   1 Pet. 2:11

365   2 Kings 5:20-27

366   Matt. 26:14-15

367   Matt. 27:6-10

368   Paraphrase of quote attributed to Oliver Wendell Holmes, Sr. (Specific source unknown.)

369   Gen. 19:17, 26

370   Phil. 4:19

371   Matt. 6:24; Luke 16:13

Chapter 22—Calm Before the Storm

372   Ps. 65:9; Ezek. 47:1-12

373   Rev. 22:1-3

374   Ps. 23:2-3

375   Heb. 2:1

376   Exod. 20:12

377   1 Tim. 4:12

Chapter 23—Death's Door

378   Isa. 53:7

379   Job 7:15-16

380   John 18:10

381   Exod. 20:13

382   John 6:44

383   Occurred in 73/74 AD. [Titus Flavius Josephus, *The Wars of the Jews*; or, *History of the Destruction of Jerusalem*. Translated by William Whiston, (Rome, 75; Project Gutenberg, 2001), www.gutenberg.org/ebooks/2850.]

384   Deut. 31:8; Ps. 18:2

385   James 1:12; Rom. 5:3-5

386   Ps. 55:22; 1 Pet. 5:6-7

387   1 Kings 13:4

388   Matt. 7:13-14

Chapter 24—Satisfaction Mountain Park

389   Rom. 8:29-30; 2 Thess. 2:13

390   John 10:11

391   Isa. 43:1; John 10:3

392   Heb. 13:1-2

393   Hos. 14:9

394   1 Tim. 1:18-20

395   Prov. 21:16

396   Rev. 20:14-15

397   Gen. 25:29-34

398   Matt. 26:14-16

399   Acts 5:1-11

400   Matt. 7:21-23

401   John 6:39

Chapter 25—Another Decision, Another Mistake

402   Titus 3:4-5

403   John 10:1-6

404   John 10:7-10

405   Prov. 26:12

406   Eccles. 10:3

407   Heb. 12:16

408   Ps. 23:1-6

409   Exod. 33:15-16

410   Ps. 3:5-8, 27:1-3

411   Prov. 29:5; Dan. 11:32; 2 Cor. 11:13-14

412   Rom. 16:18

413   Deut. 8:5

414   Heb. 12:5-11

415   Rev. 3:19

Chapter 26—Not Dissuaded

416   Eccles. 10:15

417 Prov. 26:11

418 2 Cor. 4:4

419 2 Cor. 5:7

420 Prov. 19:27

421 Heb. 10:32-39

422 Eph. 6:12

423 1 John 2:20-23

424 Heb. 6:17-20

425 Luke 10:1

426 Robertson, Robert, 1758. "Come, Thou Fount of Every Blessing."

Chapter 27—Testimony

427 Rom. 6:20-23

428 Eph. 5:6-14

429 James 1:18; 1 Pet. 1:3

430 Gal. 2:16

431 Luke 3:8-9

432 Ps. 119:105; Rom. 8:28

433 1 Kings 19:11-12 (KJV)

434 Ps. 86:15; Rom. 5:8

435 Luke 19:39-40

436 Isa. 64:6

437 Rom. 6:1-23; Eph. 2:1-10; Heb. 10:1-39; 1 Pet. 1:1-25

438 Rom. 10:9

439   Luke 7:41-43

440   Ps. 95:6; Jer. 29:12-13

441   Heb. 4:16

442   John 6:39

443   Acts 16:30-31

444   2 Cor. 12:9

445   1 Tim. 1:15a

446   Rom. 4:25

447   Rom. 8:1

Chapter 28—Ignorance

448   Prov. 13:4

449   Jer. 17:9

450   Prov. 28:26a

451   Rom. 3:11-12

452   Mark 7:20-23

453   Gen. 8:21

454   2 Cor. 5:10

455   Ps. 139:23-24

456   Eph. 2:8-9

457   1 John 1:7-10

458   1 Cor. 1:18

459   Matt. 11:27

460   Eph. 1:17-20

461   Eph. 2:8-10

462   2 Cor. 4:3-4

463   Rom. 1:20

464   Prov. 1:7

465   Heb. 10:14

466   Matt. 5:48

467   Heb. 10:14

Chapter 29—Backslider's Story

468   Matt. 7:21-23

469   Prov. 29:25

470   Rom. 2:1-4

471   Prov. 27:5-6; Gal. 6:1

472   Prov. 12:26,13:20; 1 Cor. 15:33-34

473   2 Chron. 7:13-14

Chapter 30—End of the Road

474   A reference to the historically inaccurate but philosophically
       true portrayal of Hernán Cortés's landing in Mexico in 1519,
       where his ships were scuttled for building materials and to make
       it impossible for his troops to evacuate when things became
       difficult. (One was kept intact to send sought-after riches to the
       King of Spain.) So, while not literally burned, the troops were
       "all in" with no effective means of retreat. (Glenn Stanton, "Fact
       Checker: Burning Your Ships for Jesus," thegospelcoalition.org,

The Gospel Coalition, March 13, 2013, www.thegospelcoalition.org/article/ factchecker-burning-your-ships-for-Jesus/.)

475   Isa. 62:4 (KJV)

476   Isa. 62:11-12

477   Rev. 21:9-21

478   Ps. 46:10a

479   Isa. 26:1-4

480   One definition of common grace is, "The grace of God by which he gives people innumerable blessings that are not part of salvation." [Wayne Grudem, *Systematic Theology, Second Edition* (Michigan: Zondervan Academic, 2020), Chapter 31, 1242.] Or, simply, the blessings enjoyed by all people, including those not included in God's plans for salvation.

Chapter 31—Final Challenges

481   The travelers share their experiences several times through the story. The most obvious reason is that each person they meet would want to hear their stories. But there are two additional reasons: 1) As a reminder of God's faithfulness. Reference Josh. 4:1-7, 19-24. God has Joshua build a mound of stones to remember what he did for the Israelites for many generations. 2) To enrich and complete the experience. Reference C.S. Lewis, who said, "A pleasure is full grown only when it is remembered." [C. S. Lewis, *Out of the Silent Planet* (New York: HarperOne, 2012), 75. Kindle.]

482   2 Kings 2:11-12

483   Gen. 5:21-24

484   Luke 24:50-51; Acts 1:9-11

485   1 Cor. 15:51-52

486   Prov. 3:5-6

487   Rom. 8:1

488   Mark 9:24

489   Isa. 43:2

490   Ps. 40:2

Chapter 32—Celestial City

491   Heb. 12:22-24

492   Rev. 2:7, 3:4

493   Isa. 57:1-2, 65:17

494   1 Cor. 9:24-25; 1 Thess. 2:19; 2 Tim. 4:8; 1 Pet. 5:4; Rev. 2:10, 4:10-11

495   1 John 3:2

496   Rev. 4:6-11

497   Rev. 19:9

498   Rev. 22:14

499   Isa. 26:2; 2 Cor. 5:21

500   Matt. 25:21

501   Rev. 5:13b

502   Rev. 21:21

Chapter 33—Not Welcome

503   Luke 18:9-14

504   2 Thess. 1:9-10

Chapter 34—Awakened Challenge

505   Matt. 7:21-23

Questions

506   Matt. 5:9

507   Wayne Grudem, *Systematic Theology, Second Edition*, Chapter 4.

508   Chesterton, *What's Wrong with the World, 7th Edition*. ibid.

509   Ps. 127:2; Mark 6:31

510   Gal. 5:22-23

511   For a dramatic example of this, read Ivan Mesa, "The Missionary Legacy of Jim and Elisabeth Elliot," imb.org, International Mission Board, April 1, 2019, www.imb. org/2019/04/01/missionary-legacy-Jim-Elisabeth-Elliot/.

512   John Piper, "Episode 999: How Do I Pray the Bible?," February 6, 2017, produced by *Desiring God*, podcast, MP3 audio, www.desiringgod.org/interviews/how-do-i-pray-the-bible.

513   1 Tim. 4:12

514   Matt Smethurst, "6 Pillars of a Christian View on Suffering," thegospelcoalition.org, The Gospel Coalition, June 2, 2013, www.thegospelcoalition.org/article/6-pillars-of-a-christian-view-on-suffering/.

515   Todd Billings, "My Incurable Condition," christianitytoday.com, Christianity Today, accessed April 16, 2022, www.christianityto-day.com/pastors/2015/spring/my-incurablecondition.html.

516   Grudem, *Systematic Theology, Second Edition*, Chapter 32.

517 Olan Stubbs, "Conviction vs. Condemnation," campusministry.
org, Campus Ministry Today, January 20, 2020, campusministry.
org/article/conviction-vs-condemnation.

518 For a more thorough discussion of regeneration, visit www.
preceptaustin.org/regeneration.

519 Gal. 5:22-23

520 Rom. 8:37-39; 1 Cor. 1:8-9; Phil. 1:6

521 Taken from www.dbsguide.org/.

Changes and Additions

522 John 4:53; Acts 11:14,16:15; 1 Cor. 16:15; *et al.*

About the Author

David Harakal lives in the Middle East/North Africa. In 2020, he left his 30-year career in corporate finance and marketing (including over 20 years at IBM) to work with Christians outside of North America. Before leaving, he served as an elder at the Austin Stone Community Church in Austin, Texas, averaging 8,000 in weekly attendance. He and his wife have two grown, married children.

David can be reached at www.DHarakalAuthor.org or by e-mail at DHarakalAuthor@gmail.com.